ESCAPE FROM HELL

Escape from Hell

MARY IRVING

Chapter 1

Sochi crept soundlessly through the forest on bare hooves. Her breath fogged the air. She wiped her sweating palms on her heavy woolen pants, then clutched her winter jacket, which was pinned at her shoulder, to keep out the chill. Her long ears swiveled at every sound. Her horns curved back over her short brown hair, shining in the moonlight.

This forest had become intimately familiar to her; she'd studied it until she knew it as well as the forest around her home. A clearing in the basin between three hills had been filled with tents and temporary wooden structures for weeks. She was familiar with that camp now too, after months spent watching and following these humans. At first, she was unfamiliar with stalking humans — until recently she'd gone out of her way to avoid them. Humans were dangerous. It was legal and encouraged for humans to kill satyrs. To hunt them. The High Commander paid for satyr hooves and horns. Until a few months ago, Sochi felt uncomfortable if she saw a trail of campfire smoke in the distance, for fear it could be hunters. A lot of good her caution had done her. She'd still lost everything.

Sochi reached the edge of the forest at the top of a hill overlooking the human camp. A sea of peaked tents spread out before her, their smoke holes breathing dark plumes into the night sky. Horses and oxen were stabled at the back of the camp, near the latrines. Sochi could hear their soft noises even from her distance. A dark row of wooden sheds housed their supplies.

Banners furled out by an autumn wind indicated this was the High Guard's camp, the battalion under the direct command of the High Commander herself. The colors were washed out by the night, but Sochi could still see the crown and sword silhouetted in silver against a maroon background, the symbol of the Galilia's ruler, the High Commander. The image sent a thrill of fear down Sochi's spine. She looked away from the banners and saw signs that the humans were planning on leaving this location soon. Carts were being loaded with supplies. Many of the wooden structures were half torn down, although some were still in use. In a few days, the humans would pack up and move on.

But she already knew that. It was why she was here — time was running short. The humans wouldn't set up another camp like this. After they pulled out of this location, they would go back to the capital city, Highdel, and hide behind their walls for the winter, like a bear in a den. They would be dug in and safe until they emerged again in the spring to spread more destruction and grief. If the satyrs were going to attack, they had to do it now.

Sochi's heart raced. In addition to the terror of sneaking into the High Commander's own camp, she also held a deadly weapon pinned to the roof of her mouth by her tongue. A rough pouch filled with a deadly poison. Sochi would deliver the poison to the High Commander, even though it would likely cost her life; the only thing she had left to sacrifice.

Sochi slunk down the hill. This was the most dangerous part of the plan. It was a dark night, but she was exposed while she moved down the slope. She stuck close to bushes and stray trees that would disguise her shadow and her form, but an alert guard could spot her, and then the mission would be over before it was begun. Fortunately, the guards weren't alert tonight.

She slipped behind the first tent she came to and hid in its shadow. The canvas snapped in the breeze, further helping to disguise the slight sounds of Sochi's movement. She could smell the animals, packed too closely together on the other side of the camp.

The military camp was helpfully arranged in a neat, logical grid. Sochi knew exactly where she needed to go and how to get there. She moved between the tents silently, shrouded in darkness. The sound of footsteps and conversation ahead froze her in her place. The organized camp made it easy for her to navigate, but it also left little opportunity for concealment. She cast around frantically for a hiding place, but there was nothing. Her pulse pounded in her ears as she pressed close to the nearest tent, hoping the shadows would be enough to camouflage her. Her tongue cradled the pouch in her mouth, and she closed her eyes, willing the humans not to notice her. To her great surprise, they didn't turn down the path where Sochi was hiding. Instead, they made for a tent with warm lights and the hum of music and laughter. Sochi inched away from that tent.

She crouched low as she scuttled between the temporary structures to the storage shed, one of the few wooden buildings. It was well-guarded, but the guards were distracted by the warm light and laughter from the inviting tent Sochi had passed. It wasn't hard to sneak past them.

Sochi slipped into the storage shed and looked around. She found an empty sack which had been filled with grain, and threw it over her shoulder as she hurried between the shelves. The humans' supplies were beginning to dwindle at the end of their campaign. They would make it back to their city on what was left in the shed, but it was sparse enough that they would notice what Sochi took. Distracted by the crunch of soldier's boots outside the shed and the ominous weight of the pouch on her tongue, Sochi didn't pay attention to what she shoved in the sack. It didn't matter; the supplies wouldn't make it out of the camp. They were just bait in a trap.

Sochi gently pinned the pouch to the roof of her mouth with her tongue and swallowed. *She* was bait in a trap. She had to kill the High Commander if there was to be any hope of ending her mission to exterminate all the satyrs in Galilia. Even the sanctioned settlements — villages where satyrs were supposed to be allowed to live, as long as they didn't leave or cause an inconvenience for humans — weren't safe. No one warned the settlements when they'd lost their sanctioned status. Humans just showed up with fire and steel and destroyed everything. They killed everyone, on the High Commander's orders. The High Commander who was here, in this camp. She was here, and Sochi would kill her.

When her sack was full of random food supplies, she hoisted it onto her shoulder. Everyone knew there were few greater crimes for satyrs to commit than stealing the supplies they needed to live. With a sack full of food, Sochi guaranteed her death, but she also improved the chances that the High Commander would want to question her personally. It was the only way to get close enough to the woman to deliver the corrosive poison.

Her breathing was shallow, and her heart raced. It was almost time. She stood in front of the door to the supply shed, fear freezing her in place. Her long ears twitched as she listened to the soldiers walking past the door. She closed her eyes and clenched her fists. She was scared. She was going to die, and as hard as the last few months had been, she didn't want to die. She thought back to why she was here.

She remembered coming home to her village, a sanctioned settlement. She'd spent the winter season looking for work, and after two months living on foraged scraps and the odd jobs she could pick up in the satyr-friendly mountain towns, she was looking forward to seeing her family again. Leaving the village was dangerous. Humans were *supposed* to kill any satyr who strayed away from the sanctioned settlements, but there wasn't enough food at home, so Sochi took the risk and left so there would be more for the people she left behind. The village was supposed to be safe — until it wasn't.

Sweet lilacs perfumed the air, announcing spring. Sochi hoped she'd be home in time for the planting festival, but when she reached the village, it was gone. The buildings were burned. The people — all the people, men, women, and children — were left to rot where they died, cut down on the streets, in their homes, and in their beds. The lilacs mingled with the odor of decay, and Sochi retched.

She found loved one after loved one amongst the ash. Metal stoves were the sole survivors of the fires, standing alone in destroyed homes. She found her sister's body, already beginning to decay, cut open and left to rot, her horns and hooves chopped off. She'd died in her garden with rakes and shovels scattered around her. She hadn't been bothering or threatening anyone, but they'd cut her down anyway.

Sochi opened her eyes, tears glistening on her cheeks. She was going to die, but she was going to take that monster with her. She was going to finally catch the prey she'd been hunting for months. She was going to kill the High Commander. Fear still coursed through her, but the fire of her anger pushed her forward. She wiped away her tears, listened until the patrol's shuffling footsteps had passed, and then pushed out of the shed. She stuck to the shadows, but she was careful not to be fast enough to escape. She waited until a guard saw her before she slipped between buildings.

"Hey! Stop!" the guard shouted.

Sochi clung to the sack and ran, leading the guard on a chase. She couldn't let him catch her too easily or the humans would suspect a trap, but she couldn't get away, either. She allowed the weight and awkward bulk of the sack to slow her down.

A rope coiled around her ankle and pulled tight. Sochi resisted the impulse to cry out as she fell to the ground, dropping her sack and spilling the briefly stolen supplies everywhere. She held her jaw and tongue carefully. She couldn't break the pouch now; she was too close to her goal. She kicked her hooves, but the rope was tight. Before she could reach with her hands to free herself, a foot slammed into her back, knocking the air from her lungs and pinning her to the ground on her stomach.

"I got it!" shouted the guard on top of her.

Pain lanced through Sochi's shoulders as her arms were wrenched back and tied behind her.

"Looks like it was stealing supplies," another guard said.

"You think the High Commander will want to hear about this?"

"We should see what we can get out of it first."

Sochi's heart sank. The stolen food was supposed to be the key. They were supposed to take her straight to the High Commander when they saw it. She must not have taken enough. If they were going to question her first, they might cause her to break the pouch in her mouth and accidentally kill herself.

The guard finished tying Sochi up and stepped off of her. She couldn't move; her arms and legs were bound too tightly. A guard grabbed her by the horn and lifted her off the ground.

"Ahhh!" Sochi cried as pain spiked through her head from the strained horn. Horns were sensitive, and the humans knew it.

Sochi saw the guards grin through her tears of pain. "You gonna play nice, little goat, and tell us what you're doing here, or are things going to get messy?"

Sochi glared at him through the pain. She was tempted to bite the pouch and spit its contents in his face. She would like to hear him scream in pain as he died. If they were going to torture her, it was likely she wouldn't live long enough to deliver the poison to her true target, but she couldn't give up hope that she might still kill the High Commander herself.

He lifted Sochi higher by her horn, eliciting another gasp of pain from her before laughing and dropping her to the ground. "I guess this is going to get messy. Get her to the workshop and tie her to the drying racks." The guard stepped on Sochi's horn, sending pain shooting through her and forcing her to turn her head and look up at him. "We can add these horns to the High Commander's collection. Don't worry, little goat. You'll get to see them one last time before we turn them in. I'm going to cut them off and show them to you bit by bit."

Fear cut through Sochi as the guard removed his boot. She was hoisted onto the other man's shoulder and carried away. She knew she couldn't get free, but she writhed against her restraints anyway. Cutting off her horns was the most painful thing Sochi could imagine, and logic couldn't overcome her fear of it. In blind panic, she flailed for freedom, but the guard carried her easily. Through her tears, pain, and terror, Sochi clung to the hope that she would be able to deliver her poison to the High Commander. She could die, but she needed to take the monster down with her.

Chapter 2

High Commander Rin Tallow sat behind her camp desk. It was one of the few solid pieces of furniture in the mobile camp, but it was still a camp desk. The writing surface was half the size of her desk in the palace, and she'd crowded that space with books, documents, and correspondences, leaving herself only a narrow square to work on. It was claustrophobic, and she hated it. Of course, this late in a campaign, she hated everything. A chill seeped into her quarters despite the thick wall hangings and the fire in the stove behind her. Rin sat back from her work and rubbed the cramp out of her fingers as she reread what she'd written.

It had been a disappointing harvest for many across Galilia, and she was writing their neighbors to the south to request a trade, supplementing Galilia's grain in exchange for surplus yield from the mines. The exchange should have been straight-forward, but Galilia was on rocky terms with their neighbors and Rin had to walk a delicate line. Galilia was a small country tucked in the northern hills and mountains. There was enough wealth in the mines to draw the attention of her neighbors, but not enough wealth in the fields to draw their military might.

Rin glared at the letter. It wasn't right. She hadn't addressed their concerns about the growing satyr refugee population in their northern province. They blamed the refugees on Rin's Satyr Removal Act. Rin agreed that the satyrs were fleeing south, but if the southerners didn't like it, they didn't have to allow the satyrs in. If the south met them with steel, they would go somewhere else, or they would die as they should. But Rin couldn't say that in a letter requesting a trade agreement, so she was stuck trying to delicately dance around the satyr issue while making a convincing case for the trade deal.

She pushed aside the correspondence for now and pulled a report from the stack of work that needed to be done. She hadn't even finished reading the introduction before someone knocked at her door. She had requested not to be interrupted, but secretly she was grateful for the break. Putting off her work was tempting; it would be easier to do in a few weeks when she was home, anyway.

Rin stood and went to her door. It was late, and her support staff had already been relieved for the day.

"Yes, Captain Delton?" she snapped.

The captain stood rigidly at the door to Rin's quarters. He knew she'd ordered no disruptions, so if he was interrupting her work, it must be for something important.

"High Commander, there's been an incident."

"What kind of incident?"

"A rebel satyr was caught in the supplies."

"I'll be right there."

Rin left the captain at the door. Her office and her sleeping quarters occupied one large tent in the temporary camp. The space was divided in half by a large maroon curtain with the silver crown and sword emblazoned on it. Rin pushed through the curtain into her living space. Her bed was one of the other few pieces of real furniture in the camp, but like her desk, it could not compare to what waited for her at home. Her wardrobe stood open. She'd already removed her uncomfortable chest plate and shoulder guards for the night, but she still wore her bracers and leg plates. Rin went to the vanity and pulled her straight black hair back into its customary bun. She checked her reflection for stray hairs before pinning the bun in place. Her skin was pale, and dark bags stood out below her eyes. She needed sleep, another thing that would come more easily when she was home.

Although she wasn't wearing all of her armor, she was still in full uniform with all the appropriate ornamentation of her rank. The crown and sword were embroidered prominently on her crisp, silver-trimmed maroon jacket, reminding everyone of the power she held. Her pants were clean, and still pressed despite the day's wear. Rin inspected her reflection. She never left her quarters with a sloppy appearance. Finally satisfied, she threw her cloak over her shoulders. It was too cold to walk across camp without it.

Rin stepped out of her quarters, and Captain Delton snapped to attention.

"Take me to the goat," said Rin.

"Yes, sir."

He led the way through the camp. They stepped around carts being loaded up for the last leg of the journey to Highdel. Rin wanted to be home in her palace before the first snow of the season fell. She could see her breath on the air as she walked, and her boots crunched frozen ground. They would need to hurry if she was going to get what she wanted. Winter was approaching faster than usual this year. An early frost was part of the reason Rin had to ask the southern kingdom for grain.

"Right around here, sir," the captain said.

He led her past the barracks to the workshops. A contingent of tradespeople — carpenters, tailors, and metal and leather workers — kept the soldiers protected, clothed, and armed. The tools they used in their crafts also happened to be quite helpful for convincing tight-lipped satyrs to talk.

The workshops were a small cluster of buildings; most of the work was done outside in a large shared courtyard, defined by a fence. Within the fence, the dirt was packed down by workers moving back and forth with heavy loads. Bright lanterns lit up the workspace despite the dark. Large tables were pushed to one side, piled high with tools. There were poles driven into the ground, with rails strung between them to create drying racks.

Soldiers were milling around the space, all of whom stopped and came to attention when they saw Rin. As they moved aside, Rin saw the satyr. It was female, and a bloody mess. She was slumped on the ground, held up by her arms, which had been lashed to the drying rack. Her horns had been sawed off, and blood still flowed from the wounds. Rin's soldiers would have cut down the satyr's horns piece by piece, sawing off a new, painful chunk every time she had refused to answer a question.

Rin turned to the highest-ranking soldier among the blood-soaked men and women standing around the satyr. "What did you get out of her?"

The sergeant stood straighter at being addressed by the High Commander herself.

"Sir, her name is Sochi. We haven't gotten anything else out of her yet, sir."

"Just a name?" asked Rin, glaring down at the satyr. She was annoyed with her soldiers. They should have reported the creature when they realized she was being stubborn. Now there were no horns left for her more skilled interrogators to work with.

The satyr met Rin's eyes with a fiery defiance.

"Sochi, are you going to tell me what you're doing here, or am I going to have to introduce you to one of my more creative interrogators?"

The satyr continued to glower up at her.

Rin shook her head. "Go get Tine," she said to one of the bloody soldiers.

"Yes, sir," he said.

Rin turned her attention back to Captain Delton while a murmur ran through the gathered soldiers. They all knew Tine's bloody reputation. He could get any satyr to talk, even with the horns wasted.

"Did you find anything on her?"

"Yes, sir. Stolen supplies," said the captain, pointing to a small sack on the ground behind the rack.

Rin smiled. That made this satyr's actions a raid. There was a sanctioned satyr settlement a few miles away. If it weren't for the contingent of satyr sympathizers in her court, there wouldn't be any satyrs left in Galilia. Rin wouldn't have to make deals for grain. None of it would be wasted on the half-breeds, so there would be more than enough for the people of her lands. The goat-lover commanders from the mountain towns protected the animals over their own people. Until Rin rooted them out of her government, she couldn't touch those few sanctioned settlements, unless they were connected to an attack against a human. Rin went out of her way to pass these villages in hopes that one starving satyr would choose to steal from her and give her an excuse to wipe them out. This Sochi might be good at holding her tongue, but she had fallen for Rin's trap all the same.

"While we wait for Tine, begin arranging an extermination squad. We'll wipe out the nearby satyr settlement in the morning," Rin told Captain Delton.

"Yes, sir."

"Dismissed," she said, and the captain left to carry out her order.

"Sir, the supplies have all been accounted for," one of her soldiers reported, bent over the sack.

"Good, have them returned to the storage shed." Rin turned to follow the captain.

"No," said the satyr at Rin's feet.

Rin stopped and glanced down at the satyr. "Oh, so you've found your tongue."

"That village did nothing wrong. They have nothing to do with this. I'm not with them," said the satyr.

"Then who are you with? Why are you here?" demanded Rin.

She had no intention of calling back the extermination squad and Tine would have his fun with the goat, but any information would be helpful.

"I was hungry," said the satyr, looking down and away from Rin.

A wave of suspicion washed over Rin. Something was wrong. Why was this satyr talking now? She had endured a great deal of torture, only revealing her name. She hadn't interrupted Rin when she gave the order to exterminate the settlement. She only spoke up when Rin turned to leave. Rin followed the satyr's line of sight, but a soldier was blocking her view. She took a few steps closer and looked where the satyr was looking. There was something in the shadows. Rin squinted and took a step closer to the prisoner.

"Soldier, do you-" Rin was cut off by the satyr whipping her head up and spitting on Rin's leg.

Surprised, Rin stumbled away from the creature. She looked back at the shadows and saw a glint of metal.

"Enemies to the east!" shouted Rin, pointing at the glint as something whistled past her face. "Archers! Number unknown!"

Rin dropped to the ground behind the table. Her leg was in pain, and she looked down at it. Whatever the satyr had spat at her, it wasn't saliva. It had gone through her plate armor. The pain she felt was from it eating into the flesh of her leg. Puss and blood foamed from her shin. Her leg wouldn't hold her weight.

Rin glared up at the satyr. Bloody and bruised, it smiled — an angry, hate-filled smile. Rin needed medical attention, but she wasn't going to get it under a hail of arrows. She shouted orders to establish a defensive perimeter, and soldiers raced to carry out her commands. She clutched her leg, trying to stem the flow of blood from her injury. The satyr in front of her laughed. Blood stained the corners of its mouth.

The pain in Rin's leg began to diminish, but not because the wound was lessening — it was getting worse. Rin was losing feeling in the leg. She glared at the laughing satyr.

Suddenly, everything stopped.

Rin looked around in confusion. The satyr was frozen in manic laughter. A soldier's boot was poised above her head, stopped mid-kick. It took a moment for Rin to notice the arrow hanging in the air inches from her face. She lifted her finger and tapped the arrowhead. It fell to the ground at her feet. Rin hissed in pain. Whatever had caused the world around her to stop had not stopped the poison from eating through her leg. She examined the wound, but before she could establish any-thing more constructive than the fact that it was disgusting, there was a loud popping noise and a strange figure appeared in front of her.

It was a shiny yellow creature, with a reflective panel for a face, and it towered over her on two legs. Its hands looked like large gloves, and Rin realized the yellow material and face panel were some kind of armor. The strange armor was bulkier than plate, and made it difficult tell anything about the figure, other than the fact that it was too tall to be a satyr. It must be human. There was another pop, and another yellow figure appeared next to the first. Then two more loud pops and two more figures. Most of the face plates were directed toward Rin, but one turned toward the satyr. It tapped the figure next to it and pointed at the half-goat.

"What do you want?" demanded Rin, projecting as much authority as she could while lying on the ground with a geyser of fizzing blood and puss streaming from her leg.

The yellow figures said nothing. One of them grabbed the two who were distracted by the satyr and dragged their attention back to Rin. They began approaching Rin. She pushed herself back with her good leg, and the movement sent spasms of pain radiating out from her injury.

"I'm warning you!" she snarled from where she sat, cornered. "I'm the High Commander. Come a step closer and you will be executed!"

The yellow figures seemed unaffected by her threats and continued to lumber towards her. It took only a few steps for them to catch her as she slowly scooted away. Rin howled in agony when a firm hand grasped her ankle below the wound. Any numbness that the injury had caused was erased as the hand caused damaged muscles and tissue to flex, sending pain shooting up her leg. The figures ignored her, snapping silver bands around her wrists and ankles before stepping back. Rin was confused. The bands looked decorative. She examined the one around her left wrist more closely. A blue light pulsed within it. The pulsing grew faster until a solid blue light glowed from the heart of the material. There was a hiss from the band. Rin held it away from her face just as it burst open and a thick fabric enveloped her.

Buried in the fabric, Rin struggled and kicked, crying out as she moved her injured leg. The fabric covered her face so she couldn't see, and she struggled to breathe as the heavy material pressed around her. An unseen hand grabbed her arm. Then another hand grabbed her on the other side, and she was hoisted off the ground.

There was another pop, and a sensation of being squeezed. Then everything went black.

Chapter 3

Rin woke lying on her back on a hard table. She cracked her eyes open, and bright light flooded her vision. Squinting, she tried to raise her hand to shield her eyes, but her arm was pinned down. Her leg had stopped hurting. Had she been hallucinating before she passed out? Was she in the medic's tent? Had they fixed her up so efficiently that the pain in her leg hadn't even lingered as a twinge? That was unlikely. Whatever that satyr had spat on her would be unfamiliar to the doctor; satyrs were notorious for their strange poisons. And Rin had seen the injury. No matter how skilled her doctor was, it should still hurt.

Slowly her eyes adjusted to the light in the room, and she looked around from her reclined position. There wasn't much to see. The room was completely white. Even craning her head around as much as she could, she couldn't find a door. Just four white walls, a white ceiling, a white floor, and a black rectangle on the wall across from her. It shone like polished metal or a mirror, but was too dark to give a good reflection.

Nothing in the room seemed immediately threatening to her, so Rin turned her attention away from her surroundings and examined her restraints. She was pinned down at her wrists and ankles. If she strained her neck, she could glimpse manacles around her wrists, but they didn't budge when she strained against them. They must have been welded to the table. Chains would have given more freedom of movement.

In her effort to see how she was restrained, Rin saw her clothes. She wasn't wearing her uniform anymore; instead she was dressed in a strange, lightweight outfit. The top was powder blue with a V-shaped neck and sleeves that cut off before her elbows. The pants were the same color and cut off above her knees. She strained to see her injured leg, but couldn't lift her head high enough to catch more than a glimpse of dark scar tissue.

After examining as much of her situation as she could from her position, Rin realized she should be cold. She was wearing almost nothing, and although it wasn't the harshest part of winter, even the milder cold of autumn could kill her in such a state of undress. But the room she was in was well-heated, despite the lack of a stove or fireplace to provide warmth. Where was she? How had she gotten here? What was going on?

Rin thrashed against her restraints. Every weld had a weak point. If she could twist just one limb free, she might be able to get a better view of the room she was in. The manacles didn't move. Rin expected pain in her leg as she tried to move it, but it felt as though it had never been injured. What was going on?

When Rin stopped thrashing, the black rectangle across the room flashed, going from a simple reflective surface to one alive with movement. Noise filled the small white room. The pictures moving in the black frame were of her, and it was her voice that filled the space. The images were of her in her throne room, late at night. The candelabras were lit, and the room was empty except for her and one adviser.

~*~

"It's the 'High Commander' now," snapped the tiny Rin on the wall.

"Yes, High Commander, I realize that, but even a high commander cannot order the extinction of an entire species—"

"Did I say *a* high commander?" asked Rin, cutting off her adviser.

Light glinted off her elegant palace armor as she shifted positions. The sound coming from the black square captured the soft clinking of the plates as Rin moved. The Rin in the black frame glared at her adviser, Belvain, making it clear that she was not happy waiting the few seconds it took him to recall her exact words.

Her parents' will had saddled her with the obtuse adviser for two more weeks, until the end of her first two years as High Commander. He had slowed her down the entire time they'd worked together. She had been twenty-four when her parents died, too old for a regent, but her parents had tethered her to the man all the same. Their will insisted that he would provide guidance through a difficult time as Rin learned how to use her power in the event that her parents were unable to teach her themselves, but all he managed to provide was frustration and obstacles.

"You said *the* High Commander," said the adviser, "but that-"

Rin interrupted him again. "Yes, I am THE High Commander. There are other commanders, but I am the High Commander. It is well within my power to issue an order; the commanders can veto it if they see fit."

"You are abusing the system! You know that the commanders are on recess and won't be able to vote in time."

"I am using the system in place. It's not my fault that system is flawed."

"As your adviser, I cannot allow you to do this," said Belvain, taking a firm step toward her. "I am also part of this system."

Rin pinched the bridge of her nose and moved closer to her throne to impress upon the impertinent man exactly how much power she had. Her armored boots clacked smartly against the polished marble floors, and her elegant dress swished with her movement. The large pillars were so well-polished they reflected a muted image of her as she waited the requisite amount of time for Belvain to lose his nerve.

"Rin," he said. Rin smiled; that was the gentle tone she expected. "You're under a lot of stress right now. I don't think you should make such a monumental decision without the other commanders. That's all."

"I know," said Rin. She watched the adviser in the reflection from a pillar, not turning around to face him. "I need to do this. I need to know I can do it. With my parents..." She bit her lip. It still wasn't getting easier to talk about them, but she needed to control the adviser, and bringing them up was the quickest way to shut him down. "With my parents gone I need to know I can put something right."

Belvain was silent for a moment. "I know it's hard, Rin, but I simply can't let you go through with this." He turned to the door. "Until next month, you cannot enact a single law without my signature. I intend to use that power to stop you until your commanders return from recess."

He turned down the hall and disappeared from view. Her window of opportunity was closing. If Belvain prevented her from enacting her laws during this recess, she would have to wait nearly a full year before she would have this chance again. Her forty commanders represented the regions and provinces of Galilia. They all bowed to her crown, but they were of their lands. Some would see her bill as a power grab, and the goat-lovers from the mountain towns would try to protect the satyrs. They couldn't stop her directly, but they could water down the law with addendums and limitations until it was completely toothless. Rin had to enact the law now or lose her chance. She turned to her guard.

"Kill him," she said quietly.

The guard nodded and followed the adviser out of the room. Rin turned away from the door and the guard. Belvain had been a close friend and confidant of her parents. He'd helped raise her. Why couldn't he get out of her way? Why did it have to come to this? She had to do what was right for her people; she couldn't let sentimentality for her adviser stop her.

Satyrs were vicious creatures. Only two years ago she'd cowered in fear from them as they slaughtered her parents. She knew the palace and its web of hidden passages better than anyone. When she'd heard her mother's shriek of pain, she'd raced into hiding, trusting the palace guards to rescue her parents. It was only as her parents' anguished screams continued that she realized with horror that no guards were coming. They'd been killed or bought out in advance. The attack had been well-coordinated.

Rin had listened, frozen in place, as her parents died, their cries echoing through the passageways. She heard the satyrs and the traitorous guards searching for her, and she knew it was only a matter of time before they stumbled onto her hiding place. She'd clutched the dagger her father had given her in trembling hands. As it happened, the city guard arrived before the satyrs found her, and the attackers fled.

Two years ago she'd been too weak and too frightened to act. Not anymore.

Rin withdrew to her study, a small room behind the throne. Tapestries on the walls showed scenery from across her lands and tableaux from ancient stories. Bookshelves stood between tapestries and windows, stuffed full of old leather tomes. One window looked out over gardens, which were bathed in the full moon's light. Rin had spent more time in the study than in her own quarters lately.

She pulled off her uncomfortable shoulder guards and placed them on the reading bench under the window, then sat down behind her desk. It was stacked high with paperwork, the legislation she'd worked on since her parents' death. Much of it had been written in secret. She didn't want her adviser and his goat-loving friends within the government learning of her plans and taking steps to stop her. Now was the time to strike.

The bill she'd been carefully crafting since her parents' death sat on her desk, waiting to be signed. She sat down across from the controversial pages and pulled them close. This was her revenge. She'd painstakingly penned every word. There were no loopholes or work-arounds — it was air-tight. She pulled the summary page off the top and read the title: The Satyr Removal Act. This would do it. This would ensure that she no longer had to share her lands with those disgusting goats masquerading as humans. The satyrs who had assassinated her parents would regret their actions when they had to watch their entire people get wiped out. She would secure Galilia for humans. Only humans.

Plucking the quill from its inkwell, Rin signed her bill into law with a flourish. As she watched the ink dry on the page, she smiled. She would put everything right. The satyrs would die.

Chapter 4

The real Rin blinked and stared at the wall hanging, which now displayed a still portrait of her smiling at the paperwork on her desk. What were her memories doing in a picture frame on a wall? The shock began to wear off, and Rin realized that whatever was happening, she was in trouble. A memory she'd thought had occurred in private was somehow captured and playing before her eyes. An entity that could do that was dangerous. As panic took hold, she thrashed against her restraints in earnest. She had to find the weak point in the shackles that held her to the table.

It didn't take long for Rin to run out of energy and lie there panting and tired, sweat dripping down her back and soaking her strange clothes. The manacles that held her to the table were stronger than her. The moment she stopped moving, a section of wall across the room from her opened, and a tall woman with olive skin and straight hair cropped along her jawline entered the room. She wore a strange, close-cut garment with buttons down the front.

"Is the woman on the screen you?" asked the stranger, staring at a board in her hand rather than at Rin.

Rin just stared.

The woman glanced up. "Are the translators not working?" She addressed the corner of the room. "Jason! How many times do I have to tell you? I can't do my job if the subject doesn't understand me."

There was a pause, and then a disembodied voice replied, "The translator is on and working. I think she's in shock."

Rin strained against her manacles. Was there someone else in the room?

The woman clicked her tongue. "I do not have time for this," she said. She walked to Rin's side and slammed her fist down on the table next to Rin's head, causing her to twitch violently. "Is this you or isn't it?" she demanded.

"Yes. It's me. Where am I? What's going on?" Rin was completely lost, and confusion could be deadly.

"You are a war criminal, and you're here to pay for your crimes. Would you like representation or will you be presenting your own case?" The woman held a stick above the board. Up close Rin could see that the board was emitting light, which created shadows on the stranger's face despite the brightness of the room.

"I don't know what you're talking about. Where am I? Why am I tied down?" demanded Rin. War crimes? She was definitely in trouble. She needed to get as much information from this woman as possible.

"Representation it is," the woman said, writing on the board. "Do you have any known allergies or other major health concerns our doctors should know about?"

"I will not answer another of your questions until you answer mine!"

"I'll put you down for a no. Not that I would expect anyone from your time to know what an allergy is."

"I demand an answer to my questions."

"I have everything I need. You are restrained to prevent further injury to your leg, which has been repaired — you're welcome. As to *where* you are, prison. But I think the more interesting question, which you haven't asked, is *when*. Welcome to the twenty-third century."

The woman left the room and the door slid shut behind her. The outline of it disappeared into the white expanse as if it had never been there.

Rin stared up at the ceiling. The twenty-third century? That had to be a mistake. It was the end of the sixteenth century. Was the woman saying she'd traveled seven hundred years into the future? That was impossible!

While Rin was contemplating the meaning of the woman's words, the door opened again. Rin looked up, planning to ask her more questions. Had she misspoken? Had Rin somehow been transported somewhere that measured time differently? She knew some distant lands used different calendars, but the journey to those places would take months. How had she traveled that far while unconscious?

Her questions died on her tongue. It wasn't a woman who walked through the door; this time a short bald man with pale skin entered.

"Hello Rin. I'm the doctor who fixed your leg," the man said as he approached her.

Rin watched him as closely as she could from her restrained position. A doctor. Was that why she'd been taken to this strange place? She had been severely injured. Had she somehow been knocked unconscious and transported to a place where her injury could be properly treated? The woman said they'd repaired it, but if she'd been brought here for treatment, why were they talking about war crimes?

"Let's just have a look," said the doctor, bending over Rin's leg.

Rin stiffened, preparing herself for the pain, but when he prodded her it didn't hurt at all. The doctor studied her leg, periodically tapping and scraping on a board similar to the one the previous stranger had carried. Then he straightened and stepped away from Rin.

"It looks good," he said, looking up from his board. "I think you should be ready to walk on it."

He turned toward the door.

"Wait, how did I get here? What's going on!" called Rin.

The doctor ignored her and left.

Rin dropped her head back against the table. She was frustrated. No one would answer her questions. The woman's words made no sense. What she'd said was impossible, but none of the explanations Rin could come up with could account for everything she had experienced. How had her leg been healed? How had the rectangle on the wall been able to replay a moment from her memory? Why had the woman made the absurd claim that she was seven hundred years in the future? Who was accusing her of war crimes, and what did that mean? What was going on?

A few minutes after the doctor left, there was a small pop and Rin's wrists and ankles were released. She jumped off the table and fell promptly to the floor. Her legs were weak with disuse. How long had she slept?

Sitting on the floor, she took a better look at her leg. An angry scar was all that remained of the dire injury she'd received from the satyr. A dark blotch marked the place where the poison had made contact with her skin a quarter of the way up her shin, and angry dark tendrils of scar tissue webbed up her leg towards her knee. A wound like that should have been incurable.

Shakily, Rin used the edge of the table to drag herself into a standing position. As she stood, the strength came back to her legs. She took a few tentative steps. Nothing felt tight or stiff. After the initial weakness wore off, she found she could walk easily. The injury she'd sustained from the satyr should have cost her leg, if not her life. Now she didn't even have a limp.

Rin looked around. There was nothing surprising or different on the wall that had been out of her line of sight while restrained. She crossed the room and felt the wall where the door had been. There was a crack, but it was incredibly thin, narrower than the width of a hair. Rin ran her fingers along the hairline crack, but couldn't find anything that suggested a way to open the door.

She stood where the woman had stood and looked in the direction she'd faced when she spoke to the other voice — Jason. There was no one there. Rin paced over and examined the other wall, but no matter how closely she looked, she couldn't find a seam outlining a second door or window. Where had the second voice come from?

Rin turned her attention to the only object in the room aside from the table: the black frame with moving pictures of her memories. It was still displaying her smiling face. She climbed onto the table. The room was small, and the table reached close enough to the picture frame that she could touch it from the height it provided. She felt the edge of the picture's frame, but it was embedded in the wall. A similar seam, again the width of a hair, separated the frame from the wall. Rin ran her hand along it, but couldn't get her nails behind the frame to try prying it off the wall. She brushed her fingers from one edge to the other, and to her surprise the hanging came to life.

The pictures ran in reverse, before starting to play again halfway through her memory. Curious, Rin repeated the motion. This time the picture was displaying the beginning of the memory. After one more swipe her memory shrank to a small box among many other small boxes. Rin recognized at least two dozen images of herself from various points in her life. She couldn't place each picture, but they were all familiar to her.

"What are you doing?" demanded the disembodied voice of Jason.

Rin whipped around, but the door had not been opened; there was no one else in the room.

"Who are you?" she demanded.

"Jason. I step away for a minute, and you start messing with the screen."

Rin turned back to the wall hanging. "This is a screen?"

"Yes! Stop touching it."

She looked over the newly named object. A screen. "How are you watching me?"

"The camera in the corner," said the voice.

"Camera?"

"In the corner, above the bed."

Rin looked. There was a small black spot the size of a coin nestled in the corner. She walked across the table toward it, but couldn't reach it.

"Yes, that."

Rin walked back to the screen. She frowned at the small pictures of herself, then ran her hand over the screen in the same gesture that had brought her to the gallery of small pictures. This time the image shook, but didn't change.

"I told you to leave it alone!"

There had to be more she could do with the screen. Jason from the camera wouldn't tell her not to touch it if she couldn't use it. Rin tried a different gesture — she swiped across the screen from bottom to top. The pictures raced in the direction she'd swiped. It was like spinning a wheel of images. Picture upon picture of her life spun past, too quickly. Dizzy, she placed a hand on the screen. The images stopped spinning and the squares beneath her hand turned shades of blue. Rin swiped the screen again more slowly, and the wheel spun slowly enough for her to recognize the images she was seeing. There were hundreds of images stolen from her life on this strange screen.

"Stop it!"

"What are you going to do about it, Jason of the Camera?" asked Rin, not bothering to look at the spot on her wall.

"This, you genocidal maniac," he said, and the screen went black.

Rin whipped her head around and stared at the camera. "Did you do that?"

"Yes, I have master control of the holding-cell tech."

Rin frowned. She didn't understand what he'd said, but she didn't like the idea of someone else being in master control of a holding cell she was trapped in. Well, if she couldn't use the screen, she would take advantage of the other item in her cell. The camera.

"Where am I, Jason?" she asked, addressing the spot in the corner of her cell.

"You're in hold cell 02B. Does that help you?" Rin was irritated by the smugness of his voice.

"Where is holding cell 02B?" She needed her questions answered, and getting angry would not help her situation.

"Parvada."

"Parvada?" Rin rolled the strange word around on her tongue. "What is a Parvada?"

"It's a state."

"I've never heard of this state. Who is the monarch?"

"Angela Benvia is our Head of State."

"Head of State," murmured Rin.

She'd never heard of that title. Most of Galilia's neighboring countries and territories were ruled by monarchs. Her own title of High Commander was considered unusual, too.

Rin paused to plan a new line of questioning. She'd gotten off-track with the Parvada angle. Her hopes of being able to gain freedom through negotiations had significantly diminished. She knew nothing of Parvada, but it was clear that she was not respected in this land. The next most important course of action she could pursue would be to learn about the people around her. So far, she'd only seen humans, but she'd only seen the woman and the doctor. Were satyrs involved?

They had to be. No reasonable humans would call her actions crimes. The humans she had seen must be goat-lovers.

Was she really in the future? She looked back at the screen, which had returned to the reflective black surface it had been when she woke up in the strange room. The more she learned, the more it seemed that was the only explanation, but what kind of explanation was it? It was impossible that she could be seven hundred years in the future. Her mind couldn't begin to comprehend how it had happened. But what else could explain the screen in front of her? How else had her leg been healed? The satyrs were known for their deadly poisons, but even they didn't know how to cure them. The camera. The door with the vanishingly small outline. The people in yellow armor. The way time had stopped, freezing an arrow in the air before her face. None of it made sense.

"So, Jason, why did that woman say I was in the future?" Rin asked, trying to keep her voice calm and casual, so as not to betray the panic that was building in her chest.

Rin waited for a reply, but none came.

"Jason?"

After a few more moments of silence Rin realized he must have stepped away again. She turned her attention back to the screen. If he wouldn't answer her questions, maybe she could get answers out of the screen. Her swipes did nothing to reawaken the device, but after running her fingers around the edge of it she found a button that blended in with the wall. She pressed it, and the screen reawakened, but it no longer displayed the tiles containing pictures from her life. Instead she was looking at a large picture of a cat, with squares she did not recognize hovering above it, and a large block covering much of the cat's lower half which portrayed a stylized picture of the sun and a collection of numbers.

Rin experimentally swiped her hand across the screen and the squares spun like a wheel. She used her finger to stop the wheel, but when she touched the screen, the cat was covered with a new picture. It took a moment for Rin to decipher that the new picture was a map. Clean lines denoted roads and rivers. It lacked many of the cartographic conventions Rin was familiar with, and she didn't see a legend or any notations in the margins. This map didn't have margins at all — it stretched across the screen from edge to edge. Parvada was labeled on the map, with a blue line indicating a path across it. She stared at the image. She didn't recognize any of the rivers or labeled places. Wherever Parvada was, it was far from her home. An uncomfortable feeling grew in the pit of her stomach. There were no maps like this in her time.

"What are you doing!" demanded Jason.

The screen went black again. Rin pushed the button, but it didn't turn back on.

"How did you come to be Master Controller of the holding cells?" asked Rin, turning her attention back to the camera.

The technology was foreign to her. If she was in the future, it would be difficult for her to learn how to get anything useful from the screen, but people would remain the same. She could work to get what she wanted from Jason. She was familiar with people.

"I'm good at pushing buttons," he answered.

Pushing buttons? So it was an easy job. "How many holding cells are there?"

Jason laughed. "A lot. Technically the answer to that question is a national security secret."

Rin frowned.

"Look, are you hungry?" asked Jason.

Rin snapped her attention back to the camera. Food would have to be brought by someone. The more people she met in this prison, the more chances she would have to find someone who would be sympathetic or gullible enough to help her escape, or at least answer her questions.

"Yes."

"What do ya' like?"

Rin frowned at the strange question. "Whatever's available."

"Literally anything you can ask for is available. We've got food fabricators in every cell."

Rin didn't know what he meant, but he clearly wanted her to make a request. "I'll have a game hen."

"Veggies?"

Rin frowned. Last she'd checked, it was almost winter, although her clothes suggested otherwise. Still, it was probably best to request a seasonal vegetable. "Squash."

"Game hen with a side of squash coming right up," said the voice.

Rin wondered how long it would take for her food to be prepared, but before she could ask, there was a loud whining from the wall below the camera. Startled, she moved toward the noise. Upon examination, she found another fine outline in the wall. After a few seconds the whining stopped, and a hatch popped open. Her empty cell wasn't as empty as she thought.

There was a still-sizzling game hen, steamed squash, and a glass of water sitting behind the hatch. Rin ran her hands around inside the compartment but couldn't find any more seams. Where had the food come from? She pulled the plate and food out and began eating. The hatch stayed open.

"Put the plate back when you're done," said Jason.

"Where did the food come from?" asked Rin.

There was no reply. Her noncorporal watcher was gone again. She ate in silence. The food was good, but tasted odd. There was a strange, almost burnt taste to it, despite the fact that it looked perfect. When she finished, she replaced the plate and the hatch slid shut. She stared at the closed hatch. Could she really be in the future? How else could she explain food materializing out of nothing?

"When you need to use the toilet, it's over there," said Jason.

Rin looked around. A circle glowed on the floor next to the bed. "The floor?" asked Rin. For some reason, she didn't think people seven hundred years in the future had developed fancy screens and food compartments only to revert back to doing their business on the floor.

"There are bio-disposing plates in the floor there. It will clean up after you. You'll see. I'll leave the light on so you know where it is."

Rin looked around the room. She tried to turn the screen on again, but the button no longer worked. Whatever Jason had done, he'd disabled it entirely this time. Eventually, Rin had to use the bathroom. She squatted over the circle on the floor the way she would in the forest on a long march. To her amazement, all of her waste sank through the floor and disappeared. Rin pressed her hand against the spot where it had gone. She didn't want to crawl out of this prison through a sewer, but she would if it came to that. Unfortunately, no matter how hard she pressed, her hand didn't find any give in the floor. Somehow the floor knew to let her waste through, but not her hand.

~*~

The next day, Rin was sitting on her bed, looking around for something that could help her escape. Jason had opened yet another hatch in the wall of Rin's cell, revealing a thin mattress, blanket, and pillow, which she'd been instructed to use to turn the table into a bed. It wasn't comfortable, but it was serviceable.

Jason's voice filled the cell. "Put one of your wrists in the restraint."

"What?" demanded Rin.

"I'm about to admit your legal counsel. I can't open a door unless you're restrained. I only need one hand."

"I am not putting my own hand in a manacle!"

"Then you're not going to meet your legal counsel."

Rin glared at the camera for a moment before resting her wrist above the nearest manacle. The more people she was able to meet, the more chances she had to find an ally. There was pop, and the table grabbed her hand.

The door opened and a middle-aged woman walked into the room. Her dark hair was long, pulled away from her face and twisted behind her head before falling loosely down her back. Her dark eyes were set in a round, pale face that was bent over yet another board.

"Are you former High Commander Rin Tallow?" the woman asked.

"Former?" asked Rin indignantly.

The woman rolled her eyes up to take in Rin's face. "I don't know what impression you've been given, but you are unlikely to leave this building for the rest of your life. You are, indeed, the former High Commander. Is that your name and title?"

Rin glared at the woman. "Yes, what is your name and title?"

"I am your attorney. You may refer to me as Ms. Riviera. I am going to ask you questions, which you are going to answer fully and honestly. The faster this goes, the sooner you will get out of this room."

Ms. Riviera held her board at an angle and Rin could see that it was a screen, like the one on her wall, but small and hand-held. The woman swiped down a page of text before stopping at a place where the text changed color.

"Rin Tallow, were you aware that the decree you signed into law would result in the deaths of thousands of innocent satyrs?"

Rin glared at the woman. "I wouldn't call them innocent."

"Were any trials conducted to determine the guilt or innocence of a satyr before execution?"

"No, that is a right reserved for humans."

"Were you aware that satyrs possessed human-comparable intellect?"

"Only humans possess human intellect."

"Could the average satyrs express themselves through speech and writing, form complex philosophical and creative thoughts, and empathize with others?"

"Yes, but-"

"Is this not comparable to human intellect?"

"I guess it's comparable."

"It is my duty to inform you that you have been brought here on charges of genocide. The legal definition of genocide is the purposeful, orchestrated mass murder of a population with human-level intellect, based on a common characteristic. You have been identified as the instigator and orchestrator of a large-scale genocide in the-" Ms. Riviera paused and swiped her screen. "—the years 1593 to 1596. You were assassinated, but were brought here first."

"What are you talking about?"

"Assassination? Do you know where you are?"

"Parvada?"

The woman shook her head. "Someone was supposed to brief you. You are in Hell. This is what you would perceive as the future. This is the year 2287. You were removed from your time seconds before your death. Our doctors, who possess far more advanced techniques than those in your century, repaired your injured leg. You will be held here until your trial. From your trial you will be escorted to the Pit, which comprises the lowest levels of this building. This building is called Hell. You will work there until you are too old or unwell to work; then you will be returned to your time with the requisite wounds to leave history unaltered."

Rin stared at the woman, trying to comprehend what she was being told. Hell? She was in Hell? How was that possible? She wasn't perfect, but she didn't belong in Hell! Genocide? She'd killed satyrs, not people!

"Any questions?"

"What if the trial finds me innocent?"

"It won't. We have extremely accurate history books due to our utilization of time travel. The trial is just a formality."

"Why bother with it at all, then?"

Ms. Riviera shook her head and turned toward the door. "I am not going to stand here and explain due process to you."

"Wait!" said Rin, but Ms. Riviera had already left.

The manacle holding Rin's hand released her with a pop. She rubbed her wrist and glared at the closed door. Hell. She was in Hell. She'd died, or she was supposed to have died. She remembered the arrow hanging in the air in front of her face when everything had frozen and the figures in yellow armor appeared. That must have been about to kill her. These people had stopped that and taken her from her time, for what? To punish her? For genocide? No, these were no spirits or gods or whatever things people believed could judge them after death. These were just people, and she wasn't dead yet! It was slowly sinking in that she had been taken from her time and somehow transported seven hundred years in the future, but she wouldn't stay here. These people had saved her from assassination; they'd cured the satyr's poison. She would not waste that gift. She would escape and return to her time. She would not remain in Hell.

~*~

The next day, Rin examined the cell again and found a few more seams in the wall that she hadn't noticed the first time she'd looked. The lines were impossibly thin. She asked Jason about them, but he didn't respond. She poked and prodded and tried to squeeze her nails into the cracks to pry open the hatches, but nothing worked. Eventually Rin gave up. She would have to find another way out of Hell. Maybe her trial would provide an opportunity to escape. She didn't know much about the future, but she doubted they would hold a trial in her cell.

"Thanks a lot, you mass-murderer," said Jason's voice.

Rin jumped. "Thanks for what?" she asked.

"You told her I didn't brief you!"

"You didn't."

"Doesn't mean you have to go telling people. Besides, the processing officer told you about time travel. I heard her. So did the doctor."

"They said I was in the future. They didn't explain anything," said Rin, turning to glare at the camera.

"You got me switched to Pit duty!"

"What's Pit duty?" asked Rin.

"You'll see," he said. "I'm leaving a note for my replacement. You're trouble."

"I didn't know you'd get in trouble," said Rin.

"Too late," he said, "memo sent."

"What is a memo?" asked Rin.

There was silence. "Jason?"

More silence.

Rin shook her head and turned her attention back to her cell. She was bored. She poked the screen a few times, but it didn't do anything. Standing on her bed, she tried to reach the camera, but it was too high and the bed was too far away from the wall. She climbed to the floor and tried to slide the bed closer to the wall, but it wouldn't budge. Closer examination of the feet revealed they were welded to the floor. Rin sat heavily on the bed.

She had gathered all the information her small room would provide. She mulled over what she'd learned. She was being accused of war crimes, of genocide. She tried to wrap her head around the meaning of that. The people here thought it was wrong for her to kill the satyrs, but she hadn't seen a single satyr since she got here. Why did humans care?

She looked up at the screen. It held hundreds of images from her life. She'd scrolled through the pictures; now she wished she'd looked at them more closely. They must not know what it was like back then. They must not understand why she had to do what she did. Plenty of people in her own time had also questioned her methods, but they hadn't understood either. She had kept the details of her parents' death a secret. No one knew they'd been murdered by satyrs who wanted to overthrow the reign of humans. No one could know how palace security had failed. No one could know how Rin had cowered in fear while her parents died.

She'd had to exterminate the satyrs, to make up for her weakness that night. It was the only way to ensure that what happened to her parents didn't happen to anyone else. The satyrs had started the killing; Rin would finish it. Still, the words 'war crimes' and 'genocide' filled her mind. She'd never heard of war crimes, but genocide was a term she was familiar with. Was it really possible to commit genocide against satyrs?

Chapter 5

Days passed. A woman's voice replaced Jason's, and she was even less interested in talking to Rin than Jason had been. She only spoke to bark orders. Rin asked her questions, but was ignored. She didn't even learn the woman's name. Rin kept looking for an opportunity to escape. Every time the word genocide drifted to the top of her mind, she pushed it down and buried it with a fresh round of scheming. She chased her thoughts in circles. What did she know? How could she use that information? Had she committed genocide? *No.* How could she escape? Could a human really commit genocide against satyrs? *No.* How could she get out of Hell? Rin agonized over the information she'd gathered, but she didn't have enough knowledge to devise a plan of action.

After twelve meals, Ms. Riviera returned.

"We have a court date for tomorrow," said the woman as she examined Rin's appearance. "Have you showered at all since you got here?"

Rin was about to explain that she didn't know showering was an option, but the last time she informed her legal counsel of a similar oversight, she'd lost Jason and been stuck with the less-communicative watcher in the camera. "The water here tastes strange."

"I don't care if it's laced with poison. You will shower before tomorrow's trial and sentencing. The taxpayers put a lot of money into these facilities and like to know they're being used to their fullest potential. You got that?"

"Yes," said Rin.

"Hey! Laurie!" called Ms. Riviera.

Rin quickly filed the name away.

"Yes, Ms. Riviera?" asked the woman.

"Make sure this one showers before tomorrow."

"Yes, ma'am."

Ms. Riviera left, and Rin was alone again.

"Laurie?" she asked.

"What?" snapped the woman.

"Laurie, I don't remember how to take a shower."

"Take off your clothes," Laurie growled.

Rin didn't hesitate. She had never been a self-conscious person. Her mother had blamed it on swimming in the palace garden's pond naked at far too old an age.

"Drop the clothes in the box."

A hatch opened near the floor. Rin had found the hatch while inspecting the cell, but it hadn't been opened for her before. Rin dropped her clothes in the box. The moment her hands were free of the door, it slammed shut.

"Stand on the toilet."

Rin stood on the patch of floor that felt like all the other patches of floor in the cell, but swallowed her excrement like raisins on top of bread dough. A few moments later a torrent of freezing rain poured down on her. She howled as the cold water stung her skin, and scurried out from under the cascade. Looking up, she saw that the rain came from the ceiling. A crack had opened up, and water flowed through. Rin hadn't found that seam. She wondered how many more compartments were in the ceiling. She wouldn't be able to find them. The ceiling was too high, and she wouldn't see the tiny cracks from that far away.

"Something wrong?" asked the woman.

Rin glared at the camera. "It's cold."

"Hot water costs money. No one wants to waste money on the likes of you."

"I cannot get clean if the water is that cold," Rin said. "I'm sure Ms. Riviera wants me to be clean."

There was silence.

"Try it now."

Rin took a cautious step towards the water. Drops landed on her skin. The water was still cool, but bearable. She stepped fully into the stream and allowed the temperate water to flow over her skin. A shower was just what she needed.

Without warning a thicker substance joined the water. Rin instinctively closed her eyes, but not before a drop sneaked in and stung them.

"What was that?" she demanded, clutching her eyes and racing out of the stream again.

"Soap. Get clean."

Rin scrubbed the runny soap over her skin.

"And the hair," called Laurie.

Rin obliged the voice and slathered herself with the soap. Eyes clenched shut, she followed her ears to the water and removed the suds.

"You're clean," said Laurie.

The water cut off, and yet another compartment opened. Rin had found this hatch too, but had never seen it open. Inside was a towel, which Rin used to dry herself. Beneath the towel was a folded set of clothes identical to the ones she'd taken off, along with socks and heavy-duty boots. She pulled on the clothes and socks. As she was lacing up the boots, she saw that a stretchy circle of fabric had been beneath them.

"What's this?" asked Rin, holding the circle up to the camera.

"To tie back your hair."

Rin frowned. She used pins to hold up her hair, sometimes ribbons. She'd never seen a device like this. It took her a few tries, but she managed to pull her hair back into a messy approximation of the bun she usually wore. It was nice to get her hair off her neck.

"Sit," ordered Laurie.

Rin climbed onto her bed and placed her hand in one of the manacles, curious who was coming to see her. The manacle snapped shut around her wrist. She waited. The door stayed shut. Ten minutes later she realized this was her punishment for learning Laurie's name. Rin glared up at the camera and made herself as comfortable as she could while manacled to the bed. She wasn't very successful. It wasn't long before the lights went out for the night. The manacle didn't release, and Rin got very little sleep.

~*~

When the lights came on in the morning, Rin's wrist was finally released from its restraint. She snatched back her hand and rubbed her raw skin, massaging feeling back into her wrist. The food hatch opened and Rin quickly pulled the warm plate out of the compartment, afraid Laurie would take it away if she wasn't fast enough. She ate and put her dishes away.

"Sit," said Laurie's voice.

Rin glared at the camera. Would she be restrained all day now that she'd eaten her breakfast? She considered not putting her hand in the manacle, but she didn't want to lose an opportunity to talk to her legal counsel. Against her better judgment, Rin laid her hand on the cool metal, and the ring closed around her wrist. No one entered the room, and Rin's heart sank. Then the door swung open.

"Your trial will be at ten a.m.," Ms. Riviera announced, walking into the cell. She didn't look up from her screen.

Two guards followed Ms. Riviera. The door closed behind them, and the manacle on the bed released its grip on Rin.

The guards put a box on the bed and opened it. Inside were metal rings. They looked similar to the restraints stuck on the bed, but these rings weren't attached to anything. One of the guards took Rin's hand and clasped the first ring around her wrist.

"What kind of defense will we be mounting?" Rin asked as the guards attached the rings to her wrists and ankles, pulling down her boots to get them around her socks.

"Defense?" asked the woman, glancing up from her screen. "There is no defense for what you've done. This trial is merely a formality."

Rin glared at the woman. "Isn't it your job to help me?"

"It is my job to see that justice is served," Ms. Riviera said, returning her attention to the screen in front of her.

"Stand up," ordered one of the guards, as the last ring clicked around her ankle.

Rin stood. The guard manipulated a screen, and the rings around Rin's wrists drew together as though a cord between them had been cinched closed, although there was nothing between them. Her hands were forced together in front of her. Rin yelped as the manacles on her ankles pulled together, yanking her feet inward and throwing her off-balance. She caught herself on the bed with her restrained hands. The guard chuckled at her distress. Then he changed something on the screen, and the pull between Rin's manacles reduced. Her hands were able to hang a foot apart, and her ankles were given enough room for her to walk, but the restraints were still held together by an invisible force. Rin couldn't move her hands farther apart or lift her feet high enough to run.

"We're done down here, Laurie," said one of the guards.

Rin's arms tingled with excitement as her cell door opened. Ms. Riviera left, and the guards prodded for Rin to follow. She shuffled out the door and into a stark hallway. It wasn't as bright as her cell had been. The walls, floor, and ceiling were all made of metal. There were screens along the walls, showing views from the cameras inside the cells. Rin craned her neck to see as many of the screens on the walls as she could. Every prisoner she saw was human, as were the guards she passed in the halls. Still no satyrs. Why did these humans take such a strong stance against killing satyrs? *Genocide*. No. She needed to take advantage of this opportunity. Seeing the halls outside her cell might help her devise a method of escape. She needed to get back to her time. She focused on memorizing the route they took.

The guards pulled Rin to a stop in front of a door, and Ms. Riviera pushed a button next to it. They waited, and eventually the doors slid open. Rin shuffled in with Ms. Riviera and her guards. The room was small and metal. From waist height up, the walls were reflective, and Rin saw her appearance for the first time since waking up in a prison cell. Her hair was more disheveled than she liked, but she looked alright, all things considered.

Ms. Riviera pushed another button on the inside of the room as the doors closed. Then the entire room fell. Rin stumbled back into the wall, terrified that the building was collapsing. The guards laughed at her. The attorney ignored her, not even glancing up from her screen. Rin's heart raced, but then she realized the room was supposed to fall. She forced herself to let go of the wall and stand calmly as the room plummeted downward. The guards continued to snicker, and she felt the heat of embarrassment in her ears.

After a long descent, the box came to a stop. Rin stumbled, and the guards laughed at her again. Her anger flared — in her own time, no one would dare laugh at her. But her anger was gone as quickly as it came. She wasn't in her own time. She had no power here. Guards could mock her, and she could do nothing about it. The doors opened and Rin stumbled out of the room behind Ms. Riviera. The guards followed, still chuck-ling.

"If you need to vomit, there's a can over there," said the lawyer.

Rin's face burned hotter. Her stomach was unsettled, but she didn't want to admit she needed to throw up. It would only make the guards laugh harder.

"I don't need it," she said, swallowing the bile that climbed her throat, contradicting her.

Ms. Riviera shrugged and led the entourage down the hall. Rin pushed down her nausea and looked around. They were in a new set of halls. Here the walls were a crisp white, similar to the walls in her cell. They were adorned with incredibly real-istic portraits, evenly spaced between large wooden doors. Rin didn't recognize the people in them. She wondered if they were actually screens. She'd never seen a painted portrait that was as true to life as these, but the image of her on the screen had been this realistic. All of the figures in the portraits were human. As they walked down the halls, they began to pass people. At first, those they passed just glanced at them and continued walking, but as the crowd grew thicker, people's at-tention lingered on them. The crowd parted for Ms. Riviera and the guards. Rin overheard fragments of conversation. Her name. Trial. Hell. They knew who she was. Rin was used to be-ing recognized, but she was used to that recognition coming with respect, or fear. Here it came with derision.

Ms. Riviera entered through a large wooden door, and the guards pushed Rin after her. The hall had been crowded, but it was nothing compared with the loud press of people on the other side of the door. There were hundreds of spectators in a space only big enough for half that number. They were shout-ing and talking all at once. A ripple of quiet passed through the room as Rin walked in, but then they erupted in conversation again. Rin heard her name. Insults she barely understood were shouted at her along, with others that were clearer. *Monster. Murderer. Genocide.*

A wad of paper bounced off Rin's head, and she raised her hands to protect her face. For once, she wasn't scheming. She couldn't think about escape. She couldn't even think about what they were saying. She'd had her detractors in her own time, but she had never entered a room with hundreds of people who hated her while she was powerless. She had seen crowds gathered for public executions, and these people had that same energy. They were there to see Rin bleed. How had her actions resulted in people hating her this much, seven hundred years in the future?

Rin was propelled towards the front of the room. She stumbled in her restraints, and the crowd laughed and jeered. She was vaguely aware that this room was different from the others. Rather than clean white walls and metal surfaces, here there was wood, and rugs in deep, warm colors. She was ushered through the screaming crowd, pelted with paper and other light projectiles, and delivered to a seat in the front of the room. When she sat, her manacles clung to the chair, holding her wrists to the armrests and her ankles to the legs of the chair. In front of her was a tall, imposing podium of rich oak with images of trees engraved on it. To her left was a table surrounded by people in clothes similar to Ms. Riviera's.

Ms. Riviera spoke to Rin. "This is the courtroom. You will be silent and this will be over soon. You will be sentenced to life in the Pit. I will not counter. We should be out of here in five minutes, tops."

"Why don't I get to make any counter-arguments?" demanded Rin.

"Because if you counter, they will play footage of your massacres for two hours and you will receive the same sentence as if you'd said nothing."

Rin glared at the woman, but nodded. The idea of getting out of this room as quickly as possible was more appealing than the chance to defend herself. If her own lawyer believed conviction was a foregone conclusion, Rin didn't think she stood a chance of being found innocent.

Rin cringed as a crumpled piece of paper connected with the back of her head. "Are these trials always so lively?"

"One of the papers said you planned to mount a defense. They all want to see what kind of defense you could possibly present."

Rin didn't look over her shoulder at the crowd, worried that it would rile them up even more, but she could hear them. Hundreds of people shouted their hatred at her. Rin felt very small strapped into her chair. The two guards seemed like scant protection against the throngs of people who wanted to see her suffer. Had what she'd done really merited this level of hate? *No.* They didn't understand. Rin wanted to clench her hands over her ears. She wanted to close her eyes and run. She wanted to get away, but she was tied down, on display for these people to hate.

Finally a figure came to the podium, and the crowd quieted to a low, angry murmur. The person was a man in black robes. He carried a wooden hammer in his hands.

"Let's get this over with," he said. "How are you, Ms. Riviera?"

"I'm well," she answered.

"That's good. It looks like the people are expecting a show. What are we doing here today?"

"The trial of Rin Tallow, former High Commander of Galilia."

"How do you intend to plead?" asked the judge.

"Guilty," said Ms. Riviera.

There were groans all around the courtroom in response to her answer.

"Well, that's a disappointment to our audience, but I'm glad you decided not to ruin my day's schedule. I'm still backed up from the Jackson debacle," said the judge. He turned his attention to the people sitting at the table to Rin's left. "Any rebuttal?"

One of the people stood. "No."

"Looks like we're done here," he said. "The defendant has pled guilty and will be sentenced to a lifetime in the Pit."

He banged the wooden hammer on the podium and the room exploded in swarming, shouting people. In a handful of words, Rin's fate had been sealed. Despite Ms. Riviera's remark, Rin was quite familiar with the concept of due process, and this did not feel like justice. It was a sham trial, and a waste of everyone's time.

"The next session will begin in ten minutes," shouted the judge over the clamoring crowd. "Be out of here by then."

Ms. Riviera walked over to the other desk to talk to the people seated there. To her horror, Rin was made to stand from her seat and then pushed toward the crowd. It was bad enough walking through the room when the spectators had been contained in their seats. Now her guards were trying to maneuver through them, while the people were also trying to leave the courtroom. Rin hugged close to her guards. They shoved her, and she stumbled forward. People laughed and shouted at her. She couldn't hear most of their words over the din, but she flinched as paper and pens bounced off of her. People jeered when she cringed. Her face and neck heated in humiliation. The guards pushed people who stood in their way, clearing a bubble around them, but they did nothing to stop the shouting or the objects being thrown.

Rin finally emerged into the hall, but the courtroom was exiting into the same space. Shouting voices and thrown projectiles followed her out. One person got past her guards and shoved Rin, who stumbled and would have fallen if a guard hadn't caught her by the elbow.

"Alright guys," shouted one of the guards, resting a hand on his baton. "Let's back off now. We want her to get to the Pit in one piece."

This elicited a round of cheers from the crowd. Rin felt sick to her stomach. *The Pit. Hell. Genocide.*

The guards made their way down the hall, and slowly the crowds thinned. They stopped in front of a door with the now-familiar buttons on the wall. Rin was happy to climb into the falling metal room. She didn't look at her reflection; she knew what she would see. The projectiles had knocked her hair out of place, and her face was red with embarrassment. She didn't want to see herself in this state. The guards pushed a button on the wall, the door closed and the room fell. Rin stumbled to the side, but she was prepared for the motion this time and didn't cling to the wall.

She hung her head, ignoring the guards as they talked and staring down at her manacled hands. Words spun in her head. *Genocide. Guilty. Hell. Murderer. The Pit.* She closed her eyes. No. They didn't know. They didn't understand. She hadn't had a chance to defend herself. There was no defense when a crowd was that hungry for blood. They hadn't been there, in her time.

The box fell, and Rin fought back the feeling of helplessness and fear. She hadn't managed to learn as much as she should have in the courtroom. She'd been too overwhelmed by the crowd. *Genocide.* No. She had to collect herself. She had to focus. She was going to the Pit of Hell. Escape — she had to focus on escape. She had to learn what she could, gather as much information as possible, learn what she needed to know to gain her freedom. She took several steadying breaths, preparing herself for what awaited her. She had plenty of time to center herself — the box traveled down for a long time.

Chapter 6

Eventually, the moving room slowed its decent and stopped. The guards stood, and Rin tensed. She pushed down thoughts about the trial. She stopped trying to word her defense in her head. She would never be given a chance to explain what happened; these people would always think they'd locked away a vile monster. They would never know what the satyrs did to her family. She had to focus. She had to find a way out of this place and back to her own time.

The door opened and a wall of heat rolled into the room. Rin was pushed out into a hallway that was incongruous with her experience of the future so far. Gone were the clean, crisp lines. Here the floor was some kind of stone that had no seams. The walls were paneled in wood and were showing neglect and, in a few places, rot. Metal trimmed the walls and floor, but it wasn't shining and smooth as Rin would have expected after her holding cell. It was dented and starting to rust. A short distance down the hall, half of the wall on one side gave way to a window. It was dingy and coated with a layer of soot and grime, but Rin could see out. The hall overlooked an enormous pit. The Pit was as broad as a lake, but looked far deeper. She couldn't gauge how deep it was from the hall. There were lights around the rim, and light filtered up from its depths.

Dread began to sink in as Rin was pushed down the hall. She hadn't thought about what the Pit would be like. She hadn't allowed herself to think this far ahead. She was in Hell. What would she be expected to do here? She had to escape! She had to get out of this place! She'd seen the mob in the courtroom. They hated her. They wanted to see her bleed. She was marching towards the fate that the mob had wanted for her. Only now did it sink in that she was deeply and immediately in danger. Her name and her titles would do nothing for her here. She wasn't High Commander. She was Rin, the genocidal murderer! What could she expect from people who believed that of her? This was Hell. Rin's breathing grew shallow, and her hands began to shake as panic set in. She was in Hell!

One of the guards noticed her anxiety. "Looks like the princess finally worked out what's going on."

The other guard laughed. "Let us know if you're going to faint, Your Royal Lowness."

The guards continued to make up joking titles, but their mocking comments dragged Rin out of her thought spiral. No. She was still High Commander Rin Tallow. She didn't have her armies or her authority here, but she was still the woman who had commanded a country. She was in the future, not the afterlife. She was in a worse position than she'd ever been in, but she would figure this out. She would escape. She would get home. The men next to her were idiot guards. She'd dealt with hundreds of idiots in her life, and she would survive these future idiots too. Through force of will, Rin pulled herself together. She had to focus.

At the end of the hall, the guards ushered Rin through a pair of metal doors, which opened into a decent-sized office. It was cooler in the office than it had been in the hall. Rin looked around the room, searching for any clues that might help her escape. Fear and panic lingered at the edge of her mind, and she needed to smother them with information. She didn't recognize the matte white material of the walls, and the floor was made of the same strange seamless stone as the hallway. In the center of the room was a large metal desk, with piles of papers and books surrounding a large screen. Metal drawers and brown boxes lined the walls. In front of the desk were three metal chairs, and behind the desk was a balding middle-aged man with gray hair sprouting behind his ears. His skin was a shade darker than Rin's, and he glared at her as he stood.

"Well, well, who do we have here?" he asked.

"Rin Tallow," volunteered one of the guards, "sentenced to life in the Pit."

"Life in the Pit of Hell," said the man. "Do you know what that means?"

Rin held her silence. This man had authority here, and she didn't know what words could get her into trouble. She needed to escape, and speaking before she knew her situation could make that objective more difficult. She'd already learned the unexpected consequences her words could have when she got Jason in trouble and had been stuck with Laurie.

"That means a life of hard labor. The better behaved you are, the longer you'll be with us. Some of the jobs are harder than others." The man started to pace, and his welcoming speech began in earnest. "Everyone here comes in with a clean slate and starts at the top of the Pit. This is good for you in particular. If we were organized by severeness of crime, you'd probably start in the Deep Pit. Your sentence would last a week if that were the case." He chuckled.

"I am the head warden of this prison. You will not see me again unless you're in trouble. You do not want to see me again. You will interact directly with your block warden." He paused and glanced at the screen on his desk. "Your block warden is Jason, who just came back down from the Tower."

Rin blinked. The Jason she'd gotten in trouble?

"Any questions?" asked the head warden. His tone suggested a question was a bad idea.

"No," said Rin.

"Here you'll address any non-inmate as sir," he snapped.

Rin swallowed down what remained of her pride. "No, sir," she said.

"Take her to block 207." He waved a hand in dismissal.

Her guards hurried her out of the office through a side door. They entered another hallway, similar to the one that had led from the moving room to the head warden's office: dingy stone floors with wood-paneled walls, and a window looking out over the Pit. The heat came back when they left the office. As they walked, they passed metal doors on the opposite wall to the window overlooking the Pit. Above the doors were numbers, ascending from Block 001. At the end of the hall the guard led her down two flights of stairs and stopped her in front of a pair of doors marked Block 207.

They walked into another office with cool air, much smaller than the one they'd left. Rin was told to sit in a chair in front of the desk. Her manacles clung to the chair as they had in the courtroom. Her escorts left, and Rin looked around, trying to drink in every detail while she could. This room had a smaller desk, which was made of a similar metal to the one in the previous office. There were more metal drawers and cabinets lining the walls, and more brown boxes. There was paperwork everywhere and another large screen on the desk. From where she was restrained, Rin couldn't see the screen or read any of the documents. If Jason was new here, he'd either made a quick mess of the office, or inherited a mess from his predecessor.

A door opened behind her. "It's you," said a familiar voice.

Rin looked over her shoulder. The voice matched the Jason she'd gotten in trouble. Now she could put a face to it. He was tall, with tan skin and black hair cut short.

"Jason, from the camera?" asked Rin.

He glared at her. "It's Jason, the block warden now. Do you know how long it took me to get that job? All I had to do was push buttons! Then you had to go and get me reassigned down here."

Rin held her silence.

"This is just like the head warden," Jason grumbled as he sat down behind his desk, across from Rin.

He swiped his screen a few times, his eyes moving as he read. Then he looked back up at Rin. "You're number four in cell C. You'll have a bunk and a locker. The locker is already full of the supplies you'll need: clothes, soap, toothbrush, that sort of thing. You get one day off each week. Since you're coming down on a Wednesday and you won't have time to get to work today, I'm putting you on the Wednesday break schedule. Laundry day is Friday. You must have your clothes in the hamper by Friday if you want clean clothes delivered on Monday. Any questions?"

Rin felt much more comfortable asking questions here than with the head warden. "What is the Pit? What am I supposed to be doing here?"

Jason sighed. "Someone was supposed to explain this to you, but are they going to end up down here? No."

Rin waited.

"The Pit is a forced-labor prison specifically for time prisoners. This cell block digs up ore and sends it down the Pit." Jason wheeled his chair away from his desk, rifled through one of the metal cabinets, then wheeled back. He held up a chalky black rock, which shimmered as it moved in the light. "This is ore." He held up a pickaxe and pointed to a meter on the handle of the axe. "This is what you'll use to dig up the ore. When you dig ore, this meter will fill. You are expected to fill it every day."

"I don't know how to mine," she said. Galilia's mountains were rich in mineral wealth, and Rin was adept at trading the yield from the mines. She'd even visited them when her campaigns brought her to the region, but she had no knowledge of how the actual mining was done.

"Lucky for you, you have the rest of your miserable life to learn."

Jason stood and put away the ore and pickaxe. Rin's restraints were released from her chair. She stood also. "Come with me."

Rin followed Jason through a metal door. They walked into a room with similar gray stone flooring and matte white walls. There were two metal-framed bunk beds, four metal closets, and four desks.

"Welcome to your new home. If you're lucky, this will be your home for the rest of your life. Trust me, you do not want to be sent deeper into the Pit, and that is the only way you move out of here."

Jason shut the door behind them. When the door closed, Rin's manacles loosened. They no longer pulled towards each other, and hung slack on her wrists and ankles. She spun one around her wrist.

"You will wear those at all times. When you're not in a restricted area, they'll be loose. You should be able to fit cloth under them if they irritate you," said Jason, noticing Rin examining her restraints.

She nodded.

Jason pointed at a number plate attached to one of the top bunks. "Like I said, you're number four. Anything that you can use is marked with your number."

Rin looked around. The closets each had a number, and so did the desks.

"There's a toilet and shower through there," said Jason, gesturing to a door. He pointed at another door. "And that's the common room. You eat in there. Through the common room is the entrance to the Pit. You won't go out to the Pit until tomorrow. I have office hours, but usually my office is off-limits. I monitor these spaces, so I'll know if you're looking for me."

"Camera?" asked Rin.

"You catch on quick for a genocidal maniac," Jason said. "You'll be awakened at exactly five a.m. and escorted to the Pit by a guard tomorrow morning. Don't give the guards trouble, or you'll be in trouble. Understand?"

"Yes."

"Good," said Jason.

He turned and walked back through the door to his office. Rin's cuffs tightened when he opened the door, then loosened again when he shut it behind him. She was alone, in Hell. Despite her desperate attempts to tamp down her fear, Rin felt a trickle of sweat roll down her back which had nothing to do with the heat.

Chapter 7

The panic began to well up in Rin again. She was in Hell. Her hands shook. She had been convicted of genocide and sent to Hell. *Genocide. Guilty.* No! No. No. She would escape. They didn't understand. She didn't understand. She hadn't gotten a good look at the people in the courtroom, but she hadn't seen a single satyr in the angry crowd. Why did so many humans care so much about satyrs, and yet there weren't any satyrs among them? Rin stilled her trembling hands. Reliving the trial was useless. It was over. She was in the Pit now. It didn't matter why she was here. All that mattered was that she would escape, and to escape she needed information.

Being alone was a good thing. She could explore her surroundings before the rest of her cellmates got back. She walked over to the locker with her number on it. When she grasped the handle, there was a flash of blue light under her fingers before it opened. Inside the locker were the things Jason had promised. Clothes, towels, soap, and other bathroom essentials. Rin shut the locker and tried to open the one marked 'three.' There was a flash of red light around her fingers, and the locker refused to open. Good, there was a lock. The handle seemed to know who she was by her touch.

She walked over to the desk with her number. It had a drawer, which also glowed blue before she could open it. Inside the drawer was a pad of paper and some pencils and pens. On top of the desk was a screen. Curiously, Rin experimented with swiping and tapping it. She figured out that each little picture opened a new window. The screen could have kept her busy all day, but she wanted to explore the rest of the rooms before the other residents of her cell returned. Moving kept the fear at bay. Moving made her feel like she was doing something. She would have plenty of time to explore the screen later.

Rin opened the door to the common room. The handle glowed blue. The common room had the now-familiar gray stone floors and white matte walls. The space was split into two distinct areas. Directly in front of Rin's cell door was a long metal table with metal chairs. She assumed that was where food would be eaten. On the other side of the table, a metal rectangle was embedded in the wall. It looked like a window, closed with a metal plate. Rin tried to open the window, but it wouldn't move. There was a screen on the opposite wall, with a worn sofa and three worn chairs facing it, and a cabinet beside it.

She opened the cabinet with the familiar blue glow under her fingers, and found an assortment of games within. She poked through them for a pack of cards, but didn't find one. Closing the cabinet, she turned her attention to the other four doors in the room. Two of them had letters above the door: A and B.

She tried one, and it glowed red, denying her access. She had expected as much. People weren't allowed in cells unless they lived there. A heavy metal door on the other side of the room also glowed red when she tried to open it. She suspected it led to the Pit. An unmarked door glowed blue, but it was only a closet containing cleaning supplies.

Rin returned to her cell and explored the bathroom. There were four toilets, which looked like a more compact version of the latrines she was used to. That was a relief; she didn't enjoy crouching over the floor to relieve herself. There were two showers and two sinks. Everything seemed to operate with levers and knobs, unlike the shower in the holding cell, which had been operated entirely by a second party. With a little experimentation, she figured out how they all worked.

Rin settled in the chair in front of her desk. She was feeling better, having gotten a read on her surroundings, but fear still threatened to close a fist on her chest. She was in Hell, accused of genocide.

It wasn't the first time the accusation had been made. Rin remembered a particular mountain town early in her campaign to exterminate the satyrs. The town was often cut off from the rest of Galilia by particularly harsh winters and a ridge of steep mountains. It was accessible in the summer months, but not outside that brief window of warm weather. The town had a large satyr population, but despite her monetary incentives, they didn't send any horns or hooves to her palace.

Mountain towns in Galilia tended to be lawless places, often pushing the bounds of Galilian control, so when the passes cleared in the summer, Rin took her battalion to the mountains to determine why the region had failed to kill any satyrs. When they arrived, they found the human inhabitants of the town hostile toward Rin and her command. They had called the satyrs their neighbors and hid them. They had accused Rin of genocide, too.

It didn't take long for her soldiers to round up the hidden satyrs and dispatch them. Any humans in the town who put up too much resistance shared the fate of their neighbors. The bodies were left in the streets, as a reminder of Galilia's might. No one from the mountain towns openly accused Rin of genocide again. Periodically, she sent a battalion to those towns, to ensure no satyrs were being harbored and quell any dissent in the unruly region.

Rin focused on the present. There was no more use dredging up memories of old campaigns than there was in dwelling on her trial; both were in the past. She needed to focus on her present, and plan for her future. She pushed aside her fear and began experimenting with the screen on her desk. Tapping pictures opened them, and she figured out that she could pinch the screens to close them. She wasn't sitting behind her desk long, however, before there was a commotion in the common room. Voices. Her cellmates were back from their day's work. Fresh fear washed over her. She was in Hell. What kind of cellmates would she have in here? Her hands shook as she walked towards the door to the common room. Taking a deep breath, she forced them to still before opening the door to meet her fellow denizens of Hell.

There were eleven tired-looking, grime-covered people waiting in front of the metal window. Men and women with a variety of skin and hair colors, all of them human. The youngest among them looked to be in their teens, and the oldest had white hair. They were all wearing clothes identical to Rin's: baggy shirts with V-necks and short pants. Rin crossed the room and took her place at the end of the line.

Jason walked into the room through the door marked 'B.' He had a small screen in his hands, similar to the one Ms. Riviera had used. All the inmates looked up at him.

"Everyone, Rin," he said, pointing to her. Rin held her chin high as every eye in the room flickered to her before turning back to Jason.

"What happened to Hugo?"

"Moved down for stealing meds out of the clinic," answered Jason. "Anyone know who they were for?"

Silence.

"I thought not. I'm supposed to offer you an extra day off each week for a month in return for information."

He paused, but no one took him up on the offer.

"Whatever," he said. "My office is open for the next two hours."

With that he walked back out through the door that led to his office. A few seconds after Jason left, the metal window slid open. The line moved past the window quickly, and Rin discovered it was a food fabricator. It was like the one she'd had in her holding cell, but large enough to create enough warm food for twelve people instead of one.

When Rin had collected her plate, piled high with unfamiliar food, she turned to the table. There was one seat empty near the end. She settled into it.

"When are you from?" asked an older man sitting next to her. He had olive skin, gray hair, and a scrawny frame.

Rin's heart raced at being addressed by one of her fellow prisoners, but she needed information. She had to talk to these people to get that information. "1593. You?"

"I'm told I died in what is now called 43 First Era."

Rin coughed on her bite of food. She'd thought she was far from her time — this man was born over a thousand years before her! Rin took a drink of water to clear her throat.

"The name's Gaius. You can call me Gai."

"What cell are you in?" asked a woman from across the table.

"C," she answered.

"In Hugo's bunk, duh," said another inmate, farther down.

"That's our cell," said Gai. He pointed to the end of the table. "With Cleo and Charlotte."

Two women glanced down the table. One woman was younger than Rin, early twenties, with curly black hair and dark skin that Rin associated with foreigners who had traveled a long way; traders and dignitaries. The other woman was Rin's age or slightly older. She had pale skin, fairer than Rin's, and thin brown hair.

"Cleo is from 2063, both of our futures, and Charlotte's from your time actually."

Rin looked down the table again. She didn't recognize either of the women he had pointed out and couldn't guess which one was from her time and which was from the future.

Rin tucked into her warm food. She wasn't hungry; the stomach-flipping rides in the moving rooms and the nerve-wracking ordeal of her trial and sentencing had combined to kill her appetite. The fervor with which the other inmates ate, however, left her wondering how often food was made available. She made sure to eat every last crumb, for fear that she wouldn't be able to eat again for a while.

Rin carried her plate back to the window and placed it on a pile of dishes. She turned nervously to see what the other inmates were doing. The screen on the wall was displaying a talking, moving picture, like the screen in her holding cell had done. The seating area in front of the screen was full, so Rin turned towards the door marked C. The handle glowed blue, and she passed into the room only accessible to her, Gai, Cleo, and Charlotte.

Rin slumped into the chair in front of her desk. Her eyelids were heavy after the night of poor sleep before her trial, but she didn't want to climb into her bunk yet. She wanted to watch her cellmates. What did they do before bed? Was there something she should be doing?

"Have you figured out how to use that yet?" asked Gai, nodding toward the screen on Rin's desk.

"I understand the basic idea," Rin answered, flicking the screen and sending the small pictures spinning.

Gai collapsed on the bunk below hers. His number was two. He fell asleep immediately, without showering or changing his clothes. Rin turned her attention back to the screen. She tapped a square. It was a calendar. The highlighter that encircled the date amazed her. May 19th, 2287. She would be celebrating her 724th birthday in two months. She swiped the screen experimentally, and the calendar flipped to the next month. She swiped again and tapped her birth date. A new screen opened and asked her about the day's event. Rin filled out the information about her birthday and saved it. She pinched the calendar closed and committed the square to memory. She tapped another square. A white bar appeared on an off-white background. She tapped the bar, and a collection of letters appeared below it. She tapped a letter, and it appeared in the bar. She typed the word 'hello,' but nothing happened.

The cell door opened, and the younger woman Gai had indicated walked in. She looked over Rin's shoulder as she peeled her clothes off.

"You have to send the search," she said.

Rin looked back at her screen. Nothing said 'send.'

"With the magnifying glass."

Rin saw a small icon next to the white bar. She tapped it. The screen blinked, and a list of things related to the word 'hello' appeared.

"You can ask it questions and it'll answer them, but be careful. The block warden can see everything you do on that screen. So don't do anything he might take issue with."

Rin pinched out of the question screen and remembered its picture as well.

"Are you Cleo?" she asked, turning to speak with the half-naked woman. She sounded like she knew what she was talking about, so Rin suspected she was the one from her future.

"Yes, nice to meet you."

How had she earned a place in Hell, and how long had she been here?

"You're one of the satyr nuts, aren't you?" asked Cleo.

Rin frowned. "What?"

"You went mad and tried to kill all the satyrs. You were in my history books," said Cleo.

Rin felt a trickle of dread. These people had more information about her than she had about them.

"It didn't work. There were still satyrs around in my time, although not many lived in Mniotia, where I'm from. There don't seem to be any here, though," said Cleo.

Rin frowned. "There aren't any satyrs here? In Hell?"

"No satyrs in Hell or anywhere in this time. They're extinct this far in the future, so I guess you won eventually."

Rin filed that piece of information away for later. "You know why they brought me here. Why did they decide you should be in Hell?"

"I killed a bunch of people in my quest for power," answered Cleo.

Rin's eyes widened in surprise at her blunt answer.

Cleo laughed at her reaction. "In my time Mniotia had been suffering from political unrest for decades. I always thought I was very clever. School came easily to me, and I could see patterns and connections that other people missed. I was fascinated by politics. Mniotia's stability was so fragile. I could see the strings I could pull to bring it all tumbling down. When I was thirteen, I thought it would be fun to rule the region. I pulled on those strings and everything crumbled as I expected, allowing me to step into the vacuum of power. Millions died, but I got what I wanted. Eventually it all caught up with me, and I was assassinated just before my fifteenth birthday."

Rin blinked. That was incredibly young. There had been a child monarch on the throne of a nearby kingdom in Rin's time, but he had been controlled by his regents. Rin hadn't been allowed complete freedom to rule on her own when she'd taken power, and she had been twenty-four.

A thought struck Rin as she tried to envision the politics of a completely foreign land. "I've never even heard of Mniotia; it must be far away from Galilia. How are we speaking the same language? You don't have an accent or anything."

Cleo grinned. "You noticed? There's a translator. You've got a chip in your head. We all do," she tapped her forehead. "I get the impression that they're popular in this time. The chip translates language, written and spoken, for you. In reality everyone is speaking different languages — you, me, even the guards."

"You know a lot about this time. How long have you been here?" asked Rin.

"Sixteen years now, in this very cell."

Rin's jaw dropped. "I thought you said you were killed when you were fifteen."

"Fourteen," corrected Cleo. "It was before my birthday. Yes, I've lived longer in this time than I did in my own."

"You don't look thirty years old!" She looked to be in her early twenties, maybe twenty-five at the oldest.

"No, it's something to do with the Pit. No one ages right here, even the guards. We all grow older, but at a much slower rate. Time locals like that. It means we get to suffer longer in Hell before we actually die."

"If they put us back in the time we were taken from, how will they explain that you died a child, but were buried as an old woman?"

"They can fix up our bodies to look whatever age they want. For your time, it's pretty easy. With me, the forensic science will be harder for them to fool, but we're far enough in the future that they can trick the people of my time, too."

Rin was still digesting what she'd learned when Charlotte entered the room. She didn't even glance at Rin, just walked to her locker, grabbed an armful of clothes and her towel, and went to the bathroom.

Cleo sank into the chair behind her own desk. "You should get some sleep. It's an early start in the morning."

"You don't need sleep?" asked Rin.

Cleo grinned. "Tomorrow is my off day. I get to sleep in."

Rin tapped a few more of the pictures on her screen, but her heavy eyes begged her to take Cleo's advice. She'd learned a lot about Cleo and a little about Gai, and she could use the question box on her screen to learn more about them later. It was time to get some rest.

Chapter 8

Bright lights woke Rin abruptly. Her bleary and confused brain forced off sleep and she quickly sat up. Her head slammed into the ceiling, forcing her back onto her elbows. Clutching her throbbing head, she slid out of bed.

After she finished in the restroom, Rin shuffled into the common room. The food fabricator window was open, but there was no line. Several people lounged around the room with food. Rin stepped up to the window and took a bowl of warm porridge. She sank into the chair she'd been left with the night before and ate her breakfast.

Before she finished eating, the door to the Pit opened. Heat flooded the common room as two uniformed guards entered.

"Rin," said one, looking at a screen in her hands.

Rin stood. Fear stirred in her chest, but she forced it down. Instead, she focused on the opportunity to learn what was beyond the doors.

"This way."

Rin snuck a glance over her shoulder as she followed the guards. None of the other inmates were watching her; no eyes followed her out the door with curiosity. Good. That meant that wherever she was going, it was normal for this place.

The heavy doors swung shut behind her. She was standing at the edge of the Pit. A great expanse yawned open in front of her, heat rolling up from its depths. She couldn't see the bottom of it. Sweat pricked her temples.

The Pit was a quarry. There was infrastructure built along the Wall, reminiscent of what Rin had seen when visiting mines in her own time. Metal chutes clung to the stone walls. Terraces were carved in rings, receding into the black depths. Stairs connected the terraces, and on the outer edges there were tracks with beat-up metal carts.

"Work groups are organized by cell blocks. Your group works in this area," said the guard, leading Rin to a point at the edge of the quarry.

She handed Rin a pickaxe identical to the one Jason had shown her in his office. It was heavier than it looked, and Rin's arms strained to hold it.

"Get to work."

Rin glanced at the stairs, but before she could move towards them, the guard kicked her in the back. She tumbled down the slope, frantically clawing at the wall with the pickaxe, terrified of falling all the way down to the unseen bottom of the Pit. At the same time, she struggled not to cut herself with the sharp pickaxe. The terrace was wider than Rin had guessed, and her downward motion was stopped by the tracks that held the metal carts. Rin shakily pushed herself to her feet. She looked over the edge and felt woozy. There was a lot farther to fall.

"Dig!" shouted one of the guards from the rim of the Pit. "And put the ore in the cart."

Rin looked at the wall in front of her. The brown-and-gray stone was striped with shimmering black veins. The black veins looked like the black rock Jason had shown her. She looked down at the heavy pickaxe in her hands. She'd never used a tool like this before. She knew how to use a sword and a dagger, and had a passing ability with a bow, but she had never been trained with tools like a pickaxe or a spade.

"Don't make us come down there!" shouted a guard.

Rin glanced over the edge of the ledge. She could see another terrace below her, but it looked like a long distance to be kicked. She turned back to the wall and lifted the pickaxe above her head, her elbows trembling with the weight. She brought the sharp implement down on the wall. It bounced off the stones, dislodging a shower of pebbles, none black and shimmering. Rin hoisted the pick again and brought it down. Nothing black came loose. The third time, the axe bounced off the black lump she'd been aiming for and slammed into her leg, taking it out from under her. Rin cried out in pain as she fell to the ground.

She pushed herself up, hissing in pain, and sat with her back to the wall. She examined her leg. It was the same leg that already bore the web of scarring from the satyr's poison. Now it also had a long gash above the older scar. Fortunately, Rin hadn't managed to put a lot of force into her swing, so the cut didn't go too deep, but it was still bleeding a lot. The dirt on the ground mingled with her blood and resulted in a sticky mess. Remembering the pile of socks in her locker, Rin kicked off her boot and pulled off a sock. She tied it around her wound and pulled the boot back onto her foot.

"Why aren't you working, inmate?" demanded a guard.

Rin didn't say anything. She pushed herself to her feet, ignored the stinging pain in her leg, and lifted the axe again. A few swings later, the rest of her cell block descended from the rim. More practiced than Rin, they slid down the slope gracefully. Some walked down the incline and settled into the work. Those who were friends chatted quietly. Too much talking attracted a shouted reprimand and threat of punishment from the guards, but their quiet murmuring was largely ignored.

There was a ten-foot radius of isolation around Rin. She ignored this and lifted the axe again. This time it ricocheted out of her hands, making a solid gonging noise as it collided with the cart. The people near her inched farther away. Thoroughly embarrassed, Rin limped over to her axe and dragged it back to her place at the Wall. She tried to dig her fingers around the shimmering black protrusion, but it was still embedded in rock.

"Having trouble?" asked Gai, coming up next to her.

"I'm a bit new at this."

He laughed. "You shouldn't lift the pickaxe so high until you get used to using it. Hold it here, near the middle of the handle, for now. Try it like this."

He lifted his pickaxe to his shoulder. Rin mimicked his action, moving her hands farther up the handle of the pickaxe.

"Focus on the rock, and swing."

Rin did as he said, and hit the rock. It wasn't enough to dislodge the ore completely, but it was loosened and Rin's blow had landed where she intended.

"There you go. In a few days you can try the over-the-head thing again. Holding the axe near the base and lifting it higher gives you more power, and it's faster, but you won't lose control and take out your own leg this way." He glanced at the blood soaking through the sock around Rin's shin and dripping down her leg.

"Thanks," she said.

"No problem." He stepped a good eight feet away. "If you don't mind though, I'm going to work out of your range."

Rin's face heated with embarrassment as she returned to her work. She focused on a rock and swung again, and again, and again. Finally, her blow knocked it free of the wall. Her axe glowed green as the rock skittered to her feet. Victoriously, Rin grabbed a piece of ore the size of her two hands clasped together and chucked it into the cart. A trickle of green seeped into the meter on her axe. The bar went from the handle to the head of the tool, and a sick feeling settled in her stomach when she realized how little it had filled. After all that work, she had only earned a small fragment of color. Jason had said she was supposed to fill the meter every day. How was that possible? She focused on the next lump of black. After four strokes and a few barely controlled ricochets, it came loose and slid to her feet.

Shaking and exhausted, she threw the rock into the cart. Using the axe to support her weight, Rin hunched over to catch her breath. Sweat was pouring off her body, and the green bar on her axe had barely filled with the second rock. She looked around. Her fellow inmates were steadily hammering away at the wall. One of the men, from a cell she hadn't met yet, paused and kicked the gray-and-brown rubble into a chute behind him. Rin looked over her shoulder; there was a chute near her as well.

"Inmate! Get back to work!"

Rin looked up — the guard was talking to her. She kicked the rubble at her feet into the chute behind her to buy a few more moments of rest for her already tired arms.

She raised the heavy axe to her shoulder and swung. Lift, swing. Lift, swing, slip. Rin staggered as the axe wrenched her shoulder and dragged her to the ground. She attacked the wall again, knocking loose yet another small, shimmering black rock, which her axe acknowledged. She gasped for breath, leaning over her axe for support. Before the guards could yell at her, Rin kicked the rubble into a chute and attacked the wall yet again.

Hours later, pouring sweat and limp with exertion, she nearly fainted with relief when a bell sounded and the other inmates stopped working. They climbed the slope, and Rin followed. At the top of the slope, they each presented their axe to a guard. Rin fell into her place at the end of the line.

When Rin reached the guard, she handed over her axe. The guard held it up to the screen in her hands. Where the others had dinged with a green glow, Rin's axe gave out a heart-sinking beep and flashed red.

"Not enough for a break. Back to work," ordered the guard, shoving the tool back into Rin's hands.

Rin wrapped her arms around the axe as the guard's shove threatened to send her off-balance and cause her to stumble over the edge of the ledge. The guard let go of the axe and gave her another push. Rin slid down the slope with barely enough awareness to hold the axe away from her face. She slumped into a pile as she slid to a stop on the terrace. She didn't have the energy to push herself to her feet.

"Don't make me come down there, inmate."

Rin tried to stand, but the gash in her leg from the morning had opened again, and the sock bandage had slid to her ankle. She physically couldn't stand. The guard was making her way to the stairs. Rin struggled to find her feet again, but her injured leg gave out. On one knee and supported by her axe, she looked up at the guard standing over her.

"I said back to work!"

The guard kicked Rin, and the little ground she had gained towards standing was lost. She fell away from her pickaxe and landed in a pile near the chute. She fought again to stand. She didn't want to be kicked down to the next terrace, far below. She managed to make it to her knees before the guard kicked her again, hard. Rin collided with the chute behind her. Her head cracked against the metal, and she lost consciousness.

~*~

Rin opened her eyes and was assaulted by bright lights. Groaning, she tried to shield her eyes, but her arms and legs were restrained. Where was she? What had happened? Had she fallen off her horse? That would be embarrassing. No. It wasn't a horse. Hell. She was in Hell. Her still-woozy mind drifted off to imagine the guards on horses patrolling the rim of the Pit. No horses in Hell.

A dark silhouette moved into Rin's field of vision. Squinting, she made out Jason's face.

"How are you doing in here?" he asked, towering over her.

Rin couldn't form words, so she just grunted in pain.

"You seem to have managed to make nearly half your quota. I'm here to decide if that's enough to avoid losing a strike."

Rin tried to marshal her cognitive abilities, pushing aside the idea of horses in Hell. Something important was happening. What was a strike?

"Well, what do you have to say for yourself?"

"I don-" Rin said, trying and failing to speak.

"Looks like they cracked her pretty hard," said Jason, turning to someone else in the room.

"She'd already lost some blood, but yes, it was quite a blow to the head."

"Will she be good to go for tomorrow?"

"Yes, but she's not clear for today. The treatment should take hold soon. The concussion is already fading."

"What do you think?" asked Jason.

"Doesn't sound like she was trying to pull anything. She actually did better than most on her first day in the Pit."

Jason looked down at the screen in his hand. What had he said? What was a strike? Rin tried to find her tongue to ask, but her jostled mind couldn't pull off the feat.

Looking up from his screen, Jason said, "So, I've decided not to take a strike, but I wouldn't get used to it if I were you."

Rin's mind slowly cleared. "What's a strike?" she asked. Her words slurred like a drunk's, but she'd managed to speak.

"Strikes are how we manage misconduct in the Pit. Every inmate starts with three strikes. If you lose all your strikes, you're sent deeper into the Pit." He paused. "You don't want to be sent down, trust me. You're replacing Hugo; he lost his final two strikes for trying to steal from this room. Most of the people in your cell have behaved and have been here a while."

Rin frowned.

Jason continued, "Most minor infringements, like not reaching your quota, are worth one strike. A strike can be earned back by achieving a double quota. A lot of the prisoners in my block have a healthy buffer. The more strikes you earn, the more strikes you have to lose before being sent down."

Rin struggled to wrap her head around the idea of filling the bar on her axe, much less doubling it. "But I didn't lose a strike today?"

"No. Sounds like you were trying to reach quota, and I tend to be more lenient in the first week."

The restraints holding Rin's hands and feet to the table released, and she sat up. The manacles were still snug around her wrists and ankles, the way they were in Jason's office, but they didn't draw together as they had when she walked through the halls to her trial.

"This way," said Jason.

Rin slid off the table. She was in a room with sleek metal floors, and metal walls lined with counters and cabinets. Rin knew she should be looking for a way to escape now that she was outside of the cell block, but she was still fuzzy from the blow she'd received to her head. For a moment, she allowed herself a break from planning her escape and just followed Jason with her head down. He led her out of the clinic and into the familiar hallway of wood-paneled walls, strange stone floors, and windows looking out over the Pit.

She was in Hell. The Pit was her punishment for committing genocide, for killing the satyrs. Were they right? Were the things she'd done that terrible? She had wanted to wipe out the satyrs. She rubbed her hand along her arm. Was that genocide? They weren't human, but were they close enough? Had she done a terrible thing? She felt an emotion welling up inside her which she hadn't felt amid the fear and panic; something much worse. Something she didn't want to name, but couldn't ignore: guilt. Dread that she was wrong. That she was the monster the people said she was. No. No. They didn't understand. They didn't know about her parents. They didn't know what it was like to watch people starve while half-goats ate their fill. She'd done what was necessary.

She pushed back against the guilt. She had to get it under control before it overwhelmed her. These people didn't understand. She had to get out of here. She had to escape.

Jason led Rin into his office. He stopped in front of the door marked C.

"You're not going on the Wall for the rest of the day, but you're going back out tomorrow," he said.

Rin nodded.

Jason opened the door and she walked through. As it closed behind her, her manacles relaxed.

Cleo was lounging in her bed with a book. She looked up when Rin walked in and smiled. "Didn't make it through your first day?"

"No," Rin said, holding a hand to her head. It still hurt.

"You look terrible."

Rin went to her locker, where a mirror on the door allowed her to observe her reflection. She did look terrible. Half of her hair had fallen out of her bun and hung loose around her shoulders. Her clothes were smeared with blood and dirt. She frowned. She didn't look as bad as she knew she should. There had been a gash in her leg — the blood staining her shorts and socks was evidence of that — but the cut was gone. As were the bruises she should have received when the guard kicked her around.

"What's wrong?" asked Cleo.

"Nothing," said Rin. "It's just that I took a chunk out of my leg with the pickaxe, but it isn't even bruised now. My clothes are covered in blood, though."

"They fixed you up."

"What do you mean?"

"The doctors here can completely heal almost anything."

"I still feel sore, and my hands are blistered. They only healed the cut and the bruises." Rin looked at her tattered hands.

"It wouldn't do you any good if they healed your aches and blisters. You need to build up muscle and calluses to do this work. You won't get any stronger if you're being healed too much. Besides, you shouldn't expect any kindness from the guards, or any time locals."

"What do you mean?"

"Time locals? The people from this time period. You were brought here because history saw you as one of the greatest evildoers in human history; we were all brought here for that reason. They were taught how evil you were their entire lives, and now you're here."

"If everyone here is evil, why are they focusing on me?"

"You're new. We all got it especially bad when we were new. They'll get used to you soon, and you'll stop being the evil person from their history books and become the annoying inmate from work. Then they'll loosen up."

Rin shook her head and closed her locker door. Cleo went back to her book, and Rin sank into the chair in front of her desk. She rested her elbows on her desk, then dropped her head into her hands. She was overwhelmed. Fear and guilt stood ready to wash over her, and she could only hold them back with the effort she spent planning her escape. She shouldn't have to explain herself to these people. Who were they to judge her? They didn't know what it was like in her time.

Rin jumped at the sound of the door opening on the other side of the common room, and then the chatter of voices.

Cleo stretched and stood, leaving her book on her bed. "The others are back. Time for dinner."

Rin stood from her desk and followed Cleo into the common room. She was tired and emotionally drained, but she needed to eat.

Chapter 9

Rin's pickaxe slammed into the wall, sending shockwaves up her arms. She struggled to hold onto it, and slammed it into the wall again. Her muscles still ached from the previous days working on the Wall, and her hands burned from the blisters. There was a thunk, and Rin looked up. Cleo was next to her, pickaxe on the ground, leaning against the rock.

"It's considered dangerous to dig too close to me," Rin warned.

Cleo shrugged. "I'll take my chances."

Rin glanced away from the wall toward Cleo and was shocked to see she had pulled off her shirt and was wrapping it around her hands. She stood in her short pants and the chest-wrapping Rin had been informed was called a sports bra.

Cleo laughed at Rin's expression. "My shirt does a lot more good protecting my hands than it would if I was wearing it. It's not like I need it to keep out the cold."

"I think we're supposed to keep our clothes on."

Cleo shrugged and swung her pickaxe into the wall. "If they wanted me to keep my shirt on, they would have given me gloves. Besides, going shirtless is much less taboo in my time than it was in the past."

Rin's eyes lingered on Cleo's taut muscles as she settled into the rhythm of her work. Sweat made her dark skin shine.

"Inmate, back to work!" a guard barked at Rin.

Rin jumped at being caught gawking. Cleo glanced over and grinned at her. Rin hoisted her pickaxe and swung it into the wall to cover the heat rising to her cheeks.

"How are you liking the future?" asked Cleo.

Rin glanced up at the guards. She'd heard them yell at people for chatting on the Wall.

Cleo saw her looking for the guards and smiled. "Don't worry. They won't come down here and smack us around if we keep working and don't talk too loud."

"I thought we weren't supposed to talk at all," said Rin, driving her pickaxe into the rock face.

"Technically we're not, but they don't care that much. So, what do you think of this time?"

"Not a fan of the manual labor," said Rin, struggling to swing her pickaxe.

"I think they had manual labor in your time too. What about the screens and the food fabricator?"

Rin frowned. She hadn't thought about the benefits of being in the future. "Those things are pretty incredible. There's so much that can be done with the screens."

Cleo nodded. "I'll have to show you some of the games. I love screens. I'm glad they let us have access to them."

"Are there any things here that you didn't have in your time?" asked Rin.

"Oh yes. We're still two hundred years in my future. In my time we didn't have food fabricators. That kind of tech probably would have made it harder for people like me to come to power. Food insecurity was a major component of Mniotia's instability."

"People like you?" asked Rin.

"Cruel opportunists," clarified Cleo.

Rin was surprised by Cleo's harsh description of her past self. "Is that what the people said in your trial?"

"No, they were more focused on the millions of lives lost in my rise to power. I've had a lot of time here to think about my past."

"And you regret it?"

"I did terrible things, Rin. Of course I regret it. You'll understand eventually."

Rin glowered at the wall as she slammed her pickaxe into it. "I didn't do anything wrong."

Cleo laughed, but when Rin looked up, she wasn't smiling. "Give it time, High Commander. The harder you hold onto that belief, the more it hurts when it crumbles in your hands and you have to face what you've done."

The conversation trailed off. Rin focused on the wall and her pickaxe. Cleo's words were more troubling than the shouts of the mob at her trial. The mob didn't know her. They didn't understand the intricacies of past politics. They were just a mob. They were overwhelming and terrifying in their potential for violence, and they awakened a guilt and doubt Rin hadn't felt before, but those feelings were easy to brush off. With Cleo, it was different. Cleo wasn't shouting accusations. She was talking from experience, and her words fed the coiled doubt inside Rin.

She *hadn't* done anything wrong. It was well within her right as High Commander to punish the satyrs for the murder of her parents. They were a blight, and they had to be wiped out. All of them.

Her mind went to one of the many satyr villages she'd seen exterminated. The formerly sanctioned settlement had lost its protected status. The humans in the region were going hungry, and the goats were using too much of the land, eating food that could have gone to people.

Her battalion had executed a netting maneuver. Squads of soldiers were posted at escape routes to catch any satyrs that managed to flee. With all avenues of escape cut off, the main battalion attacked, cutting down satyrs in their public places and breaking into their homes to kill them where they hid. There were no humans in sanctioned settlements to get in the way and make things complicated.

Many of the structures were to be left standing. Ordinarily they would have burned the village to the ground to ensure no hidden satyrs survived, but there were humans who needed the buildings, so the satyr corpses were loaded onto carts and removed from the village. After the maneuver was completed and the bodies were being cleaned up, Rin inspected the village with her officers. The exercise had been executed efficiently, and Rin had praised her soldiers for a job well done. Now they had to root out the few satyrs who remained hidden. Usually the fires would have taken them, but without the fire they would have to find them by hand.

Rin and her captains entered the largest estate in the village. Most satyrs wallowed in filth, but some had managed to accumulate enough wealth to rival humans in their living accommodations. The local people only needed the buildings, so Rin allowed her soldiers to take what they wanted from the village. By the time they reached the estate home, it had been picked over by soldiers eager to gain what little extra coin the satyr's baubles and shows of wealth might earn them. The home was a large two-story wood-and-brick structure with all the amenities Rin would expect in a vacation cabin for herself. It was wasted on a half-goat.

Rin and her officers were inspecting the home. While walking through a parlor, Rin heard a faint scratching. It could have been a rat, but Rin had grown up in a palace full of secret passages, and she knew not to overlook such a sound. She had saved her own life when her parents were slaughtered by hiding in a secret room. She gestured for her officers to walk on without her. When they moved into the next room, she heard the sound again. She snapped her head around and saw it: a panel in the wall below the window, where a corner was smudged with hand prints.

Rin sent one of her officers to get a squad of soldiers. They all gathered in front of the panel. Rin knew how secret doors worked; it took her only a moment to open. The panel in the wall fell away, revealing six wide-eyed and terrified satyr children. They screamed and cried and begged when they realized they'd been found. The squad jumped in surprise and turned their pikes on the little goats.

Rin held up her hand. "Take them outside. We don't want to get blood on the floor. It will make it harder to clean."

"Yes, sir," said the squad leader, and the little satyrs had been dragged from their hiding place behind the wall and cut open in the yard behind the house while Rin and her officers finished their inspection.

Rin swung her axe into the wall of rock. She'd forgotten that campaign. It bled into so many others. She felt a twinge of something that scared her as she remembered the fear in those wide eyes. She remembered the shouting and crying and screams that drifted in through open windows, cut short with the slice of a blade. No, satyrs weren't people. They were animals. She had done nothing wrong. Cleo didn't understand. She was from far in the future. There weren't many satyrs in Mniotia. She didn't know what it was like to live with the creatures. She hadn't seen humans going hungry while half-goats ate all the food. She didn't know what they'd done to Rin, to Rin's parents.

~*~

Every day the work got easier. Gai joined Rin and Cleo while they dug at the Wall. When it was break time, Rin climbed the slope with them, hoping that she'd dug enough to earn a break, but every day her pickaxe flashed red and she was pushed down the slope to dig while her cellmates ate and watched.

Rin was dejected, but she climbed the slope anyway. On Tuesday, the day before her rest day, her pickaxe flashed green instead of red. The guard handed the axe back and let her pass. She followed the others to a line of brown bags, took one, and sat on the rim with Cleo and Gai, looking down at the terrace. Opening the bag, she found something Cleo called a sandwich as well as a few pieces of fruit. Rin was amazed by the prevalence of fruit in Hell. In her time, fruit had been a treat that was only available during a narrow window of seasons. In larger, wealthier lands, she'd heard they had fruit in court year-round, but Rin had never visited those places. Here, even prisoners received exotic fruits all year. Cleo told her that was true even in her time, before food fabricators.

Rin sank her teeth gleefully into the sandwich and looked down at the terrace below. To Rin's surprise, there was still one person working on the Wall.

"What is she doing?" asked Rin, watching Charlotte digging through their break.

"You probably haven't noticed, since this is your first time making quota," said Gai. "She works through break and makes double quota almost every day."

"Why?"

"There's a rumor that if you earn enough extra strikes you get out of Hell," said Cleo, taking a bite of her sandwich.

Rin chewed thoughtfully, then swallowed. "Is there any truth to it?"

"No," said Gai.

"No one has made enough strikes to know," said Cleo.

"She's got to have at least a dozen by now."

"I thought you said she got double quota almost every day," said Rin.

"She loses a lot of strikes too," Cleo explained.

"She's always backtalking to the guards."

"She came up from four levels down. Maybe she's building up a strike buffer because she's afraid of going down again."

"What's down there?" asked Rin, peering into the abyss.

"I don't know," said Cleo. "I've never left this level. I've heard it's fire and pitchforks, like the stories of Hell say."

"I've been one level down for a week," said Gai. "It was just an older part of the quarry. Like this but harder. The rock face is steeper and you have to work harder to find enough ore to hit quota. I got my three strikes as fast as possible to get back up here."

Rin stared into the darkness; there was a faint flicker at its heart. Probably lights from people working at the lower levels that Gai described. She definitely didn't want to know what was farther down there. "How many levels to the bottom?" she asked.

"No one knows, but the internet says ten."

Rin was learning words like 'internet,' but the way Cleo used them still confused her.

"Back to work," shouted a guard.

Rin grabbed her pickaxe and jumped down the slope before she could be kicked.

~*~

The next day Rin woke and banged her head on the ceiling as usual.

"You get to sleep in," said Cleo. "Enjoy it."

Rin rubbed her sore head. She wanted to sleep, but the pain had already awoken her enough to slide off the bunk.

"It's better not to sleep in," said Gai. "The breakfast goes away after we head down. If you're tired, get up now, then go back to sleep after you eat."

Charlotte pushed past Rin on her way to food.

"Does anyone else have off Wednesday?" asked Rin.

"I don't know," said Cleo. "I'm Thursday and Gai is Saturday."

"There's probably at least one other person. They try to keep days off spread around evenly, so most days have two people on break."

Rin followed the others into the common room. She was becoming friends with her cellmates, except Charlotte, but she didn't know anyone from the other cells. Cleo knew everyone, but she'd been there forever. When everyone else had left, Rin was alone with a tall, lanky man.

"I guess we're the Wednesday people," she said. "I'm Rin."

"My best friend was a satyr," said the man, slamming the door marked A in her face.

"I guess I'm on my own," she muttered, turning back to her cell.

She sank into the chair in front of her desk. She hadn't had time to explore many of the pictures, although Cleo had shown her what a few of her favorites did. There was a game that involved knocking over buildings, which Rin liked as a palate cleanser for her brain. She played the mindless game for a few minutes while she thought. She needed to focus on escaping from this place, but her mind kept flashing images of little satyrs being hauled off to their deaths.

The door to Jason's office opened, and Rin's manacles tightened around her wrists and ankles.

"Rin?" Jason said from the door.

Rin turned from the game on her screen. "Yes?"

He came in and shut the door. Her manacles relaxed. "I was working on some paperwork and wanted to make sure you knew it was your off day."

Rin nodded.

"Congratulations on making it through your first week with all three strikes."

"Yeah, thanks."

"Some of your effects came through screening today."

Rin frowned. "My effects?"

"Yes," said Jason. "Things that were on your person when you were brought in. Most of them were confiscated for your eventual return to your own time, but there were a few things deemed unimportant enough for you to have."

Rin was surprised. She hadn't expected to be given anything from her time. Maybe she could use something in her effects to escape.

"You don't get them just yet. If you earn an extra strike, you can choose to spend it on an item. Some items cost more strikes than others."

"Are you going to tell me what I'm saving for?" asked Rin.

"Yes, come with me."

Rin's manacles tightened as he led her to his office. They didn't draw together, just tightened, reminding her they were there and could be pulled together if the need arose. The office looked the same as it had the last time she was there. He didn't make her sit in the chair.

"Your things were just sent down today," said Jason. He touched the handle of a cabinet, and it flashed blue before opening.

The cabinet seemed small to hold the belongings of twelve inmates, although people who had been there longer had probably already earned their things back.

"Here they are," he said, stepping away from the cabinet with a box in his hands.

Rin moved closer as he placed the metal box on his desk. "Not much would fit in that."

"You don't get much," he answered. "Plenty of people don't get anything at all."

He touched the lid and it flashed blue before he opened it. Inside the box were a few measly hairpins, a locket, and a box of playing cards. In a prison in her own time, Rin would have asked for the hairpins — she could have used them to figure out how to pick a lock. But here, where the locks were all blue and red flashes of light that recognized people on touch, a hair-pin was useless.

Rin looked up at Jason. "This is it?"

"What did you expect? I'm not exactly going to offer you your gem-encrusted knife back."

"It's a dagger, not a knife," grumbled Rin, glaring at the box's contents. Her father's dagger. It had been on her when she'd been taken, and Jason had seen it. Where were they keeping it? "This junk is absolutely useless."

Jason shrugged and snapped the lid closed. "Then you don't have anything to spend strikes on."

Rin watched as Jason opened the cabinet to put the box back. There was a large package wrapped in white paper on one of the shelves. It was too big to fit in the small metal boxes that filled the rest of the cabinet.

"Whose is that?" asked Rin.

Jason glanced at where she was looking. "That belongs to Charlotte. She's in your cell."

"I know who she is. What is it?"

"I can't tell you that," he said, shutting the closet.

"I might want to buy it, though."

"You can't spend strikes on anything other than your own effects."

"Why does she get better stuff than me?" demanded Rin.

"You don't even know what it is!"

"It's more than a locket."

"Come on, I've got other things to do. Get back in your cell."

Rin followed Jason back to her cell, disappointed in what she'd been offered.

"Is it true that we can save up strikes to get out of here?" she asked as she stepped into her cell.

"Out of here?" asked Jason, folding his arms and leaning against the door frame.

"Yeah, I heard a rumor that we could save up strikes to get out of this place."

Jason rolled his eyes. "Sometimes I can't believe how badly you people just don't get it."

"Get what?"

"You aren't in some normal prison where you can earn time off for good behavior. You are in the literal Pit of Hell! There is no getting out of here. You get out when you die. Nothing you can do will get you out early. You are a monster, and you're here to be punished. Did you really think you could just dig up some extra rocks and get out of that? Nothing you can do can ever make up for the evil things you've done."

Jason's words echoed Cleo's, and they felt like a physical blow, leaving her shocked. The image of satyrs about to be slaughtered floated to the top of her mind, unbidden.

"You don't understand," said Rin.

"What do you think I fail to understand? This is your future. You saw the clips we had of your life when you were messing with the screen in the holding cell. I know you saw how many recordings there were. What do you think we missed?"

"The satyrs were monsters. They had to be wiped out to protect humanity," said Rin.

Jason snorted and shook his head. "If that were true, how am I here, oh mighty protector of humanity? You died. Your genocide failed. Satyrs lived for centuries after you were gone and humanity continued on."

"There's no satyrs now," said Rin.

Jason glared at her. "No, and that is a tragedy."

"Or maybe you don't understand. Maybe I know more about satyrs than you do, as someone who lived at a time when the half-goats were a burden on humanity. Maybe you're the one who's wrong for condemning me!"

Jason shook his head. "You have no idea what you're talking about."

He stepped into his office, shutting the door between them. Rin seethed as she paced the cell. He didn't know what he was talking about. He couldn't know. He'd never met a satyr. He hadn't lived in her time. He didn't know what satyrs had done to humans, to her parents, to her. She hadn't looked carefully at the images they had from her life. They must have missed that night. They didn't hear her parent's screaming. They didn't see the blood. The satyrs had not been quick or efficient. Rin remembered seeing her parents' room when she'd finally emerged from hiding. They must have had tried to fight or run — blood and gore were everywhere.

Enraged by her confrontation with Jason, Rin sank into the chair behind her desk. She tapped the question box — the search engine, as Cleo called it. In the bar she tapped out her name and sent the search. It was time to learn what these people did know about her. She told herself it would help with her escape. If she knew what they knew, somehow that would help. It didn't have anything to do with the guilt gnawing away inside her. Nothing to do with the memories of dying satyrs which had been dredged up and refused to be buried again. She had to confirm that they didn't know, that they didn't understand. They couldn't understand.

Cleo had taught her how to skim through the overwhelming number of results and pick the links that would take her to the most reliable sources of information. Rin found a link to a website Cleo had told her was trustworthy.

The page opened and was headed with her name. It had a picture of her dodging thrown paper as she was hurried out of the courtroom the day of her trial. Below the picture were statistics about her: Title - High Commander; Birthday - July 6, 1563; Death day - October 23, 1593; Age at death - 30; Height - 5' 2"; Eye color - blue. The list went on. It was accurate. Beneath the statistics was a short blurb describing what she was famous for; it wasn't flattering, but it was accurate in the most uncharitable way possible. The words 'genocide' and 'murderer' were used. Fear and guilt bubbled up along with visions of piled satyr corpses, but Rin pushed them down. She already knew these people saw her as a monster. So far, she saw nothing about her secret. Nothing about her parents.

Rin skimmed the article until she reached a paragraph that made her blood run cold. All the self-righteous fury she'd felt towards Jason drained away. The heading read 'Motive' and the paragraph that followed was everything she'd thought was secret. The council of satyr advisers who had overthrown and murdered her parents in an attempt at a hostile takeover. The coup that had been foiled by city guards. Rin's escape from slaughter, hidden in the secret passages of the palace. Rin's quiet ascension to power. It even spoke of how she'd kept the details of her parents' death under wraps. Every secret Rin held dear was laid bare in this article, in cold, unsympathetic language.

Her eyes glazed over as she scrolled past secret after secret of her past. These people did know everything. They accused her of using food shortages as an excuse to slaughter the satyrs rather than focusing her efforts on increasing the amount of food available to her people. They blamed her campaigns for making the famines worse, as she'd killed satyrs who worked the land, forcing the displaced satyr population to steal from humans or starve. They knew what the satyrs had done, and they still deemed her a monster.

Her guilt and doubt surged. They knew. They had every piece of information they needed to understand her, and they still condemned her. Was it true? Was she responsible for a genocide of innocent people? According to this article, the answer was yes.

Rin pinched the screen closed and pushed away from the desk, her breathing rapid and panicked. Sweat pricked her skin despite the cool air in the cell. Had she killed innocent people? When she'd approved the hunting of satyrs, had she condemned innocent people to being hunted for profit? Those villages she'd destroyed. The children. No. No. No. Satyrs were dangerous! There had to be more to it. The people of this time didn't see the danger, but someone had known.

She grasped for something to absolve her. Satyrs were dangerous. They had to be eliminated. What she'd said to Jason was still true. Someone in the future must have known that satyrs were a threat, because they were extinct in this time. They had to have been wiped out somehow. Humans were still alive and well, so they must have killed the satyrs. Jason called the loss of the satyrs a tragedy, but what did he know? Rin sat back at her desk. She could find out what he knew. She wrestled down her guilt and opened the search engine again.

Rin's heart raced as she typed 'satyrs' in the bar and sent the search. Nothing useful came up, only description after description of what satyrs were like. She tried 'satyrs dead.' This brought up lists of humans who had tried to eradicate the satyrs, including more articles about her. Rin searched for 'satyrs extinct.' The articles that came up with that search were vague. They confirmed that the satyrs were extinct in this time, but she couldn't find an explanation for it, only that they'd gone extinct a hundred years ago. Rin searched 'why satyrs extinct.' That returned more vague explanations that the satyrs were gone, but not how it had happened. Rin tried search after search, but couldn't find a reason. There were only platitudes, one of the most common responses being that the loss of the satyrs was a tragedy. Jason had been parroting a phrase he'd been taught; he didn't know why the satyrs were gone.

Rin didn't know the details, but she'd lived with the creatures. She knew — they were dangerous. She finally managed to suppress her guilt. She could feel it under the surface, but she pushed it down. The satyrs were gone now. Her reasoning might have been flawed, but she knew by instinct that the satyrs were a threat. Someone in the future had figured it out too, and wiped them out. The logic was weak, but Rin used it to protect herself from the guilt that loomed if she was wrong.

Chapter 10

Rin spent the rest of her day off on her screen. She focused on her escape rather than the satyrs. If she thought about the satyrs, the glass shield of reason she'd constructed to protect herself from the guilt threatened to shatter. She couldn't allow that.

There were important questions she needed answered. How would she get out of the Pit? How would she get back to her time? There had to be a way back; these people were planning to return her after she died so that history wouldn't be interrupted. If they could put her back dead, there must be a way for her to get back alive. She had to get back into the upper levels. The Tower, she'd heard the guards call it.

Rin searched the term 'time travel.' Many of the links were blocked, but what she could find indicated that time prisoners never left the Hell complex. It was too dangerous to have them in the outside world. That meant the equipment used to pluck them from their time was close. It had to be in the Tower. So, getting out of the Pit would be step one. The next step would be finding the equipment and getting back to her time.

She typed in more questions. She didn't want Jason to see her reading about time travel and get suspicious. If she searched for everything she'd been wondering about, the search about time travel would look like just another case of satisfied curiosity.

She learned that Parvada was a state on a continent on the other side of the ocean from her home. There were colorful pictures of Mniotia from when Cleo had lived there, and fascinating accounts of her exploits. Gai was from a time both revered and reviled by the people who curated the search engine. Like Rin, Gai was from before computers and screens, but historians had gone back in time and taken photos of his world as well.

Rin searched for her most mysterious cellmate: Charlotte. She had been an assassin who'd overthrown stable governments, casting them into chaos. Gai was right; she'd been alive around the same time as Rin, but she hadn't been a public figure, which explained why Rin didn't know her name. She also hadn't operated in Galilia. The articles speculated that was because Rin's home was too small and unstable to draw Charlotte's interest. She'd died the same year Rin came into power.

There was nothing in the histories that suggested what might be in Charlotte's mysterious package, but Rin was interested in Charlotte's facility for getting into and out of heavily fortified locations. She was better suited for escape than Rin was, and she had motive. She'd been deeper in the Pit. Almost halfway down, if Cleo was right in her assertion that there were ten levels. Cleo and Gai thought she was saving up strikes in the hope that she could earn her freedom, but what if she had another plan? Jason had said some items in their effects cost more strikes than others. What if Charlotte was saving up for that big item in the closet, and what if she had a plan for how to use it?

Rin's searches were interrupted when she heard the door to the Pit open and the voices of her fellow inmates fill the common room. She pinched her screen until it was cleared and left the cell. She was hungry. A midday meal was only provided when a half-quota was met. Since Rin hadn't been on the Wall all day, she hadn't gotten a midday meal. Additionally, the amount of work it took to wrangle her emotions, pushing down the guilt and fear while clinging to the hope of escape, was almost as exhausting as digging on the Wall.

"So, what did you do today?" asked Cleo.

"Nothing really. I spent some time on the search engine."

Gai shook his head. "I will never understand screens."

"I think I'm getting it," said Rin.

"I can't believe it's so difficult for you," Cleo said to Gai.

"I didn't have them in my time!"

Cleo gestured towards Rin. "Neither did she, and she's picked them up easily enough."

Rin cut across the friendly bickering. "Jason showed me what's been approved for me to buy with my strikes."

"Ooh," said Cleo. "Anything good?"

"No, just a bunch of junk."

"No one gets anything useful back," said Gai.

"I don't know about that," said Cleo. "I got back a book that I love."

Rin shook her head. "Well, my box isn't worth it."

"It's not useful, but that doesn't mean it's not worth it. This place sucks. It's the Pit of Hell. It can be nice to have something from your own time. Even something useless."

"I don't have any extra strikes yet anyway. Maybe if I ever manage to make double quota, I'll buy something."

Rin glanced down the table. She'd hoped, for some insane reason, that Charlotte would join the conversation and volunteer what was in the large package waiting for her. But Charlotte ate her dinner and ignored her other cellmates, as always.

That night, Rin looked for an opportunity to talk to Charlotte while she prepared for bed, but the woman was under her covers before Rin could attempt a conversation. Rin pulled out her clothes and started getting ready for bed herself.

"So, what was in your effects?" Cleo asked.

Rin pulled on her shirt and looked over. Cleo was lounging on her bed, watching her.

"Like I said, junk. A couple hairpins, a locket, and a pack of cards," Rin replied, throwing her dirty clothes in a pile in the bottom of the locker.

"The cards could be a good thing to get back, unless the locket is sentimental."

Rin shook her head as she put her boots in her locker and closed the door. She leaned against the wall, giving her full attention to Cleo. "No, there was nothing particularly sentimental about the locket."

It had been sentimental once. She'd had it made in secret for a girl in town, not from a family important enough to warn her away from Rin. They'd spent a happy stolen summer together before Rin was old enough to understand the duties and responsibilities of her birthright. When her family found out, they'd put an end to it. Rin needed a strong match with an important family, and someone who could give her an heir. Maybe when she was older and had an heir she could take a mistress, but she had to put her duty first. The girl's family had been well-paid to leave Highdel, and they'd forced her to return the locket. Rin kept it as a reminder of her duty. Years had passed, and the girl fell further and further into distant memory. There was no need for a reminder of that duty now, and she didn't want to tarnish the memory of that stolen summer by dragging it into Hell.

Rin noticed the book on the bed next to Cleo and nodded at it. "Is that the book you got from your effects?"

"Yes. It wasn't particularly important to me at the time, just the book I happened to be reading when I was killed, but it's sentimental to me now," said Cleo. She held out the book and Rin took it.

It was different from the books of her time. The binding wasn't leather and wood like Rin would expect, only a slightly thicker paper than the pages. The cover and the pages were worn.

"It feels so fragile," said Rin, gingerly flipping the pages.

"In my time, books like that — paperbacks — were common. They were cheap to print and weren't really meant to last the ages, although you'd be surprised how sturdy they are. You can read a summary of the book on the back."

Rin flipped to the back and read the paragraph printed there. It was a mystery, with a lot of words she didn't understand. She assumed they were references to places and technologies that didn't exist in her time. Well, the places might exist. Galilia was far from Mniotia, and Rin didn't know much about the region.

"In my time, books were expensive. They did say that printing would make them more accessible, though," said Rin.

Cleo nodded. "Yes, we learned about that in our history. In my time, and in this time, printed books are easily accessible. Literacy is also universal. Digital books are common, too."

"Digital books?" asked Rin.

Cleo gestured towards her desk. "You can read books on screens, but I find that uncomfortable. I've asked, but they won't give us physical books, so we have to make do with the screens."

Rin handed the book back to Cleo.

"Do you want to read it?"

"You'd trust me with it? You said it's sentimental to you." asked Rin.

"Sure, why not? It's not like you're going to steal it."

"I could damage it." Rin thought of how fragile it had felt in her hands.

"Just use a bookmark to keep your place rather than folding over a page and I think it will be fine."

Rin rubbed her arm. She was tempted by the offer. It would be interesting to read a book from the future, and it would be nice to have something to talk about with Cleo. Heat tinged her cheeks as her mind drifted a bit too far in imagining herself and Cleo curled up together, discussing the book. Rin shook her head. No, she needed to focus on Charlotte and her escape attempts. The guilt and doubt hovered just beyond her defenses, threatening to break through. If that happened, there would no happy book chats with Cleo. There would only be anguish. She needed to escape before that happened, and to escape, she needed to focus on Charlotte and *her* escape, not getting close to Cleo.

"I don't know, even the summary was hard for me to follow. There are a lot of words there I don't understand," said Rin, which was true.

Cleo looked disappointed. She flipped the book over and skimmed the summary. "I hadn't thought of that. Well, I'll leave it on my bed. If you change your mind, feel free to pick it up."

"Thank you," said Rin. "Is that all that you were able to get from your effects? You've been here long enough to earn whatever you want."

"Yeah, that's all they gave me. Most of the things I had with me were too technologically advanced to be given back. I know nothing about technology — I can use it, but that's about it. But they don't like to give tech back to us, because they're worried we'll use it to escape."

"So the further in the past you're from, the more stuff you get back?"

"Usually, although it doesn't sound like you got much to pick from."

Rin grimaced. "It was late when they attacked us. I was getting ready for bed."

Cleo laughed. "That sucks. You'd be surprised how many people here are like that. A lot of people get assassinated in their sleep, or on the toilet, or during sex. They don't end up bringing a lot of stuff with them and get stuck without much in their effects."

Rin's eyebrows raised. "How are they going to return the bodies that were taken during sex!? Won't someone notice?"

"I don't know. I'm glad that's not my problem."

Rin laughed.

Cleo held up her book. "Read it whenever."

"Alright, thanks," said Rin, pulling herself up onto her bunk.

She looked down and watched Cleo flipping through the book's pages. Rin wanted to read it. She wanted to have something to talk about with Cleo, but she couldn't let herself get distracted. She had to focus on her escape. She looked up at Charlotte, on the bunk above Cleo. She was huddled under her blankets, with her back to Rin. Rin had to find a way to get her to open up.

~*~

"You could try digging next to her," suggested Cleo.

Rin's pickaxe bit into the wall. She glanced towards Charlotte, who was digging alone, a bubble of isolation surrounding her. "Why doesn't anyone dig with her?"

"Because she's trouble," said Gai.

"Trouble?"

"She's always doing something stupid and losing strikes. People digging too close to her sometimes lose strikes too."

"That's not it. No one works near her because she's boring; Charlie doesn't talk. But she can't get away if you're digging next to each other. You can talk to her," Cloe said.

"Charlie?" asked Rin.

Cleo shrugged. "She hasn't told me what nickname she prefers, so I picked one."

Rin sighed and turned her attention back to the wall before the guards could yell at her. "I don't want to talk to her. I want her to talk to me."

"Well, that starts with you talking to her."

Rin shook her head, focusing on her work. She kept her budding ideas of escape to herself, but she'd told Cleo and Gai that she wanted to talk to Charlotte. She framed it as innocent curiosity: she'd seen a large package in the cabinet and wanted to know what it was. Cleo and Gai found the mystery intriguing and were eager to help. Rin felt a twinge of guilt knowing that she wouldn't be including them in her escape. It would be difficult enough to get herself out of Hell; she wouldn't be able to bring two other people with her. Rin pushed the guilt down with the other feelings that threatened to undo her.

"You want me to try to talk to her?" Cleo asked.

"You said she doesn't talk to you," said Rin.

"That never stops Cleo," said Gai. "If you would believe it, I used to be a stoic, silent figure until Cleo wore me down."

Cloe laughed. "Oh please, you love the sound of your own voice."

"Well, it is the only voice worth listening to."

Rin smiled as Cleo and Gai exchanged barbs. It was nice digging with them. She looked down the Wall towards Charlotte.

"I want to do it. I'm the one who wants to know what's in her effects," Rin said.

"You have me curious too, though," said Cleo.

"It sounds like you've burned whatever goodwill you could have had with her. Let me try. If you ask first and I start asking after, she'll think you put me up to it."

"Fine, but you have to tell us what it is," said Cleo.

Rin agreed, and they went back to digging. The friendly chatter was quashed by the guards when it got too loud, but they were otherwise ignored.

Over the course of the next few days Rin tried to have a conversation with Charlotte away from the Wall, but Charlotte avoided her. Rin didn't want to dig next to her. Partly because she didn't want to give up Cleo and Gai's company — their conversation helped keep the doubt and other uncomfortable feelings buried where they belonged. But also because she was concerned about what Gai had said, that Charlotte was dangerous. She lost strikes over small things which she escalated by arguing with the guards. Rin found it easy to believe that those digging close to her could be caught up in the mess.

When all other attempts to start a conversation failed, Rin realized the Wall was the only place to pin the woman down. She accepted the fact that she would probably lose a strike. She had three. With a cavalier attitude towards strikes in place, on the day before Charlotte's break day, Rin took up a space on the Wall next to her.

"Hi Charlotte," she said, heaving her axe into the wall, splintering the rock and stone.

Charlotte said nothing.

"We've been living together for a while, but I don't think I've introduced myself. I'm Rin."

Still silence.

Rin swung her axe into the wall thoughtfully. A chunk of black rock came free, and she tossed it into the cart and swept away the rubble.

"So, when are you from?"

More silence. Rin's unwilling dig partner glared at the wall, taking out chunks at more than twice the speed that Rin could manage.

"Is it alright if I call you Charlie?" Rin asked.

"My name is Charlotte," the woman snapped.

Rin hid a grin as she swung her axe into the rock. She had suspected the woman wouldn't like Cleo's nickname for her.

"So Charlotte, I've noticed you've been getting double quotas a lot lately. What are you saving up for?"

Nothing but the steady rhythm of the other woman's digging. Rin allowed the silence to linger. Charlotte needed to know that Rin wasn't going away until she got her answers. She allowed minutes of silence to turn into hours.

"On my last break day I had to go to Jason's office to see what items I could buy with strikes," said Rin.

Charlotte didn't bite.

"I saw your item in there."

Silence.

"Is that what you're saving up for?"

There was a screech as Charlotte's axe skidded across the surface of the wall. She turned to Rin angrily.

"What do you want?"

Rin smiled. "I just want to know what it is."

"No talking down there!" shouted a guard.

"You're going to lose us both a strike," shouted Charlotte.

Rin was prepared to lose a strike. "Tell me what it is!"

Charlotte slammed her pickaxe into the wall. A shower of black-and-gray stones came rolling off from the sheer force of her swing. She didn't bother to pick out the black from the gray, just heaved another swing into the rock.

"I think I know what's going on, and I want to help!" said Rin.

"I said quiet down there!" the guard shouted again.

"Help?" hissed Charlotte. "Is it going to be helpful to lose us both a strike?"

"I just want in!"

"Alright, that's it! Both of you, up here!" the guard yelled.

The rage emanating from Charlotte made it clear that Rin had decimated whatever goodwill could have existed between them. She scrambled up the slope with the furious woman behind her.

"You were warned, and now you're losing a strike," said the guard, tapping away at his screen. "Two more and you will be sent a level down. Am I clear?"

"Perfectly," said Rin. "I'd just like to point out that-"

Rin was cut off by a boot to her chest kicking her back down the slope into the Pit. She'd been quick to jump down on her own lately and had developed a decent strategy for sliding down the slope, but being caught off-guard sent her tumbling like she had on her first day.

At the bottom of the slope she groaned and struggled to push herself to her feet. The wind had been knocked from her lungs by the kick and the subsequent fall had left her bruised and scratched, but she was relatively unharmed. Drama was still unfolding at the top of the slope, however.

"You were warned and now you've lost a strike," the guard was repeating, tapping his screen.

"You can't do this!" shouted Charlotte.

"One strike will be deducted from your surplus."

"I didn't do anything. It was Rin that was talking. I was try-ing to get her to leave me alone."

"If you keep arguing it will be two strikes."

Rin watched in horror. She had been prepared to lose a strike, but she hadn't realized Charlotte would lose two. How would she get Charlotte to let her in on the escape plan now?

"Shut up, Charlotte," said another guard, coming over and, mercifully, kicking the protesting woman down the slope be-fore she lost the second strike.

Charlotte untangled herself at the bottom of the slope. Rin reached over to help, but Charlotte pulled away. Worried that she would end up costing the furious woman another strike by accident, Rin moved down the Wall and away from her.

~*~

Rin worked straight through her break, but didn't manage to make a double quota. After dinner, she went to Jason's office.

"You want to talk on the day you lost your first strike? What a surprise," said Jason, rolling his eyes.

"It's not my strike I want to talk about," she said, standing in front of his desk.

"What is it you want to talk about, then?"

"Charlotte's strike," said Rin.

"Yeah, I heard that was your fault. You better watch out. She's a former assassin, and we all know how well your last encounter with an assassin went."

Rin glared at Jason. "I want to give her one of my strikes."

"You can't do that."

"Why not? I can buy my stuff with strikes, why can't I give them away?"

"Firstly, you can only buy stuff with surplus strikes; you don't even have a full three strikes left. Secondly, even if you did have surplus strikes, you can't give them away."

Rin decided to play the card Jason had dropped in her lap. "Look, I don't want to end up on the wrong end of another assassination."

"It isn't possible for inmates to kill each other."

"I trust her creativity. I sleep in a room with her!"

"I saw you were researching your cellmates on the screen. You're actually scared of this woman?"

Rin was careful. She couldn't push her concern too far or he'd get suspicious. "Look, we all know it was me causing trouble. It's not fair to blame Charlotte for what I've done."

Jason laughed. "This is completely ridiculous."

"Jason. Please."

He shook his head. "I'm going to do this one time. No more fighting with the assassin, got it?"

Rin nodded.

"Alright, get out of here, and be careful. You don't want to lose that last strike."

Rin hurried back to the common room, passing Charlotte in their cell on the way. The glare she shot at Rin made it clear that what she had done was necessary. Hopefully, in giving Charlotte one of her strikes, Rin would earn her goodwill, and talking to her on the Wall wouldn't be a complete failure.

Rin stayed away from Charlotte for a while. She was afraid the woman would lose her temper at the sight of Rin walking towards her and lose another strike. She settled for watching her instead. Charlotte lost strikes almost as quickly as she gained them. The woman went from quiet to enraged in a moment. Rin was baffled by how this woman had earned a reputation as a silent assassin. Maybe Hell had changed her.

When Rin decided the dust had settled from her first disastrous attempt at conversation with Charlotte, she took up a spot on the Wall next to her again. Rin focused on her work. She was still trying to achieve a double quota and earn back one of the two strikes she'd lost.

After working in silence for nearly an hour Charlotte said, "You can call me Lottie."

Rin glanced up.

"Don't look. You don't have any more strikes to lose. The block warden told me where my extra strike was coming from, and if you can convince him to transfer strikes from one inmate to another, maybe you're a good person to have around."

Rin focused on swinging her pickaxe into the wall. A black stone came free, and she kicked it into a small pile of rocks she'd felled.

"What is it?" asked Rin. "What is in the package?"

"A way out," said Charlotte. "But we can't talk about it here."

A warm bubble of pride bloomed in Rin's chest. She was in Hell, cut off from her authority and her power, but she could still get what she wanted. She could escape. She would get home.

Chapter 11

Rin worked hard to achieve a double quota, but she couldn't dig fast enough. She was still gaining strength in her arms. She waited for Charlotte to tell her a secret that would lead to her escape. Day after day Rin watched Charlotte dig, earn strikes, argue with the guards, and lose those strikes again. If saving up strikes was essential to Charlotte's escape plan, Rin could understand why her ability to give her strikes to Charlotte would be attractive. That made Rin nervous. Jason had told her he would only transfer her strikes to Charlotte once. If her value to Charlotte was dependent on her ability to share strikes, would Charlotte cut her out of the plan when she learned she couldn't deliver? She had to find a way to give strikes to Charlotte without Jason's help.

Rin drove her axe into the wall. Lulled into a rhythm, her mind drifted to her past. She remembered a campaign to the south, routing satyrs who were trying to escape to the southern border. Her soldiers had rounded up the fleeing satyrs, their horses trampling those they couldn't herd together. The satyrs begged for their lives. They said they would leave Galilia if they were allowed to live, but Rin's relationship with the southern kingdom was already strained by the number of satyrs pouring over the border. In order to maintain the necessary trade agreements she had to curb the fleeing satyrs, so they were cut down and their bodies left to rot in the road. Rin squeezed her eyes shut as doubt crept in. Could she have maintained the trade agreements without the slaughter? *The murder?*

No. Rin forcibly turned her attention away from the past. She watched the meter on her pickaxe as she dug. She needed to find a way to give Charlotte her strikes. The green acknowledgment that she had felled another rock came when her pickaxe knocked it free from the wall. The meter on the handle of her pickaxe didn't fill until the ore fell.

She turned her attention to Cleo and Gai.

"No, they wouldn't do that, it would completely end the character's arc," said Cleo.

"They ended the butler's character arc," Gai argued.

"The butler wasn't as important, and they wrapped up his story neatly before killing him off. The gardener and the heiress haven't even kissed yet!"

"What makes you think they're going to kiss?!"

"It's obvious," said Cleo.

Rin watched them dig as they argued over a television show they were both watching. She had seen a few episodes, but wasn't as invested as they were and didn't know the story well enough to engage in their debates about what would happen next. Gai and Cleo were digging together. They kicked their rubble into the same pile and they kicked the rocks they collected together into another pile. When they took a break to clean up their workspace, Cleo cleared away the rubble, and Gai took the ore to the collection cart. The ore wasn't counted by the cart. It was counted when the pickaxe knocked it down.

Curious, Rin experimented with the limits of what the pickaxe would count. She loosened the ore until it was about to fall and, checking to make sure the guards weren't watching, pried it free with her hands. The meter on her pickaxe didn't register it. Rin tossed aside the ore and picked up her axe again before the guards could yell at her. So the meter only registered ore that she knocked free from the wall with the pickaxe. She could get a chunk of ore loosened to the point where she could pull it free with her hands, but if she didn't use her pickaxe to knock it down, she didn't get credit for the work. If someone else knocked it free, would they get the credit? Rin needed to test her theory.

Cleo and Gai were still deep in their debate about what would happen next on their show, and weren't paying attention to Rin or much of anything else around them. Rin moved closer to Cleo as she worked until they were almost in each other's way. She waited until they stepped away from the wall again to clean up their workspace. While Cleo and Gai were distracted, Rin moved a few steps over to the portion of wall where Cleo had been digging and used her pickaxe to loosen a chunk of ore. There were enough scrapes in the wall from Cleo's work that she wouldn't notice Rin's addition. Rin shuffled back to her place on the Wall.

When Cleo returned, Rin watched her. Cleo raised her pickaxe over the ore Rin had loosened. It took her one swing to knock it down, and Rin saw a sliver of green illuminate in Cleo's meter. It had worked: Rin had given Cleo credit for the ore that she'd loosened. Rin smiled as she stepped away from the wall to clean up her work area, depositing the ore in the collection cart and brushing away rubble. It wasn't what Charlotte wanted, but it would work. Rin could give Charlotte her strikes without Jason's help.

~*~

More days passed. Rin had all but given up on Charlotte, when she was startled awake in the middle of the night by a hand over her mouth. The hand moved away and pulled at her shoulder. Silently, Rin climbed down from her bunk. She was pushed toward the door to the common room. Stepping into the room, she saw Charlotte behind her in the glow from the screen on the wall. Charlotte urged her forward with a steady pressure between her shoulder blades. Rin's heart raced. Finally, she would learn Charlotte's secret. She glanced around the room. Jason had said there were cameras. He would find this clandestine meeting suspicious. If Charlotte was clever enough to have a plan, did she also have a way around the cameras?

Rin was pushed into the closet full of cleaning supplies. There was an older woman with gray hair, wrinkled tan skin, and a wiry build waiting for them. She sat with her back against the wall of the closet, arms folded. Rin recognized her from one of the other cells on their block, but she didn't know her name or when she was from. Charlotte closed the door; they were plunged into darkness as the light from the screen was reduced to a faint line under the door. There was a click, and a light illuminated the room. Rin looked up. Charlotte had pulled a chain and turned on the light.

"What's going on?" asked Rin.

"Be quiet," the woman hissed. "Why did you bring her?"

"I told you. She was able to share her strikes with me. She'll be helpful."

"We wouldn't need that kind of help if you would just hold onto your strikes."

"The guards have it out for me," said Charlotte, sitting on the floor of the closet.

Rin sat and listened to the bickering. She needed to get a read on the dynamic between these two. The fewer people involved in an escape the better, so each person in this room must serve a purpose. She needed to figure out what their purposes were.

"Jason will be in here to take a strike from all of us any minute. There's cameras," said Rin, nervous about the fact that she was already down to her last strike.

Charlotte had more strikes than anyone. She could withstand losing them and did lose them often. She didn't know where the other woman stood on her accumulation of strikes, but Rin suspected she was the most vulnerable of the people in the room, and she didn't think either of them would give up a strike to save her.

"There's no cameras in this room," said Charlotte.

"Jason would have seen us leave our cell."

"I tricked the cameras to glitch at certain times each night," the other woman said. "The pattern seems random, but I know exactly when they will go out. We all came here during a black-out. The block warden didn't see us."

Rin frowned. She didn't know the word 'glitch,' but she could guess its meaning. The woman was familiar enough with the technology of this time that she could tamper with the cameras. Was that her purpose here? Knowledge of the future? That would be Charlotte's weakness. Charlotte was from Rin's time. Even if she'd been in Hell for years, she wasn't likely to learn enough to disable future technology.

"So then, how did you do it? How did you convince the block warden to give your strikes to Charlotte?" the woman asked. Rin heard her unspoken question: *Why should we include you in this operation? What makes you worth the risk?*

Rin was relieved that she'd prepared for this question. She knew how to give Charlotte her strikes, even if it wasn't in the exact way Charlotte wanted.

"I told him I was afraid you'd assassinate me in my sleep," said Rin.

The woman snorted. "Why does the block warden care if you get yourself assassinated again? Oh, I'm sorry. *Jason*. Did you give him a reason to want you around? A little incentive with that smart mouth of yours?"

Rin was thrown by that accusation. Heat flooded her neck and face. "No! I don't even like men!" she snapped.

The woman crossed her arms and leaned back. "Didn't say you had to like it."

"So, you can't actually help us?" demanded Charlotte.

Rin was still reeling from the stranger's accusations, but she pulled herself together. She'd been thrown off, but she'd planned for this. "Not in that way, but I do have an idea. Charlotte, I think I could dig rocks for you."

"We've tried. The quotas are counted by the pickaxe, not the cart. If you dig a rock and Charlotte throws it in the cart, it still goes to your quota."

"If we were to work on the same stretch of wall, and I were to loosen rocks so all you had to do was knock them down, that would count for you, right?"

Charlotte thought about it. "It isn't what we were hoping for, but it will work. What do you think?"

The other woman nodded her head in agreement.

"I need to know what's going on before I start helping you, though," said Rin.

"We're going to escape, and if you help, we'll bring you along," the woman told her.

Rin shook her head. "That's not going to work for me. If I'm going to give up my chance to build up a strike buffer, I need to know what the plan is. I'm not going to be involved in something that's doomed to fail."

"You're lucky we're including you at all. You will help us and be glad for the opportunity," snapped Charlotte.

"I will do no such thing," said Rin, glaring at her. She was the High Commander, not some underling to be bullied into submission.

"Lottie, watch your temper. The cameras are blacked out, they can still hear you if you're too loud," hissed the other woman.

Charlotte took a few steadying breaths. She glared at Rin. "I never did like you, when we were alive."

"I didn't even know who you were."

Charlotte rolled her eyes. Her anger was fading; it went as fast as it came. "I wouldn't have been doing my job well if you'd heard of me. Fine, you're right. I am saving up strikes for one of the items that's being held for me."

"What is it?" asked Rin, forgetting Charlotte's comment about disliking her. Rin wasn't interested in winning popularity contests. She wanted to escape.

"What it is doesn't matter, the key is what it's made of."

Rin frowned. "What do you mean?"

"Charlotte is saving up for an item that contains copper and silver, two substances that are difficult to come by in Hell. I can use those materials to build a device that will jam the security features of this place, buying us time to escape," said the woman.

The roles were making sense. Charlotte had the materials needed for the escape, and the other woman had the expertise. That left Rin in the uncomfortable position of being nothing more than muscle. In her own time, she would have worried about being killed after Charlotte accumulated her strikes, but Jason had said it was impossible for inmates to kill each other. She hoped that was true.

"So you can black out security. How do we get out? I'm sure they can turn off the moving room," said Rin.

"Moving room? The elevator?" asked the older woman.

"There's a ladder. I saw it when I was four levels down. The Pit is narrower down there."

"How do you know it leads out?"

"After I saw that ladder, I stole a map from a block warden. The ladder is an emergency escape hatch for the guards. It goes all the way up."

"There will be guards up there. How are you going to distract them?" she asked.

"The guards won't be there if we don't set off the alarms. We need Charlotte's effects to get the components I need to make my scrambler," said the woman.

Rin shook her head. "That gets us out of the Pit. How do we get back to our time?"

"You don't need to know that yet."

"I'm not going to help dig if I don't know the full plan. If we get out of the Pit, it will only take them a few minutes to round us up again. I don't know how to get around in this time. I need to know how to get back home or I'm not helping."

"Charlotte, this isn't worth the risk."

"We're in this deep with her," said Charlotte.

The other woman shook her head.

Charlotte turned back to Rin. "The time machine is in this building, in the lower levels of the Tower just before the Pit. It's in a library where they do their time-travel research. They use it for more than just kidnapping us. If we can get to the machine before they detect our escape, we can use it to get back to our time. None of us know how to use the time machine, but Allie can figure it out if she gets close enough."

Allie. Rin was happy to have a name for the other woman.

"How do we get from the hatch to the library?" asked Rin.

Charlotte shook her head. "You can see the map when you've done more for your end of the deal. You know the plan now. Will you help us?"

Rin nodded. She wanted to see the map, but she was not in a strong position to negotiate. She needed these people more than they needed her. Even without her help, Charlotte would eventually earn enough strikes to get her item back from Jason. Allie's technical knowledge was more useful than Rin's strikes. The greatest leverage she had over them was her ability to reveal their plan to Jason. She would help them, and wait. If they didn't show her the map soon, she would have to make threats, but she needed these people to get her out and back to her time.

"Alright. I'm in," said Rin.

Chapter 12

Over the course of the next few weeks, Rin worked on the Wall side by side with Charlotte. The woman hardly spoke to Rin, and it was lonely work. Eventually Gai and Cleo joined her at her new segment of wall, but Rin had to be careful not to let them see what she was doing. She felt a pang of guilt that her escape attempt didn't have room for them. She liked Gai and Cleo more than Charlotte and Allie, but it wasn't about who she liked. It was about who would get her back to her own time.

As the weeks dragged on, Rin managed to dig faster, but she still only barely made quota every day, giving up a majority of the rocks she dug to Charlotte so that Charlotte could make triple quota and earn two extra strikes. They would have been done faster, but Charlotte infuriatingly lost strikes as fast as she earned them. Even with Rin's help, she was slow to build up a strike buffer. It was rare for her to make it through a day without losing any strikes, and some days she lost multiple strikes in a single argument. But as much as Rin longed to take a break or slow her pace, she appreciated the work. It kept her mind off her guilt and doubt.

On one of her days off, Rin was busy at her computer. She was playing a game, trying to keep her mind from wandering into the forbidden corners where guilt and doubt festered. She focused her thoughts on the map of Hell. She hadn't convinced Charlotte to show it to her yet, and she was getting nervous. She needed to see the map before Charlotte earned enough strikes to buy back her item. Once Charlotte's item was in their possession, Rin lost all of her value. The only card she had left was the threat of revealing their plan to Jason, and that was a dangerous card to use.

Rin's attention was drawn away from her game by her restraints tightening. Jason stood in the door to his office, arms crossed, watching her.

"Yes?" she asked, turning around in her chair to talk to him.

"You've been here six months," said Jason.

Rin nodded. He was right. She was intimately aware of how long she'd been in the Pit of Hell.

"Usually at this point, inmates have lost one strike, which you've managed twice, and have earned back at least one strike. You, however, are barely making quota. Why is that?"

Rin covered her frown by pushing back her hair. She hadn't expected these questions. She didn't realize how closely Jason watched the inmates. "I just can't seem to make it past my quota."

"That isn't true," said Jason. "You were making average progress for your first few months here, but suddenly you started going downhill. I want to know why."

Rin shrugged. "I guess it's just really hard work and I don't want to do any more than I have to."

"If that were true, you wouldn't be working through breaks. Tell me, Rin. If you tell me what's going on now, I'll give you back both of your strikes and no one will know, but if I find out there's foul play on my own, remember, you're already on your last strike."

Rin's brain screamed through the calculations. If she truly believed in Charlotte's escape plan, then it was foolish for her to do something to jeopardize it, but if she didn't think it would work, she would be smart to tell Jason about it and gain back the strikes. If she told Jason, she could earn his trust and respect. He held a lot of power over her life. Having him on her side would make life in Hell more bearable, but giving up her chance at escape to get him on her side would be condemning herself to remaining in Hell. She couldn't give up her hope for escape. Without it, she would be lost in the guilt that loomed in the corners of her mind. Giving up on escape would be admitting that the people of this time were right. It would be admitting to genocide, and the innocence of the satyrs. Rin couldn't do that. It would destroy her.

"I'm just tired," she said, her heart pounding. "That's all."

Jason shook his head. "Fine, but don't say I didn't warn you."

He stepped back into his office and closed the door with a soft click. Rin's manacles loosened as the door closed. She felt the guilt pushing at the barriers she'd built.

She remembered the time her battalion had found a camp of runaway satyrs by accident. They were living in the forest, on the run from hunters. They'd given themselves away by lighting a campfire. Their clothes were paper-thin, and winter was closing in. When the scouts found their camp, they were half-frozen and nearly starved to death already. Killing them had been a mercy. Rin closed her eyes and rested her head on the back of her chair. There was more to it. The satyrs had been wiped out. They had been a danger to the world.

Rin's hands shook as she fought off her self-doubt, and her heart raced from the conversation with Jason. What if she was wrong? What if the reason the satyrs were gone now didn't excuse her actions? No. She had to escape. She had to get back to her own time and away from these people and the judgments they cast on her.

She took a shaking breath and turned her attention back to her computer, but she couldn't focus on the game. Her mind kept skittering back to the darkness where her guilt hid. She had to get a glimpse of that map. She had to know how they would escape. She needed something else to think about.

~*~

The next day at dinner there was a surprise: along with their normal food, they each had a piece of cake.

"What's this?" asked Rin, sliding into her seat next to Gai and Cleo.

"It's cake. I know you're from a backward time, but you must have had cake, even back then," said Cleo.

Rin laughed. "Of course we had cake, but what's it for?" asked Rin, before taking a big bite. It was the sweetest cake she'd ever tasted.

"It's kind of a mean joke, actually," said Cleo.

"How so?"

"They give us cake on the anniversary of the invention of time travel, which was a hundred years ago today. If it weren't for time travel we wouldn't be here, but they make us celebrate anyway."

Gai shook his head. "If it weren't for time travel we'd all be dead; I'm willing to celebrate."

Rin nodded. "I'm happy to celebrate also."

Cleo rolled her eyes. "Where's your moral indignation?"

"Maybe it's somewhere under this cake," suggested Gai.

Cleo snorted a laugh and dug into her morally repugnant cake as well. Rin was distracted by that number. Something else had happened a hundred years ago. It took her a moment to remember what. Then it clicked — the satyrs. In her frantic search for a reason for their extinction, she'd found many articles detailing when they'd gone extinct.

"What's wrong?" asked Cleo, nudging Rin's shoulder.

Rin was startled out of her thoughts by Cleo's touch. Heat bloomed in her cheeks, and she ran her fingers through her hair to cover her reaction. "Nothing. I was just thinking, according to the internet, satyrs went extinct a hundred years ago."

"You looked that up?" asked Gai.

"I was curious."

Gai shook his head. "Talk about single-minded focus! You're dead, and you're still worried about the politics of your time! One of the nice things about being dead is not needing to worry about that stuff anymore."

Rin shrugged and took a bite of her cake. If Gai wanted to believe she'd looked up the fate of the satyrs because of her lingering hatred for them, she wouldn't correct him. The guilt and doubt that were growing in the corners of her mind weren't something she wanted to share with anyone.

"It could just be a coincidence. I'm sure there were a lot of advancements being made around that time. Any one of them could have caused the extinction of the satyrs. Did you see any articles that linked their extinction with time travel?"

Rin shook her head. "No, everything I saw was vague. It just said a tragedy a hundred years ago had resulted in the deaths of the satyrs."

Cleo took another bite of her cake. "That's kind of weird. They must know what happened. You couldn't find any details? You used the search engine the way I taught you?"

"Yes, I phrased the question a few different ways and everything. There was nothing that explained how they died, just confirmed that they were extinct."

"You think the satyrs were wiped out because of time travel?" asked Gai, glancing between Rin and Cleo.

Cleo took another thoughtful bite of her cake, then shrugged. "I don't know. It could just be a coincidence. If the two were related, I don't see why Rin would have such a hard time finding that information online."

The conversation slid away from satyrs. Gai and Cleo talked about what they planned to do on their days off, and Rin's attention drifted. Her friends' laughter faded to the background while she was lost in her own thoughts. Could time travel be involved in the mysterious disappearance of satyrs? Rin wondered at the implications of the new information before carefully pushing it to the back of her mind. It brought her thoughts too close to the guilt and doubt she was so carefully avoiding.

~*~

The next morning Rin's axe bit into the wall. Her hands were calloused and no longer bled with every swing of the axe. She was excited. Today Charlotte would earn the last strike she needed to get her item from Jason. It would take time for Allie to build her device, so they wouldn't be able to escape right away, but Rin would be able to take breaks again and build up her strike buffer. Hopefully that would get Jason off her back.

The incident occurred close to break time. Charlotte's axe slipped on a stone, sending a shower of rocks and eliciting a flurry of cursing from the woman.

"What's going on down there?" demanded one of the guards.

Rin kept her head down and continued to swing away at the wall, careful to fell every rock in case the guards came down and noticed all the loosened rocks waiting for Charlotte to collect them.

"It's the damn wall!" shouted Charlotte.

"Stop messing around and get back to work!"

"That's a bit harder than it looks!" Charlotte yelled back.

All chatter along the Wall stopped. The only sounds were Charlotte's continued mutterings and the clang of pickaxes against stone. The rest of the cell block's daily entertainment was about to begin as Charlotte and the guards started their regular screaming match.

"I bet it is," shouted the guard. "But it's going to be even harder now that you're down a strike."

"What!" demanded Charlotte. "A strike? For slipping?"

"For fooling around on the Wall! If you're not careful there will be another one for mouthing off!"

"This is ridiculous!"

"Fine, another strike it is!"

Rin cringed. She wanted to hit Charlotte over the head and knock her unconscious to stop the stream of strikes slipping through her fingers, but she knew that if she interfered she would lose her last strike, and she wasn't sure she could talk Jason into saving her.

"This is an outrage! You can't do that!" shouted Charlotte.

"Actually I can, and I'll take a third strike."

Charlotte's face was red with fury.

"I didn't do anything!" shouted Charlotte.

"Shut up, inmate," called another guard. "You're on your way to losing a fourth strike."

Hearing the threat slapped some sense into Charlotte. She went back to muttering and began swinging her axe again.

Rin was furious. Charlotte had lost three strikes in a completely unnecessary series of events. Rin didn't dig for Charlotte for the rest of the day. She took her break and reached a full double quota, earning back one of her lost strikes. Hopefully, Jason would assume his talk with her had motivated her improved performance, and wouldn't make the connection to Charlotte's outburst.

"Thanks for all the help," muttered Charlotte, as they trudged back to the cell block.

"Jason's suspicious of my strikes," hissed Rin. "I can't keep digging for you if you're going to throw your strikes away!"

"You want in on the plan or not? You don't dig, we'll leave you behind."

"I want to see the map. I won't dig another rock for you until I see it," said Rin.

~*~

That night, Rin was awakened by a hand over her mouth. She followed Charlotte to the closet where Allie was waiting.

"When I planned this meeting, I thought you'd have the copper and silver for me," said Allie, leaning against the wall of the closet.

"It was the guards," said Charlotte.

"I want to see the map," Rin demanded, cutting to the reason she was there.

"No."

"Yes. I've been digging for Charlotte for months. I need to know that the rest of the plan is more reliable than she is at holding onto strikes," she said.

Allie snorted a laugh.

"It's not my fault. The guards have it out for me," said Charlotte.

"I don't care why you keep losing strikes, but the fact is you do and I need something more to convince me to keep digging for you."

"Just show her the map."

"No. She doesn't need to see it!"

Rin crossed her arms and glared at them. She didn't want to threaten exposing their operation to Jason. After all, she did sleep in the bunk next to Charlotte. Jason said inmates couldn't kill each other, but he also didn't think inmates could escape. Rin had pinned her hopes on Charlotte's ability to prove him wrong on one count; she hoped she wouldn't prove him wrong on two. It would be a dangerous gamble, but she was not going to leave the closet without seeing the map.

Charlotte glared at Rin, then heaved a frustrated sigh. "Fine!"

She pulled a folded square of paper from the waistband of her shorts. She had shoved it into the slit in the fabric that accommodated the drawstring. The paper was thin, and she was careful as she unfolded it and smoothed it out on the floor of the closet.

Rin leaned closer and examined it.

"This is the hatch where we'll come up," said Charlotte, hovering her finger above a spot on the map. She moved her finger to a complex of rooms. "This is the library where they keep their time-travel machine."

"It's so close to the Pit?" asked Rin.

"That's why we age so slowly here. We're too close to a time-travel machine. Time doesn't work right around them. Really, a lot of things stop working when brought too close to a machine like that. It's why we're here. Do you think they'd be using inefficient human labor if machines worked right here? The screens here are also archaic. They would have been considered outdated in my time, a hundred and fifty years ago," said Allie.

Rin studied the map. She traced a few paths from the hatch to the library, memorizing the twists and turns she'd have to take. If she got separated from the others, she wanted to be able to get there on her own.

"Satisfied?" asked Charlotte, once Rin had absorbed the map.

"Yes," said Rin.

Charlotte grabbed the map back up, carefully folded it closed again and shoved it back into its hiding place in the waistband of her shorts.

"Good. We'll get the last few strikes tomorrow, and I'll get my effects from the block warden," said Charlotte.

Chapter 13

Rin, Cleo, and Gai dug together on the Wall. It was a relief to build up her strike buffer after subsisting with only one strike for so long, although she was worried Charlotte and Allie would try to escape without her. Every morning, she woke up with the panicked thought that Charlotte might be gone.

"Do you know Allie?" Rin asked Cleo and Gai, looking down the Wall to where the older woman was digging.

Cleo glanced up. "Not well. She hasn't always been in my cell block. She dipped down a level or two, but I don't think she's been very deep in the Pit. Why? Getting curious about the inmates outside our cell?"

Rin nodded as she swung her pickaxe into the rock face. "Yeah, she just seems pretty old. In my time, I don't think someone her age would be able to work in a mine."

"That's part of the healing they do. I should be too old for this kind of work too," said Gai.

"When is she from? What did she do?" asked Rin.

"She's only from about a hundred and fifty years ago. They can only go back in time to before time travel was invented, so she's from one of the most recent time periods," said Cleo.

"She's from your future too."

"Yes, but I looked her up when the block warden at the time introduced her. I was curious what someone so close to the present day could have done to get pulled out of the past. One of the reasons they use for keeping us here is that we weren't punished enough for our crimes in our own time. There aren't many people here from more recent times because, by then, they felt people were being adequately punished."

"Yeah, if you ask around, most people here weren't killed in prisons or executed. If a person is punished in their time, the time locals consider that justice served," said Gai.

"So, what did she do?" asked Rin.

Cleo tapped her forehead. "You know I told you we have chips in our heads? The ones that make it possible for us to understand each other even though we're speaking different languages?"

Rin nodded.

"Before time travel was invented, there was a big boom in technology around the chips." Cleo gestured toward the ore at her feet. "They use the same material we're mining. I don't really understand it; we didn't have the technology in my time. The ore hadn't been discovered yet. Apparently it has some crazy properties. They've refined it to make it safe, but back in Allie's time it was still very experimental. The chips can be used as translators, but they also have more sinister mind-controlling applications. Allie did some crazy mad-scientist stuff. She would use the ore to make people do things they didn't want to do. A lot of her research was later used to make the ore safe, but in the process she burned through a lot of lives. She'd lure vulnerable people in by misrepresenting her work and use it to make them torture and kill people they cared about before doing them same to themselves."

The blood drained from Rin's face. She'd been sneaking out at night to meet with someone like that? She sounded horrendous, a true monster. Rin pushed down the knowledge that the time locals saw her and Allie as equally monstrous. She had seen torture before. Satyrs hid from her extermination, and once one was caught, they questioned it for information about the others. Satyrs didn't break easily, but they did break. She remembered satyrs mutilated and near death, their horns cut from their heads, their limbs broken. She remembered them begging for death after the location of their fellow runaways had been pried from them. Rin shook her head. Even with her bloody history, a device like Allie's was a step too far. She wouldn't use it, not even on a satyr.

"Why?" asked Rin.

Cleo shrugged. "The articles I found said she just wanted to see if it was possible for people to resist the chips in different configurations. Sometimes people would break out of her control in the middle of one of her horrible experiments. Even the people who survived often went on to kill themselves soon afterward because of the horrible things Allie made them do."

"And she wasn't adequately punished in her time?"

"No. In her time, she was celebrated."

Rin's jaw hung open. "What?"

"Yeah, she made incredible breakthroughs in technology. Her methods were kept quiet, and the technology built on her research revolutionized her world — it helped a lot of people. But her methods were deemed too horrible by the time locals, so they pulled her out of her own time and put her here for punishment."

Rin felt bile rise in her throat as she dug. Learning about Allie drove home exactly how the time locals saw her. They thought she deserved the same fate as someone like that. Allie's past made her stomach turn. Invading someone's mind and making them torture people — that was horrendous. Images of tortured satyrs drifted unbidden to her mind, and Rin slammed her pickaxe into the wall. No. That was different. They weren't people, and they were dangerous! She attacked the rock face with fresh vigor. She worked at a furious pace, pushing the physical ache in her arms to eclipse the panic welling up inside her — the fear that she'd done something equally horrible.

~*~

Rin sat on the floor of the closet with Charlotte and Allie, still struggling with her new knowledge of Allie's past. The woman across from her was a monster, but she fought past her disgust. Allie might be a monster, but she had the knowledge to help them escape. As unsettling as her past was, it gave Rin more confidence that Allie would be able to figure out how to operate the time machine and get them all home.

Rin set aside her disdain for Allie and focused on Charlotte. With Rin's help, Charlotte had finally managed to save up the number of strikes she needed to get her effects from Jason. The item was in her lap, still enclosed in white paper. A tingle of excitement rushed through Rin as Charlotte unwrapped the package. After weeks of working and waiting, Rin would finally know what was in it. Charlotte pulled away the paper to reveal a richly engraved jewelry box, with gems and precious metals embedded in its wood faces. It was beautiful...and not the kind of thing a person carried around.

"You died with this on your person?" asked Rin incredulously. She had owned similarly grand items in her life, but she didn't walk around with them in her arms. She left them in her chambers or on display.

"I was in the middle of a job when I was taken from my time. I took this from the target as a bit of extra payment. They took all the goodies inside, but they let me have the box," said Charlotte.

"How does a jewelry box help us?"

Allie took the box from Charlotte and pulled a fork out of her pocket. One of the tines was bent forward and fashioned into a kind of knife. She began scraping out the silver inlays. "I told you, Rin. It's not the item, it's the metals. Silver and copper are essential components for the device I'm building, and they're hard to come by in Hell, because the time locals know how they can be used." Allie turned her attention to Charlotte. "This should be enough. Where's the copper?"

"In the hinge," said Charlotte.

Allie opened the box and nodded. "Perfect."

"Do you think someone will notice the copper and silver missing? If they know how useful it can be it might raise alarms if they realize it's been removed."

"If they saw that the metals had been harvested from the box they'd be suspicious, but I'm going to hide the box in my locker. They don't think anyone in our cell could use the metals. You, Me, and Gaius are from too far in the past. Cleo is too tame for them to worry about."

Allie snorted. "Even Cleo is from too far in the past to be able to use the technology I'm working on."

"Won't they worry about this," said Rin, gesturing towards Allie. "The idea that you would give the metals to someone in a different cell?"

"They never see us interacting. As far as the time locals know, Allie and I never speak," said Charlotte.

"It's still a risk," said Rin.

"Of course it's a risk. Escaping is a risk, but it's less of a risk than staying here. I'm not going to be able to stay at the rim forever. The guards have it out for me. I cannot go back down the Pit," said Charlotte, watching Allie work on the box.

Allie nodded. "Exactly. If I don't get out now, I'm going to die here. Even with the proximity to the time machine slowing my aging, I'm getting too old."

Rin frowned and leaned back against the wall. She had to get out too. She wasn't too old, and she didn't struggle with the guards the way Charlotte did. She wasn't as afraid of the Deep Pit as she knew she should be. The thing that scared her in Hell was within her. The guilt and doubt, as if sensing her attention, struggled against the cage of reasoning she'd built around them. Her chest clenched with fear at the strength it had gained. She had to get out before those emotions broke free and consumed her.

~*~

A few days later on her break day, Rin was sitting in the common room. She'd figured out how to work the large screen, which Cleo informed her was a television. On her day off, it was nice to just sit on the couch and watch the colorful pictures.

"I see you're busy," said Jason, popping his head in from her cell.

"What do you want?" asked Rin. "I built up my strikes again."

"I noticed," said Jason. "You're still not going to tell me what took so long?"

"I already told you. I don't want to work any harder than I have to."

He shook his head. "I came in here to show you this."

He tossed a newspaper in Rin's lap. She looked down at the front page to find her own face staring back at her. Unlike when she'd searched her name on the screen and had been presented with an image of herself cringing as objects and insults were hurled at her, this picture was of her in the full regalia of her time. She looked powerful and confident. The headline read, THE ANNIVERSARY OF A REIGN OF TERROR.

"What is this?" asked Rin.

"It's an article about you. Today is the anniversary of the day you took power," Jason answered.

"You celebrate it?"

"New arrivals in Hell get special media attention for the year — you know, to remind people why they're in Hell. You're one of the highest-profile acquisitions this year."

"Well, at least I've got that going for me," grumbled Rin.

Jason laughed, then sobered. "I saw you looked yourself up."

Rin nodded.

"You read about your own history once, but you never searched your name again. Most people search their name whenever they're bored. Why did you only look it up once?"

Rin stared at her image in the paper. She looked powerful and confident, but Rin remembered this day — the day she'd become High Commander. It had been a difficult time for her. Her parents had been assassinated, leaving her to figure out what to do next, alone. She looked strong, but inside she was devastated and scared. She'd slept in her armor for a year after her parents had been murdered in their rooms. She'd used that misery, coupled with the power her parents' death had bestowed upon her, as weapon for wiping out the satyrs in retribution. Actions that this paper condemned her for, and actions she found harder and harder to justify.

She clung to the hope that exterminating the satyrs was somehow the right thing to do, but the article in her hands suggested that she was wrong. Horrendously wrong. That when she'd struck out in anger, she'd devastated and ended countless innocent lives. She couldn't face that kind of guilt; it would destroy her more efficiently than any torture Hell could devise. She clung to the hope that the satyrs had been wiped out because they posed a threat to humanity, but the article didn't leave room for that possibility.

Eventually, Rin realized Jason was waiting for an answer. Her fists clenched, wrinkling the paper. "I thought it was unsettling," she said quietly.

"Why?"

"It was all there: all of my history, all of my secrets, they were out there for anyone to see. It was unsettling to know not only that anyone could read that, but that people would decide I should be in Hell even knowing everything I knew."

"What you did was monstrous," said Jason.

"Then why did someone else finish the job?" asked Rin. She needed to know. She needed to understand what had happened. If she was going to hold onto her sanity, she needed a reason to justify her actions.

"The loss of the satyrs was a tragedy."

"What happened? I can't find an explanation anywhere," Rin said, her voice pitched with desperation.

"There was a catastrophe, and all the satyrs were lost."

"What kind of catastrophe? What happened?"

"I don't know. I'm not an expert on that sort of thing."

"Who is? I need to know. I need to understand. How did someone from the future, with all your hindsight to condemn me, find a reason to destroy them? If the satyrs were so innocent, why aren't they here today?" Rin searched Jason's expression for an answer. She needed some hint that he could see her perspective. Instead, all she found in his eyes was condemnation, and a hint of something else. Pity?

"You keep digging and I don't think you're going to like what you find. If you're looking for a justification for your actions, there isn't one. What you did was unforgivable."

"There has to be something. You said you don't know what happened. I can't have been that wrong," said Rin. Her voice broke on the last word.

"What you did was despicable, but you have the rest of your life to pay for it. You can't hurt anyone anymore here. Stop looking for justification for your actions and accept this place as your deserved punishment."

Rin stared at the paper in her hand. The glass shield she held between herself and her doubts strained. She saw that guilt threatening to envelop her. Could she do what Jason suggested? Could she admit that she'd done horrendous things? Should she come clean, tell Jason about the escape attempt and accept her punishment for her crimes? Could she survive in Hell? Digging on the Wall was hard work, but she was strong enough. She thought of Cleo's smile, the occasional brush of Cleo's hand against her arm.

No. It didn't matter how comfortable she could be in Hell. She wouldn't survive that guilt. If she let the glass shield break, she would drown. The guilt would consume her; there would be nothing left. She had to escape, had to get out of this place before it destroyed her. Rin wiped a tear from the corner of her eye. Of frustration? Fear? She didn't know what caused it.

"Well, anyway," said Jason, "I thought you'd like to read about yourself."

Rin nodded. "Thanks for the paper."

Jason left Rin alone. She withdrew from the common room and sat at her desk with her screen, tapping open and pinching closed window after window. She didn't know what she was doing or what she should be doing. Guilt gnawed at her from every angle; so many dead and dying satyr faces flitted through her memory.

Further guilt piled on when she thought about the escape. Planning it used to be her defense against the guilt of her past, but now it brought its own remorse. She was working with Allie, an unqualified monster who had stolen other people's minds and forced them to do unspeakable things. She'd thrown her lot in with that woman and turned her back on Cleo and Gai, two people who had extended a hand of friendship to her despite, in Cleo's case, knowing her as a monster from her history books.

When they realized she was gone, would they feel betrayed? Should she talk to Jason? He was watching, always watching. All she had to do was call his name, and he'd hear her through the cameras. She looked up towards the coin-sized circle in the corner of the room. She could do it.

No. She looked away from the camera, ashamed. She couldn't last much longer in Hell. She would break. The guilt would overwhelm her. There wouldn't be anything left of her to be friends with Cleo and Gai. She had to get away from the condemnation, back to her own time. She had to escape.

~*~

That evening, when the others came back from their day of work, Gai and Cleo were excited to see Rin had a newspaper.

"Where did you get this?" demanded Gai.

"Jason gave it to me. I was mentioned in it, and he wanted to show me."

"Can I have it?" asked Cleo.

"You can't have all of it!" said Gai. "I want at least one section."

Rin split the paper between them.

They perused their sections of the paper while Rin ate her warm dinner in silence. She wasn't paying attention as Cleo and Gai talked about what they were reading.

"Hey," said Cleo, touching Rin's shoulder to get her attention.

Rin's heart fluttered at the warmth of Cleo's fingertips against her skin. She looked up, hoping the pink in her cheeks would be blamed on eating hot food too fast. "Yeah?"

"Are you alright?" asked Cleo.

"Yeah, I'm fine. Just tired," she said.

"A long hard day of watching television and playing screen games?" asked Gai, still focused on his section of the paper.

Rin forced a smile. "Yeah, something like that."

She glanced back at Cleo, who was still watching her with a concerned expression.

"I'm fine. Really. It just wasn't a very flattering article," said Rin, glancing back at the paper on the table in front of Cleo.

Cleo turned the paper to the front page and skimmed the article. She looked back up at Rin. "Do you want to talk about it?"

"No, no, I'm fine. If I survived my trial, I'll survive an angry paper," said Rin.

"A trial is different. There was a lot going on. This is something that you can sit and think on. It's hard when this sort of take on what you did sinks in," said Cleo.

Rin watched Cleo's fingers on the paper. She realized she wanted to talk to her. Did Cleo feel the guilt? Was it possible to survive that? Could Cleo help her? No. She couldn't tell Cleo. If she told Cleo about the guilt and fear, it would break free. If Cleo wasn't able to help her, she would be left drowning in the emotion. No. She had to press on. Soon Allie's device would be ready. Soon Rin would be able to escape. She only had to hold out that long.

"I'm fine. Really, Cleo," she said.

Cleo gave her one last concerned look before turning her attention back to the paper, flipping to a more interior page. She laughed at something and showed it to Gai. Rin's attention drifted down the table. Charlotte had already gone to bed. Allie was talking to her cellmates. When would they be ready? She had to watch them; she couldn't let them escape without her.

Rin didn't get much sleep for the next few days. She told herself it was because she was listening for Charlotte leaving without her, but she knew it was the guilt. The things she'd done haunted her dreams. Dead and dying satyrs. Horns and hooves sent to her palace by hunters to collect their prize money. The military campaigns and their rivers of satyr blood. There had to be justification for it. If there wasn't, she truly was one of the most despicable monsters in all of history.

Chapter 14

Rin woke with Charlotte's hand over her mouth, and a thrill of excitement coursed through her. It was finally time. She climbed down from her bunk. She would leave behind the fear and guilt and doubt.

Charlotte opened the door to the common room. Rin looked over her shoulder, catching one last glimpse of Cleo in the wedge of light filtering in from the common room. She felt a twinge of remorse at leaving her behind, but with a practiced motion she repressed it and turned to follow Charlotte. They made their way across the common room, bathed in the dim light from the screen, and slipped into the closet where Allie was waiting.

"Are we ready?" asked Charlotte.

"Yes." Allie held up a strange device the size of a pack of cards. It looked like a tangle of wires shoved inside a box.

"That's going to break the surveillance?" Charlotte asked with a touch of incredulity.

"Don't let it fool you," said Allie. "It may be small, but it will jam any signal used within this prison, including the cameras and the locks. As soon as it's activated, we'll be surrounded by a blackout bubble."

"Great. Turn it on and let's get out of here," said Charlotte.

Allie twisted a few wires and toggled a switch. Rin's manacles fell from her wrists and ankles. Allie and Charlotte were also freed.

"It's working," whispered Allie.

Rin stared at the dead manacles on the ground. This was it. They were going to escape. She would be free soon.

"Stay close to me. The black-out bubble is only a twenty-foot radius around the device. If you step out of the bubble, you'll trigger the alarm and we'll all be caught."

Rin nodded. Charlotte pushed open the closet door, and they stepped out into the common room. Allie stayed between Rin and Charlotte as they crossed the common room to the door that separated them from the Pit. As Allie approached, the handle glowed blue, and it opened when she pushed on it.

Rin cringed, waiting for an alarm to sound, but the night remained still and quiet. The knot of people stepped out of the common room and onto the rim of the Pit, which gaped like the mouth of a giant beast poised to consume them. A dull, flickering light emanated from the center of it, like a campfire seen from a distance. There were no other lights around the rim at this late hour. Rin forced herself to look away from the Pit and the hypnotic flickering light at its heart. She couldn't shake the feeling that she was about to fall into it.

They slowly picked their way along the rim. Rin's heart raced. If they were caught now, they would be sent to the lower levels. She didn't know what waited there, but the warnings she'd heard were dire enough that she did not want to find out.

It took a long time for them to navigate the rim of the Pit and find the ladder. Rin looked up at where the ladder disappeared into the darkness above. The moving room had taken a long time to descend to the level of the Pit. It wasn't until Rin stared up into the blackness that she realized how far they would have to climb to escape. It was lucky that Rin's arms were strong from digging on the Wall for months. Charlotte climbed onto the ladder first, followed by Allie. Then Rin gripped the metal rung and hauled herself off the ground. They climbed. A metal cage wrapped around the ladder, giving them something to lean against when they took a break to rest their tired arms, but the cage provided little reassurance when Rin glanced down and saw how far there was to fall.

The climb was excruciating. Rin's elbows screamed as she pulled herself higher, one rung at a time. She panted for breath, and sweat poured off her back. There was nothing but her and the ladder, pulling herself up rung after rung, for hours. Rin began to worry they'd be caught out of bed by the morning call to work, that guards would notice them missing and raise the alarm. But before the lights came on to illuminate the rim of the Pit, they reached the top of the ladder.

"Ready?" Charlotte whispered from above.

"Go," hissed Allie.

Allie's device disengaged the alarm on the hatch above their heads, and Charlotte twisted it, straining against the age-rusted gears. Rin wondered how long the hatch had been there. Had it ever been opened? There was a click, and it began to open. Charlotte grunted as she pushed.

When the hatch fell open, all hell broke loose. Suddenly the hall above them was filled with harsh, blinding light. A siren screamed. Charlotte jumped out of the hatch, Allie close behind her. Rin surged upwards with a strength she didn't know she had left. She was rushing into the sound and flashing lights of an alarm, but there was nowhere else to go. She couldn't go down — her arms would give out — and she couldn't stay where she was or she'd be found and caught. So she jumped into the cacophony.

Allie and Charlotte were already pushing the hatch closed; Rin barely pulled her legs out of the way as it slammed shut. They looked at her in shock — clearly they hadn't expected her to follow. She was supposed to be trapped below. It suddenly dawned on Rin that she was meant to be the distraction. It had always seemed odd that they would include her, but now she understood. They'd invented a reason to include her, the newest inmate, in their plan. They claimed it was because she'd shared her strikes with Charlotte, but in reality she was the only one new enough and stupid enough to trust them. Well, their plan had failed. Rin would be no one's distraction.

"Come on!" shouted Allie.

Charlotte tore down the hall after Allie, and Rin followed. Allie pushed through a door, and Charlotte slammed it behind her, trapping Rin in the hall. Rin continued running. She'd seen the map. She knew the way to the library. The door Charlotte and Allie had gone through was the most direct path, but there were other ways to get there. Rin skidded down another hall, into a room that was full of tables and chairs. A dining space, probably for the guards. Rin dodged past the furniture, but almost stopped when she saw the sight across the room from her. A wall of windows gave Rin a view of the night sky for the first time in months. She was struck by the beauty of the stars and the pink tinge of morning sunlight on the horizon. There was a faint wisp of cloud passing in front of the moon. The landscape beneath that sky was alien — a flat expanse of wiry grass and shadowy rock clusters, with a range of mountains in the distance. She tore her eyes away from the windows and kept running.

Rin raced through the halls. She heard voices shouting in the distance, but they hadn't seen her yet. Charlotte and Allie had been right to bring a distraction. By splitting up, they forced the guards to choose who to chase. If they'd managed to trap her on the ladder as they'd tried to do, the guards could have spent precious time pulling her off and securing her, allowing Charlotte and Allie to escape. As it was, the guards were still forced to choose who to pursue, but it sounded like they'd decided to go after Charlotte and Allie. Rin slipped through doors, up a flight of stairs, and finally reached the library.

The library was a strange room. At the center of the it, sunk into the floor, was a cleared area dominated by a tangle of screens and wires. There was a pad on the floor among all the screens, and the strange yellow armor hung on the wall nearby. That had to be the time-traveling machine. On the level where Rin stood, ringing the machine, were shelves and shelves of books. Rin was shocked to find that a library in the future bore any resemblance to the libraries of her time.

Rin looked around. The space was dead and quiet, the screens black and hunched. The guards weren't here yet, but they would be soon. Rin climbed down to the time machine. She tapped surfaces and shook the screens, but they didn't respond to her touch. What was she supposed to do without Allie here to operate the machine? Of course they'd gone after Charlotte and Allie. Allie was the dangerous one. Allie was the one who knew how to use the technology of the future. Rin was nothing. They'd secure Allie before bothering to even look for Rin.

Panic welled up in Rin. Hide. She needed to hide. She ran towards the shelves of books. She would hide in the stacks. It was over. She wasn't getting out. No. She would hide. Rin forced down the panic and ran through the shelves, looking for something, anything, to conceal her so that she could enjoy one more moment of freedom.

Fear and dread coursed through her. She had made a supremely stupid decision. She should never have thrown her lot in with Charlotte. She hardly knew the woman! She should have told Jason about the escape attempt while she had the chance. Now she would be caught and punished! What kind of punishments would they have for her? She hadn't bothered to find out. She hadn't thought about the risks and consequences. She'd picked the first course of action that occurred to her and barreled forward, just like she always did.

As she scanned the shelves for a place to hide, a word on one of the book spines caught her eye: satyr. Rin grabbed the book off the shelf. If she couldn't escape, she would at least learn what happened to the satyrs. She would be punished in Hell, but she would know if there was any validity to the hope she used to hold back the guilt. She would know why the satyrs were wiped out, and at least she might be spared the guilt as they punished her.

Rin finally found a place to hide. The stacks of books were at least two stories tall, and near the top of one of them was a large space where books had been pulled down. A ladder was attached to a track on the bookshelves. Rin raced up it and wedged herself into the space, managing to push herself far enough back that she wasn't visible from the floor. She reached out with her leg and kicked the ladder away from her. It rolled down the track.

Wedged in her hiding place, Rin pulled out her stolen book, *The History of Satyrs*. She opened to the table of contents and skimmed the chapter headings. She needed a reason. She needed something to prove that the satyrs were dangerous. The first chapter after the introduction read *Origins*. Rin flipped to the indicated page.

She didn't understand the scientific terminology that she read, but the gist of the chapter was that the time travelers had created the satyrs. It had been an experiment. One small genetic change in a species long before the dawn of humanity; one change to confirm genetic theories of human evolution.

Scientists had found what they thought was the one difference between humans and the rest of the animal kingdom, and in order to test if they were right, they went back in time and edited the DNA of another species, hoping to make another human-like species on the planet. That change had created the satyrs, and the many human and satyr conflicts that came after; including, as Rin read it, a massive resource dispute that had threatened to destroy both species a few decades before Cleo's time.

Hope surged. That was it. Resources. There weren't enough resources on the planet for both species. The satyrs had to die in order for there to be enough food and water for humanity to survive. But as soon as she felt the hope rise, it was dashed. A resolution had been reached. After that dispute resources were shared between the two species, and although there were still disagreements, nothing threatened the extinction of humanity or satyrs again.

Rin flipped frantically back to the table of contents. What had happened to them? Why weren't there any satyrs today? She had to know. She had to understand. Skimming the entries in the table of contents, she saw a promising heading: *Catastrophe.*

Rin flipped to that part of the book and read. Any hope she had for absolution evaporated. The catastrophe was an unintended extinction event. When the timeline with the satyrs caught up with the point where time travel was invented, the satyrs and all the other things that came about because of them vanished. Satyrs and humans were living in peace around the time of the catastrophe. There was no secret reason satyrs and humans couldn't coexist. Satyrs weren't dangerous; they were innocent. The book referenced a merging of the time stream with satyrs with the one without them. The Consolidation Machine, based on the same ore technology used in time travel, held the two time streams together. It postulated that if that machine were to stop, the time streams would diverge and the satyrs would continue on in their own time stream, but scientists would lose access to their experiments. The book described the loss of satyrs as an 'unfortunate artifact.'

Rin's world stood still. This book didn't absolve her of her guilt. It shattered the glass wall that protected her. These people who had condemned her were hypocrites. They condemned her for genocide, while a machine — the Consolidation Machine — was holding an entire time stream hostage, killing all the satyrs more effectively than Rin ever could.

But their hypocrisy didn't absolve Rin. Now she saw how thin her hope had been. Why did she think finding fault with these people of the future would in any way explain away her own horrendous deeds? Remorse washed over her in waves. She'd committed a genocide. There was nothing here that absolved her of her actions. Satyrs were the result of time travelers tampering with the distant past, but humanity and satyrs had found a way to thrive together. Guilt surged through her, filling her with shame and pain. She'd killed so many people — she couldn't deny now that they were people. She'd paid hunters to kill them. How many deaths was she responsible for? The children. The villages burned to the ground. People slaughtered in their homes.

Tears streamed down Rin's face. She was a monster. She didn't deserve the mercy of the rim. She deserved the harshest punishment that Hell had to offer. She had been wrong. She'd made a mistake, and that mistake had cost hundreds, thousands of innocent lives. Why couldn't the assassins have succeeded sooner? She should have been killed on her coronation day. If only the assassins who'd slaughtered her parents had found and killed her also, as they had planned. It would have spared the world the blight of her ascension to power.

The lights came on, harsh, bright white. Rin didn't withdraw into her hiding place. She didn't try to defend herself. She was done. She wanted to be found. She wanted to be taken away and punished. She had done unspeakably awful things. If she'd had any strength left, she would have pulled herself to the edge of the shelf, would have called out, but she was empty. She sobbed, wracked with guilt, hugging her knees to her chest.

"The read on her chip is over here," called a voice from below.

Rin saw a pair of guards below her. One of them saw her. He put up his hands as though he was afraid she'd throw something at him, and ducked behind a shelf.

"Is she armed?"

"I don't know."

Another guard stuck his head out and looked at her. "I don't think so. She's just dug in back there."

"Knock her out and we'll get her down."

"Who's a good shot?"

A moment later something sharp struck Rin's arm, and darkness mercifully closed in around her.

Chapter 15

Rin opened her eyes to a bright white room, like a smaller version of the holding cell she'd been in when she first woke in Hell. She was shackled to a chair with new manacles, replacing the ones Allie's device had removed.

She wondered how long she'd been unconscious. Long enough to be transported to this room and have her manacles replaced, clearly. She didn't try to twist out of the restraints. Her head hung in shame. She was a despicable human being. Her last hope for vindication, the hope that the satyrs had posed a looming danger to humanity, was shattered. She was a monster, and she deserved to be in Hell. There was no escape attempt, no scheme to distract her in that stark white room. Just Rin and her guilt. The weight of what she'd done, the people she'd killed, pressed down on her, suffocating. She longed for the Wall. Something to distract her from the shame of her past.

Eventually the white wall across from Rin split open. She looked up to see the head warden. When she'd been sentenced to the Pit, he told her she didn't want to see him again. Now it didn't matter. She would be punished for the escape attempt. She deserved the worst Hell had to offer.

"Your friends told us everything," said the head warden, crossing his arms and glaring down at Rin.

Rin bowed her head in shame. Friends. She didn't have any friends. Cleo and Gai had tried to be her friends, but she'd pushed them away. She'd been stubbornly focused on her escape, on hiding from the guilt that now crushed her with every breath.

The head warden forced Rin's face up so that she was looking at him. His grip on her chin was painful, and tears welled in Rin's eyes. She'd done this to people. How many people? Hundreds? Another wave of remorse washed over her.

"Do you have anything to add? Want to rat on one of them? You want to try to save yourself from the Deep Pit?"

Rin didn't say anything. She didn't know more than the others. If they'd told him everything, she didn't have anything new to add.

He tossed her head aside painfully. Rin slumped back in her chair, eyes locked on the floor.

"Fine. Deep Pit it is. See how long you last," he said, storming out of the room and leaving Rin alone again.

She was left in the room for a long time; she couldn't tell how long. The bright white light was unwavering. There was nothing to indicate the passage of time, other than her growing hunger and thirst. She didn't care. How arrogant had she been to think she deserved to escape? She belonged in Hell. Assassination with a well-placed arrow was too kind for her. She had caused innocent people to suffer. She deserved to suffer.

Someone came into the room. Rin didn't look up. The person didn't speak to her, just stood behind her. Rin distantly wondered if they were going to kill her, but instead of a weapon pressed to the back of her head, she felt the person pulling her hair. They began cutting it. Rin watched as the floor around her filled with her long black hair. When the person left her alone again, her head was light and short hairs tickled her ears and the back of her neck. Rin kept staring at her hair on the floor while she waited in the white room.

Eventually, a pair of guards in heavy plastic armor entered. Their faces were covered with glass panes, and their armor looked like what the time travelers wore, except the plastic was green instead of yellow. Rin's restraints released from her chair.

"Get up," said one of the guards through the thick plastic suit.

Rin stood. The cuffs on her wrists pulled all the way together and felt welded in place. The manacles tightened, drawing her ankles together so much that it was difficult to walk. She was pushed into the hallway. It wasn't as bright as the previous room, but it had the same white crispness of the halls outside the courthouse. She stumbled down the hall and into a familiar moving room — an elevator, Allie had called it. Weighed down by her guilt, Rin didn't pay attention to the stomach-clenching drop. The room fell for a long time, longer than the first time she'd been sentenced to the Pit. She had heard nothing but dire threats about the deeper levels; now she would learn how true those threats had been.

When the room finally came to a stop and the doors opened, the first thing that struck Rin was the heat. It wasn't just hot — it was sweltering. She'd never experienced heat like this. The closest comparison she could think of was when she'd nearly burned her hands while stoking the fires in her quarters at night. Then there was the smell. Something was burning with a pungent, sulfuric odor. The smell was thick in the parched air, coating her nose and throat with every breath. Rin was shoved out of the room. She stumbled into a hall with wood-paneled walls and a stone floor. There was no window here overlooking the Pit.

The guards pushed her down the hall and into a black room. Rin couldn't see anything as she was manhandled across the room in the dark. Another door opened on the other side. The heat and the smell were worse. She was forced down a narrow hall cut from stone before stepping out into the Pit. Rin had to shield her eyes from the bright light of a roaring fire. It was huge, at least five stories tall, and surrounding it was a mountain of the shimmering black rocks Rin had mined in the upper rings. The flickering light of the roaring fire skittered off the rocks, setting them sparkling. People were standing on the pile, using shovels to push rocks down the slope and into the fire.

A guard thrust a shovel into Rin's hands. He pointed at the flames. "Dig. Feed the fire."

The guard shoved her, and Rin stumbled and fell to her knees on the mountain of black rocks. Then her manacles slackened, allowing her to move. Thick, black, pungent smoke rolled off the enormous fire, making it difficult to breathe. The smoke threatened to smother her. How was she supposed to dig when she couldn't breathe?

Rin used the shovel to push herself to her feet. She sank the blade into the mountain of rocks. She tried to scoop up a shovelful, but as she lifted the shovel, most of the rocks fell off the blade. The few small rocks left were still heavy, and Rin strained to throw them farther down the slope. They skittered down and knocked a few other rocks loose, which knocked a few more rocks into the fire. The fire flared. There was a puff of smoke, and the heat and the smell intensified for a moment. Rin coughed and covered her face with her arm.

"Work!" shouted the guard. Rin's manacles delivered a jolt of electricity, and she cried out in pain.

She bent to scoop up another shovelful of rocks, and threw them towards the fire. She coughed and gagged at the smell, and clenched her eyes shut as the smoke caused them to water. There was another jolt of electricity, prompting her to bend for another shovelful. Rin sank into a rhythm. Shovel rocks, throw rocks, cough, cry, repeat. If she stalled too long in any one step, she received a shock of electricity. The smoke and the work purged her mind. She couldn't think about her guilt or her hunger or her thirst. All she could think about was getting the next shovelful of rocks into the fire before the guards shocked her.

Hours later, there was no sign of a break. Rin staggered on the mountain of rocks. She coughed, and her eyes streamed with tears. Her lungs screamed for air. She couldn't breathe the smoke any longer. Her body was weak with hunger and fatigue. Rin struggled to stand, much less lift more rocks. The electricity raged through her, but she collapsed to her knees. She was blistered, bloody, and covered in soot and smoke.

"On your feet, inmate."

Rin tried to push herself to her feet, but she didn't have the strength. She fell to her side. Electricity burned through her, but she couldn't respond.

"I said, on your feet," the guard repeated, but he sounded mercifully far away. The fire was dim. Darkness was closing in. Unconsciousness claimed her.

Rin's eyes fluttered open in the dark; she was lying on a hard table. She expected to be dead or unable to move, but she was able to sit with relative ease. When she'd fallen unconscious, she was near death, hungry, and beyond fatigued. Now she only felt tired. The pain was gone, and she could breathe more easily. The door opened.

"This way, inmate."

Rin followed the guard. She didn't know how much time had passed since she blacked out. She was led back to the fire, and a shovel was thrust into her hands. She was forced to dig until she collapsed again. She knew days were passing as she was forced to wake and dig again and again, but they weren't marked by meals or sleep, only the insatiable fire and the occasional relief of unconsciousness. The pain and the unending heat filled her until there was nothing else. No guilt. No schemes. Only pain, fire, and glittering black rocks.

Chapter 16

Rin shoveled and passed out, and shoved some more. She had no meals to mark the days, but she knew weeks had gone by. Eventually, as Rin was being handed the shovel, she noticed that her hands were no more calloused than they had been when she first arrived in the Deep Pit. That sparked a memory of Cleo talking to her about callouses on Rin's first day on the Wall. Slowly her brain fought through the fog. There was a way of healing people. They could heal her every day, but they hadn't on the Wall so that she would build strength and endurance. Here, in this deep level, they were healing her, and apparently feeding her, while she was unconscious.

The puzzle obsessed her, forcing the pain to the side. How were they healing her? How had she not died? What happened to her when she was unconscious? She allowed the questions to consume her. She collapsed with them spinning in her brain, and when she woke the puzzle filled her mind again. Her guilt, previously suppressed by the pain, threatened to take the space the puzzle had made, but Rin forced it down. She clung to the questions: What happened when she was unconscious? What were they doing to her? Why wasn't she dead? She had to know, and there was only one way to find out. She would have to make them think she'd passed out.

Rin dug and threw rocks until she couldn't stand any longer, pushing herself close to the edge. Her faint had to be believable. Finally, she fell to the ground, closing her eyes and feigning unconsciousness. Even if she hadn't pretended to pass out, she doubted she would have been able to stagger through more than a few more shovelfuls of work. Her manacles buzzed with electricity. Through force of will, Rin held still and didn't respond to the pain. She would find out what they were doing to her.

She heard a guard crunching through the rocks. Their boot landed heavily next to her head, and she was hoisted onto their shoulder. Rin kept her body limp. Today, she would get answers.

"I've got one down," said the guard in a low voice.

He dropped her from his shoulder to the ground. Rin forced herself to remain limp despite the pain of being dropped. She was lying on a rough, taut fabric. There was a buzz, and the fabric beneath her began to move, pulling her into a dark tunnel. The fabric stopped, and a door closed at her feet. She forced herself to remain still in the tiny enclosed space. There was a blast of mercifully cool air, and the pungent smell of the Deep Pit was blown away from her. The cool air was the most welcome relief Rin had ever experienced. It cleared the fog in her brain.

She forced her body to remain limp and still. The longer she was assumed to be unconscious, the longer she would experience this glorious coolness. A door opened at her head, and the fabric under Rin began moving again, carrying her into a bright room. She was afraid to open her eyes and have her ruse detected, but she could see the brightness through her closed eyelids. Soft music was playing, and people were talking. It smelled clean. There was no smoke here. The air was soft and kind on her raw and bloody skin.

"She's one of the new ones," said a voice near Rin.

Rin remained limp as she was transferred from the rough fabric to a hard table.

The table beeped and chirped. "Looks like she's a light sleeper today. She's about to wake up."

"That's fine," an older voice said. "We'll give her something to help her sleep."

Rin didn't want help sleeping. She wanted to soak in the cool, clean air and listen to the gentle music. One of the people in the room whistled as they made a quiet clanging noise. A few moments passed. The people in the room had turned their attention away from Rin and focused on other things.

"We're almost out of her nutrient packs," said the younger voice, moving towards Rin. There was a sloshing near Rin's ear.

"That's fine," said an older voice. "We'll use someone else's while we wait for replacements. You get her dinner; I think the first-aid pack shipment that came in today is still on the loading dock."

Rin forced herself not to move or make a sound as a cold swab cleaned the crook of her elbow, followed by a sharp piercing sensation. She didn't understand the conversation going on around her, but she was happy to hear it. She hadn't heard more than a few barked orders from the guards since she'd arrived in the Deep Pit.

"Hey," called the young voice. "I think she's going to wake up on the table."

"You get the first-aid pack into her and I'll prep the sleep mask."

Rin held still as the other arm was swabbed and pierced. A soft fabric was placed over her eyes. The instant it nestled over her closed eyelids, the familiar darkness claimed her.

Rin opened her eyes in the dark. Her brain was foggy and addled, but she remembered. There had been a table, and people, and voices. She knew what was going on.

"Inmate."

Rin followed the guard, feeling fresh. She was just as pained and uncomfortable as she had been every other morning, but there was a bounce in her step. She had solved her puzzle. The satisfaction at learning what happened to her while she was unconscious kept Rin going for an entire day, but that new-found knowledge left her without a puzzle to work on. The guilt crept in around the edges of her thoughts; the puzzle had pushed away the pain and left an opening for it. Rin wrestled with her remorse to the rhythm of her digging. She was plagued by the pain and suffering she'd caused. The ghostly images of satyrs begging for their lives dogged her at every turn. The sounds of children being slaughtered on her orders filled her head. She deserved to be in Hell. She wished she could do something to atone for what she'd done.

As Rin worked to shovel rocks into the fire, the pain and smoke filled her. Slowly it pushed her guilt back to the recesses of her mind and she became nothing more than a machine to dig rocks into a fire. She wasn't Rin. She wasn't the High Commander. She had never been those things. She was just an extension of the shovel. A creature that existed to move rocks into the fire and feed the flames.

Rin waited until she had almost entirely lost herself to the fire and smoke before she faked unconsciousness again. She was afraid that the guards would catch on if she did it too often, and she couldn't lose access to that moment of cool, smokeless air before being knocked unconscious in the bright room. Every time she was back there, her mind cleared and the guilt came rushing in again. It was the price she paid for the ability to feel human. As she fed the fire, she wrestled with her guilt. She could not overcome it, but she could learn to live with it. She was in Hell; she was paying for her crimes. In her own time, she was dead. The satyrs were safe from her. She wished she could go back and fix what she'd done, but she would have to settle for paying for it.

~*~

Rin's days fell into a rhythm defined by misery. She woke, dug, and blacked out before waking again. When she'd had all she could take, she faked unconsciousness and the cool clean air purged the fog from her mind, allowing the guilt to wash over her anew. She dug and passed out until the guilt faded to just another pain in the back of her mind. On the precipice of losing herself, Rin would fake unconsciousness again, and would be reminded of who she was and of her crimes, in that cool clean room. After several trips to the cool room, Rin was familiar with the young and old voice that tended to her. Their voices were as much a comfort as the cool air. They talked about their lives and their work. Rin seldom understood their conversations, littered as they were with the unfamiliar medical terminology of the future, but kind voices in conversation were a balm to her.

It had been a long time since Rin's last trip to the cool room, and she was at her breaking point. She pretended to be unconscious, and when she was brought into the room she heard the familiar young and old voice, but there was a new, gruffer voice speaking with them. They weren't paying as much attention to Rin as they usually did when she came into the room, so they didn't notice that she was awake.

"I realize that, but this is an issue of national security," said the new voice.

"We can't make them faster," said the old voice. "Less healing would make them more durable over time, but the toxins in the smoke they breathe would kill them."

"We're already running them on shorter rest cycles than is wise," said the young voice with a defensive edge.

"It's not good enough. The Consolidation Machine needs to be at maximum efficiency for the anniversary. Why do they need to rest? Heal them so that they can work constantly."

A spike of alarm went through Rin. The Consolidation Machine. With the alertness the cool air lent her, she remembered those words. The Consolidation Machine was what held her time stream hostage. It was what killed the satyrs.

"We could cut them from five to three hours of rest, but they won't last as long. Without rest, our healing efforts will stop working," explained the older voice.

There was silence for a moment. Then the new voice spoke again. "The anniversary is always the biggest strain on the system. The machine needs to be at full capacity or we'll lose everything we've worked for." The voice paused. "I'm going to need you to burn through them. Heal them as much as you can, but cut out the sleep. We need a big push for the next few months. Go back to normal after that."

"Over half of them will die. The machine won't work at any level of efficiency without people feeding it," said the younger voice, temper mounting.

Horror dawned on Rin. They were talking about her and the other prisoners. They were feeding the machine. The Consolidation Machine. After everything, even in Hell, she was still killing the satyrs. She struggled to remain limp and unresponsive. The guilt that plagued her pressed down on her chest, making it hard to breathe. Her death wasn't enough to protect the satyrs. Even from Hell, she slaughtered them. Satyr blood continued to stain her hands.

"That's fine," said the new voice, his temper rising to match the younger voice. "We can shuffle the upper levels and bring some fresh meat down. We don't need as many people in the upper levels. I'll tell the guards to be especially harsh with the strikes."

"We're doctors," said the older voice in a stern tone. "I'm not comfortable killing people in my care."

"They are in Hell for a reason!" said the new voice, volume rising with his anger. "Grind them, doctor. We've worked too hard to develop this technology. We cannot lose it because you're worried about killing a few monsters. They're all dead already in their own time. Every second they live here is a gift. We're just cutting that gift short."

"We'll still have the technology if we lose the experimental time stream," countered the angry young voice as Rin was transferred to the table.

"Do it," snarled the unfamiliar voice. "Starting with this one."

Rin's heart stopped.

"Can't," said the older voice, the only calm person in the room. "She's still on the list."

"What list?"

"Her case is still under review. She was involved in an escape attempt that made it into the Tower. They may need her for questioning."

"Then the next one. We need to get things up to max efficiency," there was a prick in Rin's arm, "before the anniversary," another prick, "or we're all in trouble."

"We will," said the older voice. The cloth went over Rin's eyes, and she didn't hear the rest of the conversation.

The next day Rin woke with a start. The smoke and the heat closed around her as she followed the guard to the fire. She shoveled the rocks into the flame. The machine. She was powering the Consolidation Machine. Rin's guilt surged to staggering new heights. She was helping the people of the future wipe out the satyrs for no other reason than scientific curiosity. The satyrs weren't dangerous or a threat to humanity. In accepting that fact, she'd accepted the ocean of guilt that suffocated her. Now new guilt piled on top of old, as she threw shovelful after shovelful into the flames.

Chapter 17

Rin dug, fell unconscious, woke, and dug again. When she was close to losing herself in the fog and the smoke, she faked her unconsciousness for a breath of fresh air. With the reprieve from the smoke came clarity, and with that clarity came guilt. Guilt for what she had done to the satyrs, and fear that what she was doing now was feeding a machine that wiped out the satyrs hundreds of years after Rin's failed attempt. There was nothing she could do. She could let the fog consume her. She could let it wipe away who she'd been. She could let herself become nothing more than an extension of a shovel. She could die, but that wasn't fair. She'd committed evil acts. She deserved to be here, and she deserved to remember who she was and what she'd done, even if that memory caused her more suffering. She deserved to suffer.

Rin opened her eyes in the dark room. The fog had not claimed her mind since her last break from the smoke. She sat up on the table as the door opened, but it was a different door.

"Come, inmate," called a guard.

Rin walked out the door. Her manacles tightened and drew her hands together. She was in a hall. She'd been in this hall before; it must have been months ago, now. At the end of the hall was the elevator. Cool air greeted Rin as she stepped through the doors and into the room. Her mind raced. What was going on? Where were they taking her now? They went up. The motion no longer bothered her stomach. She struggled to process what was happening as they climbed. They went up for a long time, and when the doors finally opened, she was in a clean white hall. She was in the Tower.

The guards pushed her down the hall. Rin stumbled into a bright white interrogation room and was told to sit in the metal chair. Her manacles separated her hands and clung to the armrests. The guards left, shutting the door behind them. Rin wasn't left alone in the room for long, but it was still the longest she'd experienced cool, clean air while conscious since being sent to the Deep Pit.

The seamless door opened in the white wall and Jason entered. Rin stared at him. He looked the same as he had when she was assigned to his cell block. How long ago had that been? It felt like a distant memory. A happier time. Another thing she'd ruined.

He cleared his throat. "I've never had an escape attempt on my cell block before, so I've never had to do this," he said. "That's why I've been putting it off. They told me I need to hurry up though; paperwork. I need to clear you off the list."

Rin continued to stare at him mutely. He looked the exact same. It was as though she had been in the Deep Pit for an afternoon. For the first time, she was aware of her appearance. Her hair had started to grow back, but it was still short. She hadn't bathed or changed her clothes since being sent to the Deep Pit. She probably smelled like the Deep Pit, like sulfurous smoke and sweat.

"I need to ask you some questions," he said, not looking at her, focusing his attention instead on the screen in his hands.

"Do you know anything more about the escape attempt?" he asked.

Rin stared at him. There had been an escape attempt. The book. That's where she'd learned that time travel was responsible for wiping out the satyrs, finishing the job she'd started. Guilt squeezed her chest. Maybe she could tell Jason about the

Consolidation Machine. Maybe he could stop it and save the satyrs.

"I need to know any information you have about the escape attempt."

Rin continued to stare at him. Could he stop the machine? Would he stop the machine? Did he know that this place was killing satyrs? He had condemned her for her attempt to wipe them out; surely he didn't know the machine he helped feed had finished that job.

"I've never interviewed someone who's been in the Deep Pit for four months. Rin, can you speak?" asked Jason, stepping closer to her.

Rin blinked. Speaking. She hadn't done that since she was last in this room. Could she do that? "Yes?" she said experimentally. Her voice was harsh, like it was being dragged over stones, but sound came out.

"Can you tell me something about the escape attempt? Something the others didn't know?"

"The machine. It's killing the satyrs," said Rin, using her newly remembered power of speech.

"If you can tell me something the others didn't say, I can try to get you back in my cell block," said Jason. He wasn't listening to her.

"The Consolidation Machine is killing the satyrs. Time travel. It made them and it's destroying them."

"Tell me about the escape. Anything. Please, Rin."

"Rin," said Rin. That was her name. Guilt washed over her again. High Commander. Slaughterer of satyrs.

Jason put his hands on Rin's shoulders. "Rin. What did you do in the escape? If you don't tell me anything, I can't help you."

"I don't deserve to be helped," said Rin.

"If you answer my questions about the escape now, you can tell me all about the machine later," said Jason.

Rin looked up at that. Jason was looking at her, not at his screen. His eyes were scared, or sad. She couldn't tell. Maybe he could do something about the machine if he listened to her. She scoured her memory for the escape. It had been so important once. Now it was just another mistake. Something she'd done because she didn't understand. Something to distract her from the guilt.

"I dug for Charlotte," said Rin, slowly, as she dredged the memory from the shadows of her past.

Jason scrambled for his screen. "How?"

"I loosened the rocks, and she came behind me and knocked them down so that she would get credit."

Jason nodded and manipulated his screen. "Then what?"

"Charlotte used the strikes to buy a jewelry box. There was special metal in it that Allie used to break the locks and surveillance."

"We know about Allie's device. What else?"

"There were blackouts at night. Allie knew when they would be."

"Anything else? What did you specifically do?"

"Nothing. I just dug for Charlotte. They wanted to use me as a distraction so that they could get away. I didn't realize that until the end," said Rin.

Jason looked down at the screen. "We didn't know about you digging for Charlotte. I might be able to use this to get you out."

"Jason, the machine," said Rin.

"You got what you needed?" asked a guard, coming in through the door.

"You promised you'd listen," said Rin.

"I will, as soon as I get you out of the Deep Pit," said Jason. "Yes, I'm done."

The guard laughed. "Get her out of the Deep Pit? That's not going to happen."

"What do you mean?" asked Jason.

"You got what you needed. She's off the list. She'll be dead within the week."

"What if I need more information from her?"

"This was the last interview."

"Jason, the machine. Figure out how it works. Stop it!" Rin pleaded.

"Go on, I have to get her back downstairs," said the guard.

Jason took one last pained look at Rin, then left the room.

"Up," the guard barked at Rin as her manacles released from the chair. The guard forced her hands behind her back and the manacles drew together, holding them there.

Rin knew she was going to die soon. She knew the chance that she could provide information about her escape was all that had kept her alive. But rather than fear, Rin was filled with a sense of relief as she was marched down the hall and into the moving room. She'd told Jason about the Consolidation Machine. He was the only person she knew who might be able to do something about it. She would die, but at least she'd done what she could to help the satyrs. Her guilt had become her constant companion. She'd wrestled with it and learned from it. As she was walked down the hall towards the Deep Pit and her inevitable death, she felt a small portion of that guilt lift from her shoulders.

~*~

Rin dug. She passed out. She dug. She passed out. She dug. Every time she woke, she felt worse. It wasn't like before. They weren't healing her as well as they had been. Her throat was always coated with smoke and her lungs ached from the moment she woke. Her muscles felt stronger and her calluses were getting thicker, but Rin knew she was dying. She'd heard the doctors say that the smoke was full of toxins. The only thing that had kept her alive was gone. She'd told Jason everything she knew about the escape attempt. There was no reason to keep her alive any longer. She was growing stronger, just in time to die.

Fog closed around Rin's mind, and she didn't fight it. She didn't fake unconsciousness. She let the fog erase who she was and what she'd done from her memory. She was going to die. Breathing was becoming as difficult as shoveling, and every inch of her body screamed for an end. One of the other inmates threw himself into the fire, screaming as he succumbed to the only available path to rest. Rin eyed the fire, but a piece of her knew that she deserved this. The guilt wouldn't let her accept the fire's embrace.

Finally, Rin's body gave up. She fell to the ground, coughing and heaving. The sweat on her brow was cold, and she knew it was the end. Her manacles shot electricity through her, but she didn't respond, couldn't respond. Her vision was a narrow tunnel. The guard came over. He saw that her eyes were open.

"Get up," he demanded.

Electricity ripped through Rin again and again, but she couldn't get up.

The guard gave up on electrocuting her and threw her over his shoulder.

"I got one coming to you that looks like it's on its last legs," said the guard.

Rin was tossed onto the familiar fabric. She didn't respond to the pain of being dropped from the guard's shoulder. The fabric dragged her into the small cool, dark room. Rin tried to inhale the smokeless air, tried to enjoy her last breaths, but her lungs were full of smoke. She couldn't force them to inflate. She was dragged through to the bright room. For the first time, her eyes were open. She heard the gentle music and soft, familiar voices. The room was well-lit, white, and sterile. It was lined with metal cabinets, and the people wore white.

"She's pretty bad," said the young voice. It was attached to a young woman with dark skin, like Cleo's. Rin was happy to remember Cleo before she died. Cleo.

"Put her on the table," said the old voice, which belonged to a tired-looking man with gray hair.

"Can we save her?" asked the young doctor.

The older one shook his head. "She needs rest. If we could give her rest, maybe, but the boss wants them back on the line."

"She won't survive."

"There's nothing we can do. I don't know why they bothered sending her back to us."

Cleo reminded Rin of her life before the Deep Pit. Gai and Jason. Jason had come to her since she'd been sent here. He'd said he could get her out.

"Jason," whispered Rin.

"What did she say?" asked the older voice.

"Jason?" said the younger.

There was a tapping. "Do you know this one's name?"

"Rin," said Rin through her bloody, cracked lips.

"Rin? Rin," said the young doctor.

"Rin," muttered the older doctor. "There's a Jason in here requesting a Rin in his level, it's at the rim, but he's been red-taped until the end of the week."

"When?"

"Tomorrow."

"Do you think we can make her last until tomorrow?" asked the young doctor.

"We might," said the elder. "It would be nice to save at least one life this week."

"You're going to be alright," said the young doctor as a cloth covered Rin's face, and she slept.

~*~

For the first time in what felt like years, she slept well. She dreamed, and she was rested. When her eyes fluttered open, she was in a dimly lit room. The paper-thin mattress felt like a cloud to her aching muscles. She couldn't remember much from the past few months. They had been a blur of pain and soot. The first thing she noticed was that her lungs felt lighter; they were able to fully inflate and breathe in the cool, smoke-less air around her. Her surroundings were familiar. It was a room she had seen a long time ago, but she couldn't remember when. She couldn't remember anything but soot and pain and dying. Was she dead? Was that why she could breathe?

A door opened, and the room filled with a bright light. She squinted against the brightness. There was a figure in front of her.

"Hello there," said the figure.

The figure was a man. He untaped something on her arm and pulled a needle out of the crook of her elbow. She hadn't noticed it.

"You were a piece of work, but you're going to be alright now. We patched you up."

She just stared at him. Who was he? Who was she?

"It's alright, you'll be alright now."

She blinked. She'd heard that before. The pain. The dying. Someone had said that to her in that place. Did this man come from that place? Or did he belong in this wonderful place where her lungs worked and she could breathe?

"Can you try to speak for me? I need to know how well you're recovering."

She looked up at the man. "Where am I?"

He smiled. "You're a bit hoarse, but that's to be expected. And temporary memory loss is a side effect of the medicine. You should remember everything in a day or two. This is the upper-level medical clinic. You've been here before."

She was confused. Upper level? She'd heard that term before. What did it mean?

"How is she?" asked a familiar voice from the door.

"She's going to make it, but she's going to need a lot of rest. I don't think she'll be ready for the Wall for at least three days."

The Wall. Why was that term familiar?

"Can I talk to her?"

"You can try, but she's pretty out of it. I don't think she knows who she is right now."

Her mind latched onto the last statement. Who was she? She didn't know. She had a name. What was it?

The new figure approached her. "Rin?" he asked.

That was her name. Rin.

"Rin, are you alright?" he asked carefully.

Rin looked up at him. Who was he? He knew her. He looked worried. She must know him too.

"Yes," she rasped.

"You're in good hands, Lee will take good care of you."

Rin let the figure's words wash over her. She was too tired to understand them.

"Who are you?"

"I'm Jason."

"Who am I?"

"You're Rin, remember?"

"No. I don't remember."

"What do you remember?" asked the figure. Jason.

Rin frowned. She reached back into the foggy recesses of her mind, but it was dark and difficult to identify any memory beyond a shadowy form of pain and death. She concentrated.

"I don't remember much," said Rin. "Just words."

"Any little thing helps," said Jason.

"Dig, shovel, fire," said Rin, giving voice to every word that floated to the top of her mind. As she spoke, the fog began to clear and her memories grew sharper. "Death, dying, screams, the Consolidation Machine, maximum efficiency, no rest, burn through them."

Something snapped, and Rin's memories came flooding back. She couldn't speak as emotions swamped her: The guilt. The certainty that she was going to die. The hope that Jason could stop the machine and save the satyrs. The guilt. The guilt. The guilt.

"Jason!" she exclaimed, realizing who she was talking to. She tried to sit up, but she was restrained. Her manacles were attached to the bed.

"Rin, are you alright?" Jason said, relieved.

The guilt. "The machine," said Rin.

"We can talk about it later. Right now you need to focus on getting better."

The guilt. "It's important," said Rin.

"We can talk about it when you're stronger."

"I'm going to die."

"No. Not yet. Not anymore. My request went through. You were reassigned to my cell block again. You're safe. Focus on getting better."

Emotions washed over Rin. Relief. She was going back to the rim. She would be with Jason, Cleo, and Gai. The happy past she'd reminisced about in the Deep Pit would be hers again. The guilt. She didn't deserve the rim. She'd murdered thousands of satyrs. Children. She'd killed children. She'd forced others to become murderers also. She was a monster. She deserved the Deep Pit. She deserved to die. Fear. What if Jason was wrong? What if she closed her eyes, and when they opened again she was back in the black room with the heat and the smoke? She was confused, scared, tired, and weak, and she didn't know how to deal with it all.

"You should sleep. I just wanted to see you," said Jason.

"Wait, Jason," said Rin.

"What?" he asked.

"I. I don't understand."

"Don't understand what?"

"Why am I here? I don't deserve to be here. Not after what I did. I deserve to be in the Deep Pit. I deserve to die."

"You deserve to be here. Trust me. We'll talk about it later, alright?"

"Alright," said Rin.

Jason left and the doctor came back. A cloth was draped over Rin's eyes, and she slept again.

Chapter 18

The next time Rin woke, the doctor asked her a few questions. Her restraints were released from the bed, and she was allowed to sit and attempt to walk. She was able to do both. The doctor asked a few more questions. Rin answered. Guards came and took her back to her old cell block. She was given her old number. She was in her old bunk, with her old locker and her old desk. It was as though she'd never left.

Rin heard her cellmates in the common room. She closed her eyes and rested her back against the wall. She was afraid to face them. She'd tried to escape, and she hadn't said a word about the escape attempt to Cleo and Gai. What did they think of her?

Jason came into the cell from his office. She looked at him from where she cowered by the wall.

"Come on. The doctors have you on a special food plan. Since the Deep Pit feeds prisoners intravenously, you need to be eased back into solid foods. Your meal will be at the back of the food fabricator. Eventually, you'll be back to normal solid food, but for now, you're restricted to liquids," he said.

Rin nodded.

Jason led her into the common room, which was exactly as it had been when she left. There was a line of people waiting impatiently by the food window. She recognized most of the faces, though she noticed that Charlotte and Allie were missing. Rin wondered if Jason was working to scoop them up out of the Deep Pit also, or if his mercy only extended to her. She had hated this place. How could she have hated this place? How had she been willing to risk losing it? What had possessed her to try to escape?

"Everyone, Rin is back," said Jason, stepping around her to address the rest of the inmates.

The other inmates stared at Rin in silence.

"Rin?" said Cleo, breaking the tension.

Rin nodded and looked up at her.

Cleo looked confused. She left her place in line and walked up to Rin. "What did they do to you?" she asked as she gently brushed Rin's short hair with her fingers. The brief touch made Rin's chest clench with emotion. She didn't deserve this comfort.

"Rin's been in the Deep Pit for the last few months," said Jason.

"They put her all the way down at the bottom?"

"Yes, but she's back now."

"Come on," said Cleo, leading Rin by the hand to the end of the line. Cleo's spot in line was near the front, but she stayed at the back with Rin. Rin reveled in the warmth of Cleo's hand on hers.

Jason left. Cleo stayed at Rin's side. When they reached the front of the line, there was a plate of normal food for Cleo, and a bowl of broth for Rin. After months without any food, the meager broth smelled like a feast. Rin took the bowl in her hands, and Cleo took both of their glasses of water on her tray. They sat next to each other with their food. Rin stared at her plate.

"What did they do to you?" Cleo asked again, looking with concern at the bowl of broth on Rin's plate.

"Jason said I'll be able to eat normal food again eventually."

"They didn't feed you?"

Rin shook her head. "They just healed me."

Cleo ran her hand over Rin's back. The warmth was like a blanket over her shoulders, and Rin soaked it in.

"That is cruel," said Cleo, her voice tight with an anger Rin hadn't heard from her before.

"I deserve it. I did horrendous things," she whispered.

"Your terrible past doesn't excuse their cruelty."

Rin hung her head. "I think it does. I deserve far worse than what they did to me."

Cleo shook her head. Her lips were still tight with rage, but she let the topic drop. She wrapped her arm around Rin's shoulder. "Go on, eat," said Cleo, and her voice was tender despite her dark expression.

Rin took a spoonful of the broth, raising it to her lips and sipping. Warmth flooded through her as the broth filled her belly. Despite her hunger, she couldn't eat much. After so long without food, the sensation was strange. The textures in her mouth were new, and a welcome change from smoke and soot. She drank from her glass of water. The cool liquid sliding down her throat felt like a balm.

~*~

Rin woke up in her bunk, sat up, and cracked her head against the ceiling. She rubbed at it as she climbed down from her bunk to change her clothes.

"How are you feeling this morning?" asked Cleo.

Rin shrugged, pulling on fresh clothes. It felt luxurious to wear clean clothes every day. She joined the other inmates in the common room for breakfast and sat with Gai and Cleo.

"Hey, I didn't get a chance to talk to you yesterday. How are you?" asked Gai, sitting down next to her.

Rin shrugged again. Gai and Cleo fell into conversation and Rin ate her breakfast, letting their voices wash over her as she ate the soft food that waited for her at the back of the food fabricator. Conversation was especially comforting. She associated the sounds of others speaking with the cool room and relief from the smoke and the fire. It didn't matter what the others were talking about; the gentle cadence of their voices soothed her.

The plates were put away, and guards came to take them out to the Wall. Rin fell down the slope with her pickaxe like it was her first day, but she didn't care. She'd rather tumble down the Wall over and over for the entire workday than go back to the Deep Pit. She swung her axe into the wall, dislodging rock after rock. She threw the rocks into the cart, trying not to look deeper into the Pit. Trying not to think about where the rocks would go.

Rin fulfilled her quota by midday. She climbed to the top of the Wall, ate her lunch — a thermos containing soup, marked with her name among the brown bags for everyone else — and returned to her spot on the Wall. By the end of the day, she'd reached a second quota, earning an extra strike. A cushion between her and returning to the Deep Pit. Guilt gnawed at her. She didn't belong here. She belonged in the heat and the fire of the Deep Pit. Earning double quota put more space between her and moving down the Pit, but she didn't feel she deserved the protection.

Rin sat with Cleo and Gai at the breakfast table. A few days after returning to their cell, Rin was already able to share the same porridge as everyone else, despite being on her special diet for the rest of the day. Slowly soft food was being introduced, and Rin was beginning to feel better.

Cleo and Gai were trying to teach Rin a game they played, and Rin was struggling to follow it. It was a math game. For all his difficulty with screens, Gai was quick with numbers.

"It's your turn," said Cloe, resting a hand on Rin's shoulder.

"Ah, I'm sorry, what were the numbers again?" asked Rin.

Cleo squeezed her shoulder. "The numbers are 3, 7, 6, 52, and 78, and the target is 865."

Rin looked at Gai. "You've already got it, don't you?"

Gai shrugged. "It's your turn."

Rin shook her head. "I've already forgotten the numbers."

Cleo wrapped her arm around Rin's shoulders. Rin leaned toward her, hoping the contact would last as long as possible. "Don't worry. It's hard to keep the numbers straight. I struggle too without seeing the numbers written out, and I've played this game hundreds of times."

"You don't have any difficulty with it," said Rin, looking at Gai.

Gai shrugged, a casual gesture, but his expression darkened. "I have a long history of being good with numbers. This is a nice wholesome outlet for that skill compared with how I used it in the past."

"How did you solve it, then?" asked Cleo.

Gai shook off his dark mood and brightened as he rattled off his solution to the puzzle. "78 and 52 is 130, take away 6 is 124, times 7 is 868, take away 3 is 865."

Cleo withdrew her arm from around Rin and frowned, leaning on her elbows as she tried to work through the math in her head. "I couldn't even follow that to say if you're right."

"Those screens make you future people so soft-headed. Weren't you supposed to be a child genius?" said Gai with a smirk.

Rin's mind supplied her with an image of a tortured satyr with their head caved in at Gai's use of the words "soft-headed." Presumably Gai and Cleo continued their argument, but Rin lost track of the conversation. She struggled to breathe as she remembered the cruelty of her reign. She heard soldiers laughing as they called the satyrs they killed "soft-headed, once you get past the horns." Guilt turned her food to ash in her mouth. Bile climbed her throat, and she swallowed down the nausea. Rin was so lost in her spiral of shame that she didn't notice the guards come in to usher them out to the Wall until Cleo prodded her arm and, with a concerned expression, motioned for Rin to follow.

Days passed in that way. She didn't talk much. Cleo and Gai tried to include her, but the most innocuous conversations would send her into a spiral. Her emotions still swirled, and she didn't have the energy for talking when she was busy trying to understand how she felt.

When she slept, she dreamed of the Deep Pit. She saw the man throwing himself into the fire, and she remembered wishing she was him. Her shame hung on her like a weight. She had come to terms with her guilt in the Deep Pit, but now that she was away from that place, it threatened to smother her. She had been shown mercy. She'd never shown the satyrs mercy. She didn't deserve mercy. She hated herself. She deserved the Deep Pit, but every day she worked hard to earn extra strikes. She did everything in her power to avoid ever going back to that place, even though it was where she knew she should be.

~*~

"It's your off day," said Cleo, putting a hand on Rin's shoulder. Warmth bloomed in Rin's chest at the contact, before being quickly smothered by guilt.

Rin frowned. It *was* her off day. Unsure what else to do, she lowered herself back into her seat at the table and watched Cleo and the others leave for a day of work. An off day. She had forgotten about those. A day to rest. What a luxury.

After she'd sat alone at the table for a while, Jason pushed through the door to her cell. "Rin, can I see you in my office."

Rin stood and followed him through the cell, settling in the chair in front of his desk. He sat across from her.

"I talked to the doctors about you," said Jason.

Rin stared at him. Why would he do that? She was fine.

"I'm worried. You won't talk to anyone. They said it was to be expected. Very few people have ever been released from the

Deep Pit, but the doctors said it does things to people. Things that the doctors can't fix."

Rin continued watching him.

"Do you want to talk about it? I can hear you, at night."

No. She didn't want to talk about it.

Jason ran his fingers through his short black hair. Rin's hair was longer than his now.

He wheeled his chair back and opened the cabinet where he stored the inmates' possessions. He came back with Rin's pack of cards. It was from such a long time ago, from when she was High Commander. Rin stared at the worn brick of cards. She could hardly believe she had ever been that person.

"I'm giving this back to you. You don't have to pay for it. It's yours," said Jason.

He handed the pack of cards to Rin, and she took it from him with her now-calloused hands. The box felt different. She opened it and dumped out the cards, fumbling as she tried to shuffle them. It had been so long since she'd shuffled a deck of cards. It used to help her think. Think about killing satyrs.

Still. She passed the cards between her hands. Slowly her calloused fingers remembered the motions. At first, she just riffled the cards together; then she began performing the more complex shuffling tricks she'd learned as a child.

"Can you teach me a game, from your time?" asked Jason.

Rin nodded. She shuffled the cards for a moment longer, then began prepping the deck for the game she wanted to play.

"What are we playing?" asked Jason.

"It's called Pockets," Rin said. Her voice was dry. She realized she hadn't spoken in a few days.

"What are you doing now?"

"You don't play with the full deck," she told him. Her voice grew stronger as she spoke. She explained the rules to Jason. He prodded her to keep teaching him when she drifted off or lost focus.

"Do you like playing cards?" asked Jason. Rin had finished teaching him the game and they each held a hand of cards in front of them as they played.

"I did."

"Why?"

"I didn't have many friends as a child. Cards was something I could play with guards or servants."

"Why didn't you have many friends?" Jason asked as he took his turn.

"My parents were too important. Other children weren't allowed to play with me. Their parents were afraid that if I was made angry in a game, my parents would ruin their family."

"That sounds lonely," said Jason on her turn.

She shrugged.

Jason looked at his hand. "Was it lonely?"

"I didn't think so at the time. I had guards and servants. I could play in the gardens or go riding."

"Do you think it was lonely now, looking back?"

Rin was quiet for a moment as she played her cards. "I guess it was."

"Were you close with your parents?" asked Jason.

Rin played a hand, and the game was over. She collected the cards and began to shuffle them. "I was. They were my only friends. The only ones not afraid of making me angry."

"You must have been upset when they died," said Jason.

Rin wiped at the tears that formed in the corners of her eyes. "I was, but what I did... I was a monster."

"Do you regret it?" Jason asked.

"Every moment," she whispered.

"Even now that you're no longer in the Deep Pit?"

"I don't regret it because of the Deep Pit. The Deep Pit is what I deserve."

"Then why do you regret it?" he asked.

"Because it was the wrong thing to do. I hurt so many innocent people. I destroyed lives. I was a monster, and I can never undo what I did. I deserved to be in that place. I don't deserve the mercy you've shown me. I never showed anyone mercy in the past."

"I'm glad that you see the error of your ways," said Jason.

Rin wiped away more tears as she dealt out another hand to begin the game again. They played the next game in silence.

"I got these cards on a campaign," said Rin.

"You did?" asked Jason.

"Yes. We were down south, dealing with food riots, before the satyr extermination started. I had nicer cards at home in my palace, but I always took cards like these, simple sturdy ones, on campaigns. I'd lost my old pack, and stopped in a city to buy a new one."

"How long did you have them?"

"A few years. I liked them. Thank you for giving them back," said Rin.

"Gaius told me that getting your hands on something from your past might help."

"You talked to Gai about me?"

"Gaius and Cleo are worried about you. They both talked to me about you on their days off. They offered to pay with their own strikes to get you something out of your box."

"Why are they worried?"

"You haven't said a word to anyone in days. They've tried to draw you into conversation. You scream in your sleep and look through people."

They played a few more hands in silence. "I see things, when I sleep."

"What things?" asked Jason.

Rin picked up the half of the deck they weren't using in their game. She shuffled the cards between her hands. "I saw a man throw himself into the fire."

"That must have been hard to watch."

Rin continued shuffling the cards. "He screamed. He burned. It smelled of him for hours."

Jason waited.

Rin closed her eyes. "I wanted to be him. I wanted to jump into the fire and have it all be over."

Jason allowed a silence between them for a moment. "Why didn't you?"

"I didn't deserve it. I didn't deserve that freedom. I deserve to suffer."

Jason put his hand over Rin's, and she looked up into his eyes. "You were brought back here because you don't deserve that."

"You don't know the things I've done."

"I do know, remember? This is the future. We know everything about you, and I know you now. You regret what you did."

"That doesn't erase the damage I caused."

"You're not hurting anyone anymore."

"The machine," whispered Rin, remembering what she'd overheard and what she'd read.

"I'm looking into it, but you are not responsible for the machine. If it is as sinister as you think it is, it's not your fault."

"I fed it."

"You were forced to feed it," said Jason.

They played a few more hands in silence.

"Are Charlotte and Allie coming back?" asked Rin.

Jason heaved a sigh. "The only reason I could get you back here was because you served such a minor role. Allie was sent to the Deep Pit and died quickly. Charlotte was put in the Deep Pit also. I don't know if she's still alive."

"Why do you care about us? Why don't you hate us like the other guards and wardens? You should hate us. Hate me."

"I've been working here for a long time. At first, I did hate the inmates. All the worst people from my history books were paraded in front of me, and it was my job to take care of them. Eventually, I realized that I had to let go of my hatred because it was eating me up inside. I could become a hateful, bitter person, or I could care about the people I was in charge of caring for. I know that you have all done horrendous things in your lives, but you're not in your lives anymore. You're here, paying for what you've done. I try to only judge you on what you've done here, not what you did in your past."

"I did nothing here to earn your mercy."

Jason shook his head. "Charlotte and Allie took advantage of someone who was scared and vulnerable to help further their escape attempt. I know you were close to a breakthrough. I saw it when I gave you that paper. New inmates always fight it, but I could see that you were close to understanding that what you had done was wrong. They saw that same fear as vulnerability, and took advantage of it."

Rin and Jason played a few more hands while tears slid down Rin's cheeks. She didn't know if they were tears of relief, frustration, or fear.

"Thank you. I don't deserve your mercy, but thank you for it. I will do anything I can to deserve it."

"Just focus on getting better," said Jason.

~*~

When the other inmates came back from the Wall, Rin joined them in line for food. She sat at the table next to Cleo.

"How are you feeling?" Rin asked Cleo.

Cleo looked up from her warm dinner with wide, surprised eyes. She hadn't expected Rin to speak. "A little tired, but I'll be okay. How are you?"

"I'm tired too, but I think I'm getting better."

"That's good. Did Jason talk to you?"

"He did. He gave me back my cards."

"That's great! You'll have to teach me how to play one of your games."

"I will," said Rin.

They finished their dinner in silence and went back to their cell together. Rin and Cleo both got showers. Rin was still uncomfortable talking, but Jason had told her how much her silence bothered Cleo and Gai, and she didn't want to hurt her friends. In the privacy of the shower, with the divider between them and the sound of the water to protect her, Rin felt strong enough to talk.

"I'm sorry," she said, looking up into the water raining down on her from the shower head.

"For what?" asked Cleo from the shower next to her.

"For not including you in the escape attempt. For being so quiet when I came back," said Rin.

Cleo sighed. "I wouldn't have gone with you if you'd told me about the escape. I've been here long enough to know Charlotte's plan wouldn't have worked. You shouldn't be apologizing to me. I only wish you'd told me so that I could have stopped you and spared you the Deep Pit."

Rin let the water wash over her. "I'm still sorry for how I've acted since I've been back. I've been so wrapped up in my own problems, I didn't realize I was hurting you."

"I'm just happy that you're feeling better now."

"It's still going to be a while before I'm good at talking again."

"We can be patient. We're here to listen and help. Just don't shut us out anymore, okay?"

"Okay."

Cleo and Rin dried off and returned to their cell. Strengthened by Cleo's acceptance and with Cleo at her side, Rin apologized to Gai also. His response was similar to Cleo's. Gai went to take a shower, leaving Rin and Cleo alone together in their cell.

"So, why don't you teach me one of your games," said Cleo, sitting on the edge of her bed and gesturing for Rin to join her.

Heat crept up Rin's neck as she settled onto Cleo's bunk. The bed was small. Her leg brushed Cleo's as she found a comfortable position, and the close quarters felt intimate. Rin shuffled her cards and dealt out hands to herself and Cleo for another game of Pockets. She explained the game to Cleo, and they began to play. After a few quick hands, Cleo had the hang of the game and it fell into a rhythm.

"Cleo," said Rin, struggling to find words for what she wanted to ask.

Cleo looked up from her hand, brow creased with concern. "Yes?"

"How do you live with..." Rin shook her head. She couldn't think of a strong enough word for what she was feeling. She clutched her fist to her chest, where it felt like a lead weight had settled permanently. "How do you live with the guilt?" she finally asked, although she knew the word wasn't strong enough.

Cleo sighed and rested a comforting hand on Rin's knee. "I'm not going to lie, it is hard. Some days are harder than others. Some days, all I can do is focus on the things around me, ground myself in the present to avoid thinking about the past. But avoiding the past only postpones dealing with it."

"How do you deal with it?" asked Rin, looking up from her cards.

Tears of suppressed anguish stained her cheeks. Cleo and Gai wanted her to be present with them, but all she could feel was guilt. It washed over her, threatening to drown her.

"Oh, Rin," said Cleo, putting aside her cards and pulling Rin into an embrace.

Rin felt like a child as she cried, huddled in Cleo's arms.

"I know, it hurts," Cleo murmured. Her voice held an ache that echoed the pain in Rin's chest. Jason could sympathize with the inmates, and that made him kinder than they deserved, but Cleo had done terrible things also. She knew how Rin felt because she felt it too, and Rin was desperate to understand how Cleo could smile and laugh with this burden on her heart.

"I don't know how to live like this. I was supposed to die. I was supposed to die in the assassination. I was supposed to die in the Deep Pit. I keep living and it hurts so much. Jason said you and Gai want me to be present, but I don't know how."

Cleo rubbed her back and made comforting sounds until Rin's sobs quieted. "There are no easy answers. The guilt will *always* be there. No one can get rid of it, short of denial. Feeling this pain is good. It's healthy. You need to confront what you did, but you can't let it become all that you feel. You need to find a place for the guilt and a place for happiness too."

"I don't know how to do that," choked Rin.

"This helps — talking about it with someone who understands. I don't know everything, but I can help. All I want is for you to let me help."

Rin took a deep breath, and talked. She told Cleo about the ghosts that haunted her. She told her about the villages full of innocents slaughtered in the streets, and all the children. She told her about the torture and the horrible things she'd ordered others to do. She told her how she'd turned her own people against each other and soaked the home she'd wanted to protect in blood. She let Cleo see every shameful thing inside her, and Cleo listened, only speaking to encourage Rin. As she spoke, Cleo helped her find a way to live with the guilt. She never suggested forgiveness or overlooking the harm she'd caused. Instead, she helped Rin find a place for remorse, but also leave room to feel other things.

They talked later into the night than they should have, long after the lights were turned off. Gai listened, but went to sleep with the lights. He had his own way of dealing with his guilt, and hadn't come to terms with it as well as Cleo had. The conversation made him uncomfortable, but he encouraged Rin before going to sleep. When Rin was spent, she climbed into her own bunk in the dark, feeling slightly better than she had that morning.

Chapter 19

Rin worked hard to be more present with Cleo and Gai. Some days she struggled. Cleo gently reminded her when she stopped talking. Her guilt threatened to overwhelm her, but she was able to keep it from washing away who she was. Weeks passed, and Rin felt stronger. Her diet slowly returned to normal, until there was no longer special food waiting for her at meals and she was back to eating the same food as everyone else.

On one of her days off, Rin noticed Cleo's book out on her bed, and she remembered Cleo offering to let her read it. At the time, she hadn't wanted the distraction from her schemes and escape attempts. Now, she realized, it could help. Cleo was such a bulwark of support, she wanted to do something for her in return. Reading Cleo's book would give them something more lighthearted to talk about, and Rin knew the book and the story it contained was special to Cleo.

She picked up the book and turned it over in her hand. It was a mystery novel, fiction about a time unfamiliar to her. There were many strange words in the short summary on the back of the book, but she had her desk and she could look up the words she didn't understand. Learning the words and places of the future might help her provide some modicum of the support for Cleo that Cleo had provided for her.

She sat down at her desk with the book, carefully opened to the first page, and began to read. To her surprise, it wasn't as difficult for her to understand as she expected. The places and technology were unfamiliar and she had to look them up on her screen, but the story itself wasn't difficult to follow. She had not read many fiction books; they weren't common in her time. Even for someone like her, who had access to a substantial library, most books were non-fiction. As she got used to the way the story was written, she found herself absorbed into the world of the book. It was fast-paced and exciting. The detective protagonist was in constant danger. Rin's heart leapt at every turn, scared for the life of the imaginary person.

She jumped when the door to her cell opened. She had been too engrossed in her reading to hear when the other inmates came back from the Pit. She looked up from the pages. Cleo's frown of concern melted into a smile when she saw Rin huddled over the book.

"You're reading my book!" said Cleo.

Rin shuffled in her desk for a bookmark. "Yes, I remember you said I could."

"Yes! Do you like it?" asked Cleo, walking across the room to wrap her arms around Rin and peck a kiss on her cheek.

Rin's heart leapt, and her face flooded with heat. In her time, such a gesture would have been more than something casual among friends, but she didn't know about Cleo's time. The woman felt comfortable working shirtless on the Wall; clearly her norms and taboos were different from what Rin was used to. Still, Rin was left red in the face and disappointed as Cleo pulled away.

"I think so," stammered Rin, trying to recover from the heat climbing her neck and face from Cleo's brief kiss.

"You think so?" Cleo asked as they walked into the common room together.

"I don't know. I'm scared for the detective."

"It's a mystery book. That's part of the tension. It's why you're supposed to want to keep reading."

"So being worried is a good thing?" asked Rin.

"In fiction, yes. I thought you had books in your time."

"Not books like that! Books in my time were about real life. I suppose I did have some fiction books, but they weren't so stressful!"

Cleo laughed as they collected their dinner plates. "I love mystery novels. That one is pretty average for my time. It was popular when I bought it."

"I think I like it. I definitely want to keep reading it," said Rin.

"See, then it's doing its job! What part were you at?"

Rin gave her a summary of the part of the book she'd read. Cleo was excited to talk about the story and the detective character. Rin was the first person in seventeen years she'd convinced to read it. Rin asked questions, but Cleo refused to tell her what would happen next. She didn't want to ruin the story. They talked excitedly about the book. For a brief conversation, Rin was able to forget the guilt and the fear. She was able to smile and laugh and enjoy a conversation with Cleo.

When they left the common room for bed, the guilt came rushing back, but her smile lingered.

~*~

A few weeks later, Jason called her into his office to play cards and talk on her day off.

"Hi, Rin," he said as she sat across from him at his desk.

"Hi."

"How are you feeling?"

"I'm alright," Rin said. She watched Jason. He looked tired, or maybe sad. "How are you feeling?"

Jason sighed and ran his fingers through his hair. "Not great, actually."

"What's wrong?" asked Rin.

Jason glanced at his screen before looking back at Rin. "Come with me."

Rin frowned and followed Jason through a door behind his desk. She had assumed the door led to a closet, but instead it opened into a living space. She stepped into a dining room with a table and chairs. The floor was a light blue ceramic tile. Across from the table and chairs were stone-topped counters, and a sink. A kitchen. Jason led Rin through a doorway to the left. A half wall separated the next room from the kitchen, with tall chairs pulled up to it on the far side. The floor in this room was a rug that stretched wall to wall and was a uniform gray-brown. The room with the rug had a couch and a comfortable chair, similar to the ones in the common room, but less worn. They faced a wall-mounted screen.

"What is this place?" asked Rin, looking around.

"This is where I live."

"You live here? You don't go home at the end of the day?"

"No one who works in the Pit can go home at the end of the day. You've noticed that being close to a time machine slows aging?"

"Yes."

"Well, the effects of that can be harmful. We're all healed often enough to reduce those effects, but if I left the Pit, I would contaminate people in the outside world, so I'm expected to stay here."

Rin looked around the living space. It was small and cramped. "Is this why you were upset to lose your job in the Tower?"

Jason smiled. "Yes. People who work in the Tower don't have to live on-site. But I'm here now. I worked in the Pit before I got the job in the Tower."

"I'm sorry I cost you that job," said Rin.

Jason waved his hand dismissively. "It wasn't really your fault. You didn't know you would get me in trouble. It was Riviera's fault. I didn't have the Tower job for long, anyway. I didn't have a chance to get used to it before ending up back on Pit duty."

Jason sat down on the couch, and Rin sat on the chair across from him.

"I brought you in here so we could talk in private. There are cameras in my office. They aren't monitored, but the recordings could be pulled and reviewed."

"Why did you want to talk in private?"

Jason sat back in his seat. "I've been looking into the machine."

Rin sat up straight.

"You were right. It is more sinister than I realized."

"It's killing the satyrs."

Jason closed his eyes and sagged back in his chair. "Yes, it is killing the satyrs. I was able to access some classified documentation through the computer network here, and it was disturbing."

"What did it say?"

"Time travel doesn't change the past; it causes a split in the time stream. When people go back in time, we don't see the effects of the changes they make, because the changes cause a branch and a new time stream."

Rin nodded.

"That's how it's supposed to work. But scientists wanted to be able see the effects of the changes they made, so they forced one time stream to align with ours using the Consolidation Machine. When they altered the past to create satyrs, the time streams should have branched. We should never have seen the effects — we should never have known about satyrs. But the people who changed the past wanted to be able to conduct experiments and see how those changes moved forward in time. By forcing the two time streams to overlap, the machine causes the experimental time stream — the one with satyrs, your time stream — to collapse at the point when time travel was invented. You were right. The machine is killing the satyrs."

"It kills everyone?" asked Rin.

"Only the people and creatures that don't exist in this time stream, but about two-thirds of your time stream is destroyed when time travel is invented, including all the satyrs."

Rin ran her hand over her hair. It had grown out long enough now to be pulled back into a short ponytail. "And the machine at the heart of the Pit. Is that the Consolidation Machine?"

Jason looked sick. "Yes. The classified documents I found confirmed it. That is the Consolidation Machine. As long as it runs, it holds the two time streams together and causes the extinction of the satyrs."

"We have to stop it," said Rin. She owed it to the satyrs. Her guilt gnawed at her. She couldn't erase what she'd done, but she could stop the machine from finishing the job she'd started.

"After wrestling with what I found on the computers, I agree. That's why I wanted to talk about it with you," said Jason.

"What are we going to do?"

He shook his head. "I don't know. I thought you could help figure something out. You've been closer to the machine than anyone."

Rin felt a sick knot in her stomach. She wanted to start working on a plan to destroy the Consolidation Machine, but she was afraid of treading that ground again. "Scheming is what got me sent to the Deep Pit. It's what brought me here."

"This is a worthy cause."

The sick knot remained. She had managed not to lose herself to the guilt, but could she stop herself from going too far the other way? If she did what Jason wanted, if she began making plots and schemes again, could she hold onto the progress she'd made toward becoming a better person? Could she scheme without becoming a monster? She'd thought she'd been doing the right thing when she tried to avenge her parent's death, but she had ended up committing genocide.

"I don't know," said Rin.

"I can't destroy the machine on my own. I don't have the access or influence. I have as much control over the machine as you do. I need your help."

"I can try," she found herself saying.

"Thank you, Rin. What do you need?"

"Information. The more information I have, the better I can plan. We need to figure out what the machine is vulnerable to. I saw a man throw himself into it, and the machine was fine. It will take a lot to destroy a machine like that."

Jason nodded. He told Rin everything he'd learned about the machine. She listened and asked questions, but wasn't able to come up with a course of action.

"I'm going to need to talk about this with Gai and Cleo," said Rin. "They might be able to help."

"Are you sure?"

"Cleo's been here for a long time."

Jason nodded. "She's been here twice as long as I have."

"Exactly. She might know something we don't, and I still feel guilty about trying to escape without them. If I'm going to do this, I need you and them to hold me accountable so that I don't lose myself in schemes. I can't forget why I'm doing this," said Rin.

"I have faith in you," said Jason.

Rin shook her head. "I don't. I'm afraid that I'll distract myself with this problem and forget my guilt. When I first got here and was confronted with the idea that what I'd done was wrong, I used the escape attempt to bury my guilt. I can't lose sight of that again."

"Alright. If you think you need them, I'm not going to stop you."

"I won't tell them that you're involved."

"You don't trust them?"

"I do trust them, but I'm still worried. I want to protect you," said Rin.

"I can protect myself. You don't have to worry about me."

Rin smiled. "I don't want another incident like the Tower. I already got you demoted once."

Chapter 20

The day after Rin's conversation with Jason, she and Cleo worked side by side on the Wall.

"How are you feeling?" asked Cleo.

"I'm alright."

"Didn't sleep well last night?"

Rin shrugged. "As well as I ever do. Why?"

"You were screaming in your sleep again."

"Oh, I'm sorry about that."

"I just want to make sure you're okay. You know you can talk about it with me if you want," said Cleo.

Rin swung her axe into the wall in silence. She felled several more rocks before she spoke again. She didn't want to talk about what she'd seen and what she'd learned, but she needed Cleo's help. She needed to work on destroying the machine, and she couldn't do it without Cleo.

"I dream about the Deep Pit," said Rin.

Cleo quietly dug next to her. Waiting.

Rin allowed the steady rhythm of her pickaxe striking rock to push her forward and stop her from trailing off. "The Deep Pit is a terrible place. It's full of death and dying. At the bottom of the Pit is a fire. It's the heart of a great machine."

Rin paused, focusing on the pickaxe and the rocks. She forced herself to think about that place. Talking about it brought back the smell, the smoke, and the heat. "The machine is the reason there aren't any satyrs in this time."

Cleo's axe scraped the wall. "What?"

Rin focused on the wall and the work as she told Cleo about the Deep Pit. She focused on explaining the machine and how it held their time stream hostage, killing everything that made their world different from this one. In talking about the machine, Rin had to tell Cleo about the library and the book she'd found about the satyrs, and the conversation she'd overheard between the doctors and the mysterious other voice that insisted on burning through prisoners to keep the machine at maximum efficiency during the anniversary of time travel.

From there, she couldn't stop. She told Cleo everything. She told her about shoveling rocks into the fire until she collapsed. She told her about faking her unconsciousness and enduring the pain for a breath of fresh air when she was sent back to the doctors. She told her about losing herself in the smoke and the heat. She told her about wanting to jump into the fire and how, even though she would do everything she could to avoid going back to the Deep Pit, she knew she deserved that fire and pain. She didn't deserve the mercy she'd been shown.

"Rin, I am so sorry you went through that," Cleo said.

Cleo wrapped an arm around Rin, pulling her close, and the tension in Rin's chest uncoiled. She looked up, but the guards were preoccupied, talking amongst themselves. Rin relaxed and turned into Cleo's embrace.

"Like I said, I deserve it," said Rin.

Cleo squeezed her tight before releasing her and turning back to the Wall, just before the guards saw them.

"Sometimes, we don't get what we deserve. Sometimes that's a bad thing and good people go unrewarded, but sometimes it's a good thing and those of us who have done terrible things get a second chance."

"I should have died down there," said Rin.

"I'm pretty glad you didn't."

Rin looked up, and Cleo smiled at her. Warmth blossomed in Rin's chest. If her life could make Cleo happy, maybe it was worth continuing on.

Rin and Cleo continued digging. Rin didn't want to tell Cleo what she needed to do; she was afraid of it herself. What if her actions put her back in the Deep Pit? What if she lost herself in the scheming? What if she wasn't good enough, and she failed? She needed Cleo's support. With Cleo at her side, she would be strong enough to do what she needed to do, even if that meant going back to the Deep Pit. But she was afraid Cleo wouldn't stand with her.

Buoyed by Cleo's support thus far, Rin spoke again. "I'm going to destroy it."

"What?" asked Cleo.

"I'm going to destroy the machine," she said.

"How?"

"I don't know how yet, but I have to destroy it. I can't go back and undo the terrible things I did to the satyrs, but I can stop that machine from wiping them out. It's the only worthwhile thing I can do. If I'm going to be given a second chance I don't deserve, I'm going to use it to help the people I hurt."

Cleo and Rin dug in silence.

"You'll end up back in the Deep Pit. It could kill you," said Cleo.

Rin nodded as she heaved her pickaxe into the rock. "I was going to die in the Deep Pit. If Jason hadn't saved me, I would have, and I wouldn't have had the chance to do anything good to make up for the evil I've done. If I can take that machine out with me, at least my death will mean something."

Their pickaxes rang out, filling the silence between them. Rin struggled to find the words to ask Cleo for help. She didn't know how to ask anyone to take that kind of risk for her.

"I want to help you," Cleo said, before Rin could figure it out.

Rin was weak with relief.

"Thank you. I need you," said Rin.

"I don't know what I can do, but I want to make sure you're safe," said Cleo.

"I need you to help me stay grounded. I can't lose myself in schemes. I need to remember my guilt and why I'm doing this. I can't return to being the cruel person I used to be."

Cleo smiled. "You couldn't go back to that if you tried. You've changed too much."

"Still, that is my greatest fear."

"I'll help you," Cleo reassured her.

"Thank you," said Rin.

~*~

Cleo and Rin dug together until lunch break. Then they slid down the Wall again and kept digging. Gai joined them, and Cleo prompted her to tell Gai about the machine. Rin was emotionally drained from her conversation with Cleo earlier, so she told Gai about the machine without going into details about the Deep Pit.

When she finished, Gai let out a low whistle between his teeth. "That's a big problem."

"I'm going to destroy it," she said.

Gai looked between her and Cleo with wide eyes. "You are? You can't do that! What will happen to us?"

"I don't know," she said. In the midst of her fear and remorse, it hadn't occurred to her to worry about what would happen to her if she succeeded in destroying the machine.

"Don't you think you should figure that out before you destroy the machine linking us to our own time? You could make it impossible for any of us to ever go back!"

"We aren't going back. We're supposed to work here until we die."

"Won't it cause a massive change to our time stream if all of us disappear from history? I know we're all about to die, but history will be changed if they can't find our bodies!"

"That change will be better than the entire time stream being wiped out."

"What if it doesn't just trap us here? What if it kills us!"

A fresh guilt twinged to life in Rin. She hadn't thought about what the consequences of destroying the machine might be. For all her desire to be better, to do better, she was still falling into her old habit of diving straight into a course of action without thinking through the consequences. That was what had led her to commit genocide, and led her to throw in her lot with Charlotte and Allie. Now she was risking the lives of everyone in Hell.

"We're already dead," said Cleo.

Gai turned his shock toward Cleo. "You agree with this? You're usually so careful! You're the one telling me to keep my head down. You're the one who's spent sixteen years in the same cell."

"Seventeen years, almost eighteen. And yes, I believe in getting along and staying alive, but this is important. As Rin pointed out to me, we can't undo what we've done, but we have an opportunity now to do something good. When so much of the difference I've made has been negative, I want to do something positive for a change," said Cleo.

Gai shook his head. "No, I can't be a part of this. I won't stop you and I won't tell anyone what you're working on, but I can't help you. It's too much of a risk."

"Gai, this is important," said Cleo.

Gai looked between Cleo and Rin. Rin wanted his help. She needed his help. For a moment he looked like he might agree, but then he shook his head. "I can't. I'm not like you two. I was never a person who was involved in grand plans. I've changed a lot in my time here, but at the end of the day, I can't put my own life at risk even if it is for the greater good. I haven't changed that much."

"You can't turn your back on something as important as this," said Cleo.

"No, if he doesn't want to be involved, we should accept that," said Rin, although she felt his refusal to help like a physical blow.

Cleo looked sharply at Rin, then back at Gai. "You're making a mistake."

Gai smiled with sad eyes. "I'm quite talented at that. Don't worry. I won't tell anyone what you're doing, but I can't be involved. There isn't anything I could do to help anyway."

Rin's heart was heavy, but she nodded and accepted Gai's refusal. She couldn't force him to be involved, and it wasn't something she would want to do even if she had that power.

Chapter 21

A few weeks later, Rin stood in line waiting for the food window to open. She was tired and dirty from a day on the Wall and frustrated that she couldn't figure out how to stop the machine. She turned the problem over and over in her mind, but she didn't have enough information or resources to do anything to stop it.

While they waited for their food, the door from cell C opened and Jason came into the common room, followed by a new face: a man in his early twenties with pale skin, a dirty-blond mop of hair, and a long lanky frame.

"Hello everyone, this is Taylor. He's going to be joining us for a while. Office hours are open," said Jason, before turning back and disappearing through cell C.

Taylor scanned the line of people in front of him, then took his place at the end of the line behind Rin. She ignored the newcomer.

"Hey, are you High Commander Rin Tallow?" asked Taylor.

Rin glanced over her shoulder. He must be from her future to recognize her on sight. Guilt squeezed her chest at the use of her title. This new person knew the monster she'd been in life. She was the villain from his history books.

"I was her," she grumbled. Mercifully, the line started moving and she was able to step forward and away from Taylor before the conversation could progress.

Rin grabbed her hot food from the window and went to join Cleo and Gai at the table. Taylor's use of her title stuck with her as she picked at her food. It brought back memories of her past. The guilt pressed down on her.

Cleo nudged Rin's arm with her elbow. The brief contact broke her from her miserable thoughts, and she looked up. Cleo was frowning.

"What's wrong?" asked Cleo.

Rin shrugged and took a bite of her dinner. "Just tired."

Cleo looked down the table towards Taylor. Rin followed her eyes. Taylor was watching them. He caught them looking at him and turned quickly back to his food. Rin felt the guilt claw at her. He'd been gawking at the monster from his history lessons.

"What did he say to you in the food line?" asked Cleo.

"Not much. He asked me if I was me." Rin paused. "He used my old title."

Cleo put a comforting arm around her shoulder and Rin drew strength from the contact. She wondered if Cleo knew how much her touch affected her.

"That's not you anymore," said Cleo.

Rin stabbed her food. "It was me. Anyone new coming in here will know me as the High Commander and they're right to hate me. I was that horrible person."

"Everyone here is a horrible person too. Remember, this is Hell. Just because you don't know what other people did, doesn't make them innocent."

"He doesn't look like he could do anything too horrible."

Cleo laughed. "How many people here look like they could do horrible things? You remove us from our structures of power and most of us aren't very intimidating."

Rin glanced down the table towards Taylor again. He was bent over his food, studiously not watching her. Cleo was right.

She didn't know anything about him. It didn't lessen her guilt, but it made it easier to bear.

After dinner, Rin sat at her desk. She was tired, but also curious about Taylor. Her bed was tempting, but with sleep often came nightmares. She didn't mind postponing it to satisfy her curiosity. She swiped her screen to wake it up, opened the search engine and thought about how to word her question. She didn't know Taylor's last name or titles. She didn't even know what time he was from. She'd turned around to ask Cleo how to word the search when Taylor walked in. The question died on her lips, but she'd already caught Cleo's attention.

"What is it?" asked Cleo.

Rin glanced at Taylor, who was standing in front of his locker. "Never mind. I'll ask you later."

She turned back to her computer and decided she would have to figure out how to formulate the question on her own.

"So, Taylor, how did you end up here?" asked Cleo.

Rin looked over her shoulder. Taylor was fidgeting in his locker, not looking at them. Cleo winked at her, and Rin smiled appreciatively. She was curious to hear how he described his past. She could see what the screen had to say later.

"Time travel, apparently," he said.

"I mean, what did you do?"

"Oh, I played with fire," he answered.

"What does that mean?" asked Cleo.

"I was good at blowing stuff up."

"Ah, you were a terrorist," said Cleo, as though that cleared up everything. It didn't help Rin. What was a terrorist? Was that what she should search? 'Taylor Hell terrorist'?

Taylor pulled his head out of the locker and glared at Cleo. "No. I wasn't. That's a lie."

"Yes, yes. Whatever you say," said Cleo, waving her hand dismissively and turning towards the bathroom.

"What's a terrorist?" asked Rin, taking up the conversation that Cleo had abandoned.

"A terrorist is someone who commits violence to bring attention to a political cause."

"And you didn't do that?"

"No."

"Then, why did you blow stuff up?" she asked.

"I blew up evil things. Offices and headquarters for people who wanted to elevate satyrs above humans! I couldn't let that happen. You understand. Satyrs are an abomination. They should have been destroyed. I wanted to carry on the legacy of people like you."

Rin's chest clenched. It hadn't occurred to her that some people in her future could see her in a positive light. She had read about human animosity towards satyrs permeating through history, but she hadn't made the connection that people who hated satyrs would champion her. Knowing that he celebrated her past made her guilt worse. The harm she'd done to satyrs hadn't ended with her death, if people in generations after her took up her 'cause' as their own.

"I was a monster. I did unforgivable things. I'm in Hell and I deserve it," snapped Rin.

He frowned. He hadn't expected that response from her. Recovering from his shock, he wrinkled his nose in disgust. "Apparently you're not the person we thought you were in my time. You were supposed to be an incredible leader, someone who saw the satyrs for the disgusting half-breeds they are and did the right thing. Now I see you're just a cowering goat-lover."

Rin's anger flared and she leapt to her feet. She didn't have her dagger, but she had her hands and she could cause pain with them. She wanted to wrap her fists around his skinny little neck and throttle the life out of him. How dare he praise the monster she had been? How dare he call the satyrs half-breeds? She lunged towards Taylor, but was stopped by Gai, who threw himself bodily into her and pinned her to the wall.

"Woah, Rin! Stop! You're going to get yourself sent down the Pit again. Fighting is an automatic drop, it doesn't matter how many strikes you have!" said Gai, holding Rin to the wall as she struggled to reach Taylor.

Threats of being sent down the Pit cut through the haze of rage that had swallowed Rin, and she stopped fighting him. "Thanks, Gai."

Gai let her go. He watched her, afraid she would lunge for Taylor as soon as he stepped away, but as quickly as her rage had surged, it fell away. She wasn't angry with Taylor, not really. She was angry at herself. His words brought back memories of her past. She could see satyrs bloodied and dying. She could hear the taunts from her soldiers as they tortured them and burned their villages. Rin's guilt fed her anger. She couldn't hurt the woman she had been, but she could hurt Taylor, who was spewing the same ideas she had endorsed in her life.

"That's right! You're a goat-lover," sneered Taylor.

He thought his insults had caused her to lose her temper. She would give anything for that to be the worst insult that could be hurled at her. She was a monster. A despicable, vile, inhuman creature who had only made the world worse by living in it. The best thing she'd ever done was die. Calling her a goat-lover was a compliment.

Gai was hovering nervously between Rin and Taylor when the door to Jason's office opened and Rin's manacles tightened. Everyone looked up. Gai looked scared; Taylor glared at Jason. Rin just felt tired.

"Rin. In here, now."

"She didn't do anything!" said Gai.

Jason glanced at him. "I'm not dealing with you right now, Gaius. Rin, in here, now."

Gai stepped out of her way. She walked past Taylor without looking at him.

Jason closed the door behind her as she entered his office. "Sit down," he said.

Rin sat in the chair in front of his desk. For the first time since being rescued from the Deep Pit, she felt nervous in Jason's office. Gai's warning that fights were an automatic trip down the Pit rang in her ears.

Jason sat across from her. "What was that?" he asked, gesturing toward the screen in front of him.

Rin looked down at her hands.

"Was that a fight?" demanded Jason.

"Almost," whispered Rin.

"Rin, look at me."

She looked up. His expression was exasperated. "What happened? One minute, you're all getting ready for bed, the next Gaius is holding you back from attacking Taylor!"

"He called satyrs half-breeds," said Rin.

"You called satyrs half-breeds!"

"I was wrong! I was a monster!"

Jason sighed and slumped back in his chair. "I am happy that you've seen the error of your ways, but if you get in a fight with another inmate, I will have no choice but to send you down the Pit."

Rin hung her head. Her hands shook with fear. How far down would he send her? Smoke. Fire. Pain. Her vision blurred, and she saw the darkness. She felt the pain. She was going to die. She deserved it.

"Rin!" Jason's voice cut through her dark memories. "Come back to me."

Rin looked up.

"Like I was saying, we're lucky that Gaius stopped you. As it is, I still have to dock you strikes for trying to hit Taylor, but because you didn't actually hit him I don't have to send you down a level, and I won't. It's lucky you have such a healthy strike buffer. I'm docking you ten strikes, which leaves you with twenty-something in the bank."

Rin stared at Jason. Ten strikes! If she didn't make double quota as often as she did, that could have sent her down three levels!

"You have to be careful. Remember what you're working toward. Dropping levels and leaving my block won't help you with the machine," said Jason.

Rin nodded. He was right. It was hard enough working out a way to destroy the machine with a block warden who was sympathetic to her goals. How much harder would it be deeper in the Pit?

"I know. I lost my temper. It won't happen again," said Rin.

"Good. I didn't think about how hard it would be for you to have someone in your cell who idolized your past. I should have warned you."

"I was who I was, but listening to someone else parroting those old beliefs back to me without a shred of remorse was a shock. I've gotten used to people around here agreeing that I'm a monster."

"You're not the only person here who's had that problem. You should talk to Cleo about it. She was the head of a movement she now disavows, and she has to deal with people who idolized her past too."

"I will. Thank you, for not sending me down the Pit," said Rin.

"I don't want to send you down. I have a lot of leeway over who gets what punishment, but some punishments are beyond my control. I'm glad this happened in the cell and not on the Wall. If a guard saw that, you would have been five levels down before I even knew something had gone wrong."

Rin swallowed.

Jason glanced at his screen. "There's still time before lights out. Do you want to stay here and collect yourself for a minute before going back to your cell?"

Rin nodded. She focused on her breathing, and slowly the shaking left her hands.

~*~

The next day, Cleo and Gai dug close to Rin, making sure Taylor couldn't get anywhere near her to incite a fight while the guards were watching. Rin swung her pickaxe into the wall. The rhythmic beat of steel on stone did nothing to help her think about the machine. Taylor had kicked the hornet's nest of her guilt, and she was lost in the swells of emotion that washed over her. She was a monster, vile, and she had inspired future generations of monsters. She was dead, but still did harm to satyrs for centuries after her death. His admiration for her past added an entire new component to her guilt.

"How do you deal with people who were inspired by your past?" Rin asked Cleo under her breath when the guards were far enough away that they wouldn't notice the whispered conversation.

Cleo frowned. "It's hard. The things we did influenced history. That's why we're here. People born after us took up our causes and did unspeakable things in our name. It helps to take Jason's view on them."

"What do you mean?"

"You told me Jason said that the reason he can put up with us is because he knows we are dead and unable to hurt anyone anymore."

"Yes."

"That's true for everyone here, including the people who drew inspiration from us. They can't hurt people and further our legacy anymore. They are here, and they are suffering for what they did."

Rin swung her axe into the rock, mulling over what Cleo had said.

"Is it my fault? Am I responsible for the people who came after me?" she asked.

Cleo laughed and shook her head. "No. People before and after you hated satyrs for their own reasons. They may have used your name as a rallying point, but if you hadn't done the things you did, they would have had plenty of other people through history to rally around."

"That sounds like an excuse," whispered Rin. The guilt swelled and threatened to crush her.

"Did you draw inspiration from the past?" asked Cleo.

She thought back to the previous generals and leaders she'd idolized. "Yes."

"If one of those people who inspired you came back from the grave and condemned your actions, would you have stopped?"

Rin remembered the monster she had been. "No."

"Well then, what makes you think your legacy is any different? People like Taylor idolized a version of you that they invented. You weren't there to tell them what you did and didn't approve of. They did what they wanted and told themselves you would have approved. You are no more responsible for the crimes that Taylor committed any more than you are responsible for my past."

Rin continued to swing her pickaxe into the wall. She stooped to pick up the shimmering black rocks she'd felled and threw them into the cart. Then she kicked the rubble into the chute behind her. She looked down the Wall and saw Taylor struggling with the pickaxe, cursing as it slid across the wall without dislodging any rocks. She still felt a surge of guilt for the future evils inspired by her genocide, but Cleo was right. She hadn't been there to approve their actions. If she could go back to her time, she would undo the damage she'd done and prevent future generations from taking inspiration from her, but she couldn't. Her time in the past was over. Taylor was a part of that legacy, but he wasn't her responsibility. His actions and his guilt were his own burdens to bear.

Rin went back to digging. She turned her attention away from her remorse and toward the problem at hand, the Consolidation Machine. When the bell sounded and the inmates climbed the Wall for their break, Taylor was denied a break due to his low quota. He cursed and shouted. He was kicked down the Wall and lost a strike before being knocked unconscious and dragged off by the guards. He looked too scrawny to have done any real damage in his time.

"What did he do again?" Rin asked Cleo.

Cleo sat next to Rin, eating her lunch and watching the drama unfold below them.

"Blew up buildings where people he didn't agree with worked. Killed thousands of people before he was caught in one of his own explosions and died. History didn't remember him fondly. I didn't recognize him when Jason introduced him, but I looked him up on the screen. He was from around my time, a little bit before me. I knew about some of the buildings he destroyed, but didn't recognize his name. In my time, there was an effort not to reward terrorists with immortality. History didn't teach about the people who committed acts of terror, just the events," explained Cleo.

Rin stared into the Pit where the glow of the fire at its heart was faintly visible. Pieces began to fall into place, and Rin could finally see a plan coming together; unfortunately, it hinged on one very volatile element.

"I think we need his help," she said.

Cleo glanced towards Rin. The guards were all preoccupied with Taylor, so their conversation wasn't going to be overheard. "What do you mean?"

"The machine. We need to destroy it, and he's an expert at destroying things," said Rin.

"You almost started a fight with him! You really think you'll be able to convince him to destroy the machine and save the satyrs?"

"He doesn't need to know all the details. All we need is for him to build us an explosive."

"You think you can convince him to do that?"

Rin sighed. "I can convince him."

"I don't know. It's dangerous. We don't know him, and he already lost you ten strikes. What if you lose your temper again? Will Jason be as forgiving?"

"I won't lose my temper again. He'll help us. I'll let him see a bit of the monster from my past. He'll listen to the High Commander," said Rin.

"That's dangerous."

"I know. I need you to help me. I can't lose myself in that monster," said Rin.

Cleo shook her head and pulled Rin against her side. Rin's heart leapt as their bodies touched. "I think it's more likely that you won't be able to pretend to be the person from your past, not that you'll lose yourself in it. You've changed too much since then."

She looked into Cleo's deep eyes. Her lips were close enough to kiss, if only she was worthy of that kind of happiness. "Still. Promise you'll help me? I'm afraid of slipping back into my old ways."

"I promise. I'll be there at your side when you talk to him," said Cleo.

"No, I mean after. You can't be there. I don't know him. I don't trust him. If you're there, he could report you," she said.

"I'm not going to let you go through something like this alone."

"I can't be responsible for you being sent down the Pit," said Rin.

"You aren't. This is my decision. I want to be there, at your side. This is important," Cleo said firmly.

Rin didn't want to put Cleo in danger, but she did want her to be there. With Cleo at her side, she would be able to face Taylor. She would feel better about pretending to be the High Commander.

"Thank you," she said.

Cleo smiled and squeezed her shoulder before they returned to their lunch. They ate together in silence for a while before Cleo asked, "How are you going to talk to him? The cameras will see any conversation you try to have, and Jason will stop you. If you try to talk to him on the Wall, he might make a scene and get you in trouble with the guards."

Jason wouldn't stop her. She hated keeping his involvement secret from Cleo, but it wasn't safe for anyone else to know. If the plan failed and Rin got herself and the others killed, Jason would be the only one left who could do something about the machine.

"I'll talk to him at night, after lights out. Allie set up a glitch in the cameras. They stop working sometimes at night. It seems random, but she taught me the pattern. There's a black-out tomorrow night. I'll talk to him then."

Cleo nodded slowly. "That's how you three met up to plan your escape?"

Rin nodded tightly.

"Well, it worked then. I don't see why it wouldn't work now."

"Exactly," said Rin.

Chapter 22

Rin swung the axe into the wall. Chips of gray and black rock showered her in a sharp cascade. She didn't notice the small scrapes that sprouted across her neck and face as she heaved the heavy axe into the stone again and again. She had to convince Taylor to build an explosive for her. She had to pretend to be the person she once was. Then she had to get the explosive to the machine. She hauled back and slammed her axe down again, showering herself and the space around her with rubble. She knew of one way to deliver it. *Smoke. Fire. Heat.* She'd stood right next to it for months. *Pain. Guilt.* She did everything in her power now to avoid going back, but she did know how to get close to the machine.

"Hey, stop messing around on the Wall," shouted a guard.

"Rin," Gai hissed next to her.

She looked up. The guards were shouting at her. She looked around and saw that she stood in a mess of rubble and ore. Shaking her head, she dislodged a shower of dirt and rocks that had fallen into her hair, then bent to pick out the black rocks and toss them into the cart. The guards watched her for a moment before turning and continuing their patrol along the top of the rim.

"Are you alright?" asked Gai, helping Rin clean up the mess at her feet.

"Just thinking," muttered Rin.

Gai frowned and turned back to the wall. He still refused to help destroy the Consolidation Machine. He knew that when Rin or Cleo were vague in answering his questions, the real answer involved the machine, and he stayed away from the topic by not prodding.

"I wish you would leave it alone," muttered Gai.

"I can't."

"It will get you killed."

"This is more important than my life," she growled. Most things were more important than her worthless life, but she left that part out.

Gai looked up at her. "This will get Cleo killed."

Rin's chest clenched at that. Cleo's life mattered to her. She glanced over to where Cleo was working, shirt wrapped around her hands. Rin dragged her attention back to Gai. "She had the same opportunity you had to refuse."

"What if this plan of yours gets us all killed? You're messing with time travel. You have no idea what's going to happen," said Gai.

"I cannot stand by while I know that machine is down there destroying our time stream," she said, slamming her pickaxe into the wall.

"So the rest of us don't get a choice?" demanded Gai.

Rin glared at him. "You don't know it will kill you if it's destroyed."

"I know that it won't kill me if you leave it alone."

"I'm sorry," said Rin.

Gai glared and shook his head, but he let the conversation end.

~*~

After dinner that night, Rin took advantage of Jason's office hours.

"What is it?" Jason said as she stepped into his office.

"Can we talk in private?" asked Rin.

Jason nodded and led her through the door behind his desk to his private quarters. Rin sat on the high stool at the bar between his living room and his kitchen.

"I think I have a plan, but I need to know something."

"What do you need to know?" he asked.

"When I almost got in a fight with Taylor, you said you wouldn't be able to stop me from being sent down the Pit if I'd actually struck him. Does that mean someone else is watching the cameras in the cell?"

Jason frowned. "Sometimes. I'm the only one who watches the cameras live, but there are recordings of everything the cameras see. If you struck Taylor and he told someone, they would pull the recordings and send you down the Pit."

"So, no one reviews the recordings regularly?"

"No. They're only reviewed if there's an incident. Why?"

"I need to talk to people in private. Can you look the other way if me and a few of the other inmates are out of bed at night?"

"I can, but if someone else reports you, I won't be able to protect you."

"Will you be in trouble?" she asked, worried that her plan endangered Jason even with her keeping his involvement a secret.

He shrugged. "A bit, but nothing major. Maybe a write-up for not paying close enough attention to the surveillance, but that's not very serious."

"Is it true that there aren't any cameras in the cleaning supply closet?"

"Yes, that's true."

"Good. I don't want there to be any recordings of my conversations."

"What's your plan?" asked Jason.

"I'm going to use Taylor."

Jason frowned. "Taylor? The guy you almost punched within an hour of meeting him?"

"Yes. I'm going to convince him to build me an explosive to blow up the machine."

The blood drained from Jason's face, and suddenly, Rin was worried about him. It was one thing to discover a sinister machine was buried at the heart of the Pit and want to see it destroyed. It was an entire other thing to actually be a part of the scheme to destroy it. Jason was a good person. He wasn't used to being a part of plots made in the dark of night.

Rin felt a trickle of dread. What if he withdrew his support? He already looked like he was going to throw up. She was protecting him by withholding information about his involvement from the other inmates; maybe she should protect him from himself by withholding information about the plan from him. She was going to avoid the cameras by making her plans in the closet where the cameras couldn't see. She could keep the plan a secret from Jason. Yes. She would do that. He didn't need to know the details. All he had to do was ignore a few clandestine meetings in the dead of night. She wouldn't ask any more of him.

"How are you going to convince him to do that?" asked Jason.

"I haven't decided yet, but I'll get him to help," she said. She didn't think Jason wanted to hear that she would be playing High Commander to appeal to Taylor's old admiration for the monster she'd been in life.

"You're not going to get into a fight and get yourself sent deeper into the Pit?"

Rin smiled. "No. I'm just going to talk to him. All I need from you is to ignore a few people out of their bunks at night from time to time."

"I can do that," said Jason.

Rin returned to her cell and got a quick shower before bed. She lay awake after the lights went out, waiting. Her eyelids were heavy and she wanted to sleep. A long day on the Wall had left her muscles worn out and her energy drained. She listened to the breathing of her cellmates and waited until it sounded like they were asleep. Then she got up.

Rin found Cleo's bed in the dark and woke her.

"What's going on?" whispered Cleo.

"Go to the cleaning supply closet," said Rin.

Cleo stood and left the room. Rin went to Taylor's bed, and took a few steadying breaths. It was time for her to become High Commander again. Fear made her arms weak. What if she lost herself in the person she used to be? No. Cleo was waiting in the other room. She would prevent her from sliding back into that monster. Rin held herself tall, then schooled her face into the stern authoritative expression of her past. Taylor wouldn't be able to see her in the dark, but the posture and expression would help her play the part.

Rin stepped up to Taylor's bunk and woke him with a hand over his mouth. Taylor jumped and tried to talk, but his words were muffled by Rin's hand. Rin leaned close. She had to stand on her toes to whisper in Taylor's ear on the top bunk.

"Be quiet and get up. There's more going on here than you know," Rin hissed.

Taylor nodded his head, and Rin let go of his mouth. He didn't speak as he climbed down from his bunk. Rin dragged him by the arm to the door of their cell. They stepped out into the soft glow of the screen in the common room and padded quietly across the room to the closet. Rin pushed Taylor inside and closed the door behind them. Light from the screen leaked under the door, but it failed to illuminate the space.

"Do you want me to turn on the light?" asked Cleo quietly.

"Yes," Rin said.

There was movement, and a light clicked on above their heads.

"What's going on?" demanded Taylor. "There are cameras! They saw us coming in here! The block warden will be here any minute!"

Rin glared down at him. She was the High Commander, although the thought made her recoil. She pushed past her disgust with her old life. It was her past, and if she could use it to help the satyrs of the future, she would. "You don't think I know about the cameras? They have a glitch and black out sometimes. I know when the blackouts are and woke you all up in the middle of a one."

"What's going on?" Taylor asked again, with more uncertainty.

"I have decided that you may be useful," Rin told him.

"Useful?"

"Sit down," said Rin.

The three sat on the floor of the closet.

"We have been developing a plan for escape, and we think skills from your life may help with that plan."

"What?"

"I have unfinished business in my time. I will get back and finish the job I started," said Rin.

"You told me you regret your past. You said that you were a monster."

"Yes. As you pointed out, the cameras are always watching. You think I would stay on the rim of the Pit long if I didn't put on a show of remorse?"

Understanding slowly dawned on Taylor. "You were pretending, so that you would receive better treatment?"

"Obviously."

"You don't believe what you said about satyrs?"

"Of course not, the filthy half-breeds deserve to be wiped out," said Rin. Guilt, disgust, and anger welled up inside her. She swallowed hard.

Cleo's hand surreptitiously covered Rin's. She squeezed Rin's hand. Rin squeezed back, grateful for Cleo's support. She drew strength from the contact and managed to maintain the facade of the High Commander.

"I knew you weren't a sniveling goat-lover! What can I do? How can I help?" asked Taylor with an eager grin.

"We need you to build an explosive. We'll use it to escape and return to our time," said Rin.

"How will an explosive help you return to your time?"

"You don't need to know that yet. All you need to do is tell us what you need to build it."

Some of Taylor's eagerness faded. He sat back, more subdued. "I'm not going to build you an explosive and just hope you bring me along."

Rin straightened and fixed him with her best High Commander glare. She wanted to convey that she was to be trusted and feared. "We will use the explosive as a distraction. You don't need to know any more details than that. You can trust me. I will ensure you return to your time. If I fail to exterminate the satyrs, I need to know you will be there in the future to finish the job."

Taylor smiled, his eagerness returning. Rin saw admiration in his eyes and it made her stomach turn. "Yes! I can finish the job!"

"Good. What do you need to build the explosive?"

"I need a lot of things: a trigger, a catalyst, and a containment structure."

"I can expose the explosive to intense heat," said Rin.

"That takes care of the trigger, but I still need other things. I could probably come up with most of the components just from cleaning supplies and other things we have access to, but

I need something to direct the heat — something like gunpowder — and something to hold all the components together," he said.

She nodded. "I'll arrange something for you."

"Just like that?"

Rin held herself tall. "I am the High Commander. Of course I can arrange it."

Rin postured for Taylor for a few more minutes, then sent him back to their cell.

As soon as Taylor left, Rin slumped to the floor next to Cleo.

"Are you alright?" asked Cleo, putting a comforting arm over Rin's shoulder.

"I will be. I just didn't enjoy doing that, acting like that person again," Rin said. She felt cold and drained.

Cleo pulled her into an embrace and Rin soaked in the comfort.

"You did great. I really think he bought it," said Cleo.

"That's good. This entire plan falls apart without him."

"How are you going to get his explosive to the machine?"

Rin swallowed. She traced the lines of Cleo's hands. "In my experience, getting to the machine isn't difficult. I just have to stop making double quota and start a fight."

"No, Rin. You can't. They'll search you. They'll find the explosive. It won't work."

"They didn't search me the first time. They just cut my hair and sent me down."

"You said they knocked you unconscious, so you don't know. They might have searched you before you woke up."

Rin closed her eyes and leaned into Cleo's embrace. "It's not a perfect plan. If I can find a way that doesn't involve going to the Deep Pit, I'll jump on it. I don't want to go back to that place, but I will if it's the only way."

Cleo squeezed Rin close. "We'll figure something else out. We have to."

She nodded and soaked in Cleo's strength, not wanting their embrace to end. Cleo rested her chin on Rin's head, then kissed her hair. Rin looked up at her. Cleo's face was close enough for Rin to feel her breathing. Rin stared into her deep brown eyes. Her heart lurched as she realized how fully tangled she was in Cleo's embrace. Cleo leaned forward and Rin tilted her head back, and they kissed with a passion that could not be mistaken as something casual between friends in any context. Rin closed her eyes and opened her mouth, letting Cleo in, and Cleo took what she offered with enthusiasm. The coldness of inhabiting the High Commander again was forgotten as she turned to more fully embrace Cleo. Their kiss warmed her. Cleo's arms wrapped around her, pulling her in, and Rin's arms wrapped around Cleo, reaching for more.

When they finally pulled away, she stared at Cleo in awe. Her legs were around Cleo's waist, and Cleo's fingers were twined in Rin's hair.

Cleo smiled. "I've been wanting to do that for a long time," she murmured.

"I wasn't sure if you were interested in me like that or just being nice," said Rin.

Cleo laughed and pulled her into a hug.

They embraced on the floor of the supply closet, sharing smaller kisses, before finally pulling apart and returning to their bunks. Despite everything, Rin climbed into bed with a smile on her face and Cleo on her mind. As Rin rolled over to fall asleep, she felt something digging into her leg. She reached her hand into her pocket and pulled something out. It felt like a rock. It must have fallen into her pocket while she was working on the Wall. She tossed it aside before rolling over to finally sleep.

~*~

Rin woke to the lights coming on in the cell. She yawned and stretched, sitting up slow enough not to slam her head into the ceiling. The echoes of Cleo's kiss still played in her mind and brought a smile to her face. She heard Taylor's head hit the ceiling with a satisfying smack and smiled more at his quiet curses.

As she pulled back her covers she saw the rock she'd pulled out of her pocket the night before. In the dark, she'd assumed it was a piece of rubble, but in the morning light she saw that it was a black, shimmering piece of ore. She picked it up. It was a big chunk. She must have gotten credit for digging it. Her quota was counted by her pickaxe, not the cart. It offered her some small comfort that at least one rock she'd dug hadn't gone to feed the machine that destroyed the satyrs. She ran her thumb over the chalky surface. In the shadow of her bunk, the light played across the rock the same way the fire's light played on the mountain of ore around the machine. Rin clutched the rock and closed her eyes as she was transported back to the heat and the pain for a moment. If she threw the rock into the cart, it would go back there.

Rin blinked her eyes open, struck by an idea. She stared down at the rock in her hands, seeing it in a new light. If she threw it back in the cart, it would be taken down to the Deep Pit. It would be thrown into the machine. If she put something in it, like an explosive, that would be carried down and thrown into the machine. Her hands trembled with excitement. This was it! This was her way out! She didn't have to go back to that place! She didn't have to go back to the heat and the pain.

Rin raced through her morning routine. She slid the rock into her pocket and climbed down from her bunk. She ate her breakfast eagerly. She should be tired from a night spent in secret meetings, but she was too excited to be tired. The smuggled rock felt like a lead weight in her pocket. She was sure the guards would notice. They would stop her and demand to know where it came from. Jason wouldn't be there to protect her. She would be docked strikes and probably sent down a level for stealing a rock from the Wall. Nervous energy flooded through her.

The guards arrived, and noticed nothing. Rin and the rest of the inmates were escorted to the Wall, the same as every morning. Rin slid down the slope to her spot and attacked the wall. She felled a few black rocks of ore, and then, when the guards weren't looking, dropped the rock from her pocket into the pile. A few minutes later she swept the rubble away and carried the rocks, including the one she'd had in the cell, to the collection cart. Her breath caught in her throat as the rocks bounced to the bottom of the bin. She was afraid that somehow the future technology would know there was something different this time. The rocks settled in the cart and nothing happened. No alarms were triggered.

Rin's head buzzed with excitement. It had worked. No one would notice ore that went missing and reappeared the next day. She wouldn't have to go back to the Deep Pit to deliver the explosive. It would take longer, but they could throw the explosive in with the other ore and the system would deliver it to the machine for them. She would be able to save the satyrs without returning to the Deep Pit!

Chapter 23

Rin's heart raced whenever she was in close quarters with Cleo. They'd kissed a few times since that first night on the floor in the closet, but they hadn't had a chance like that again. Stolen kisses were wonderful, but Rin wanted more.

"How are you going to find those things he asked for?" asked Cleo as she kicked the rubble at their feet into the chute behind them.

Rin looked up, but the guards were standing farther down the Wall, glowering over another group of inmates.

"I have an idea for the delivery device, but I'm not sure about the heat transfer component," said Rin.

"If only we had the detective from my book here to help us," said Cleo.

Rin smiled. "The detective would be helpful. He figures out an explosion in your book and everything."

"Too bad we don't have access to a research lab."

Gai moved down the Wall towards them and their conversation died. He looked between them and sighed. "Is it alright if I dig with you?"

Rin shrugged. She didn't have anything further to say about the machine and she didn't want to alienate one of her only friends. "Fine by me."

"Of course you can dig with us," said Cleo.

"Did you see yesterday's episode?" asked Gai.

Cleo grinned. "Of course I did!"

Rin's attention drifted away from the conversation as Gai and Cleo dove into an analysis of what had happened last on their favorite television show. Where would she get the heat transfer component Taylor needed? Cleo's comment was frustrating. The Tower above them was probably full of the volatile chemicals they needed, but they couldn't access them. Jason might have that access; he might be able to help. She could ask him for the heat-transfer component. He said he wanted to help, but when she'd mentioned using explosives, Jason looked like he would lose his nerve. She didn't want to ask him to do anything other than look the other way. He'd already brought her back from the Deep Pit, saving her life. Then he'd helped her come back from the darkness in her own mind. No. Rin wouldn't go to him for help.

That evening, Rin was frustrated. She collected her warm meal of shepherd's pie from the food fabricator and sat next to Cleo, who linked arms with her and pulled her into a quick kiss before releasing her to eat her dinner.

"Aw, so sweet," said Gai with a smile. It was impossible for Rin and Cleo to steal kisses without Gai seeing. He had already teased them.

Still smiling at the quick kiss, Rin took a bite of her dinner, burning the roof of her mouth, and that's when she had an idea.

"Cleo, do you know how the food fabricator works?" asked Rin.

Cleo swallowed a mouthful of food. "I think it's an advancement from bioprinter technology. They were brand new in my time, very expensive to operate. They used cells to print tissue into whatever shape was needed. It's clearly more sophisticated now. When I was alive they used them to print human tissue for surgeries."

"How do they make the food hot?"

"Probably a heating element or something. Why?"

"I'm not sure yet. We'll talk about it more later," said Rin, worried about the cameras recording their conversation.

Rin took another bite of her dinner. There had to be a way to get the heating element out of the food fabricator. Everything could break, even in the future. There had to be a way to fix it. A way to replace the broken parts. Whatever was used to heat their food had to be something Taylor could use to make his explosive.

The next day, with their conversation disguised by the ringing of pickaxes against rocks, she told Cleo about her idea. She needed to get into the food fabricator and steal the heating element.

"There is a way to open the wall around the food fabricator. I've seen them doing maintenance on them on one of my days off, and the heating elements do need to be replaced periodically. When they burn out, we get cold meals for a few days until they get around to fixing them," said Cleo.

"Perfect! All we have to do is figure out how to get into the food fabricator," said Rin.

"How are you going to do that?"

"Maybe I can find something on the screen."

"Be careful. Jason will be able to see everything you search for. If you search for information about food fabricators and then the food fabricator breaks, he'll know you had something to do with it," said Cleo.

Rin felt a stab of guilt for hiding Jason's involvement from Cleo. "I'll be careful."

On Rin's day off, she used her free time to search for information about food fabricator maintenance. The equipment was common in this time, and Rin was able to find out a lot about it. Each model was different, but there should be a service hatch in the wall near the window. On the service hatch there would be divots, and touching those divots in the right combination would cause the panel to open. Rin went into the common room and found the service hatch. It didn't take long once she knew what she was looking for. There were four divots. She wanted to start trying combinations, but she needed Cleo to help her, so that she could try combinations and Cleo could catch the panel when it fell.

When the others came back from working on the Wall, she pulled Cleo aside and told her what she'd learned.

Cleo glanced nervously towards Jason's office door. "He didn't notice?"

Rin shook her head. "No."

"When is the next blackout?" asked Cleo, moving closer to her.

She reached out, and their fingers entwined. "There's a short one tonight."

"Good," said Cleo, and they shared a kiss before separating to prepare for bed.

~*~

That night, Rin waited until it sounded as though everyone in the cell was asleep. Then she climbed quietly down from her bunk and shook Cleo awake. Cleo found Rin's hand in the dark, and they laced their fingers together as they made their way to the common room's door. She smiled at the warm, reassuring strength of Cleo's hand in hers.

They stepped out into the common room. The screen on the wall illuminated them with a pale blue glow.

Rin glanced over her shoulder. Cleo's eyes were wide. She had been in Hell most of her life, but she'd survived by not breaking the rules; now she was following Rin into a plot that would probably get them thrown in the Deep Pit.

She squeezed Cleo's hand reassuringly. "This way," she whispered.

She led Cleo to the access panel she'd found in the wall. She pointed out the divots and explained the mechanism. Cleo nodded and held the panel while Rin began tapping out combinations. She assumed she'd be able to guess it, but she tried combination after combination and nothing worked. Her frustration mounted as the time ticked away too quickly.

"How much longer is the blackout? You said it was a short one," whispered Cleo.

Rin closed her eyes. They would have to come back for the heating element later. It would take too long to get it out now. Cleo would be suspicious of the blackouts if it lasted much longer.

"Come on. Let's get back to the cell."

Cleo held Rin's hand and they scurried across the common room to their cell. They closed the door behind them, and Cleo continued holding her hand as they crossed the cell towards their bunks. She expected Cleo to release her when she found her bunk, but instead she tugged her down towards the bed.

"Come on," she whispered.

Rin's heart raced with excitement as Cleo pulled her down into the covers next to her.

"What are you doing?" she hissed.

"There's no rule against sharing a bed," said Cleo.

Cleo pulled her into an embrace, their bodies pressed together. Rin held tight to Cleo.

"What are we going to do now?" Cleo whispered, her breath hot on Rin's neck.

Rin's thoughts were the furthest from schemes and plots they had ever been. She managed to think past her desire to pull Cleo even closer.

"Um, we'll go back at the next blackout," she answered.

"When is that?" asked Cleo. Her lips were inches from Rin's ear.

"Tomorrow."

"Have you figured out how to get the explosive into the machine?" The concern in Cleo's voice broke the spell their closeness had cast on Rin. She hadn't gotten the chance to tell Cleo her plan.

She told Cleo in hushed whispers about the rock she'd managed to steal from the Wall and her idea to use the rock as the delivery device, so no one would have to go to the Deep Pit.

"I like that plan much better. I was worried about you. I was going to suggest that maybe I should deliver the explosive, rather than you."

Rin was taken aback. "You? Why? I don't want you to go to the Deep Pit."

Cleo's hand found Rin in the dark, caressing her face. She leaned her cheek into Cleo's warm palm. Her hands were softer than Rin's, less calloused because she used her shirt to protect them while digging on the Wall. "The Deep Pit hurt you so much. I didn't want you going back there. I've never suffered like that. I figured I could spare you."

She squeezed Cleo's hand. "I would never let you do that for me. Knowing that you were down there would be infinitely worse than being there myself."

Cleo ran her fingers through Rin's hair, then pulled her in for a kiss. She reached her other arm around Rin and drew her in. Rin closed her eyes and kissed her back. Their bodies were already pressed together, but Rin dropped her hand to Cleo's hip and pulled her still closer. She wanted this more than anything. Cleo's hand slipped under Rin's clothes, and she was hit with a wave of guilt. No. She didn't deserve this. She was lying to Cleo. With an enormous effort, she pulled back.

"We can't," she whispered.

"There's no rules against it," said Cleo, tracing Rin's jaw in the dark with her thumb, one hand still on Rin's hip, under the waistband of her shorts.

"I'm, I'm not telling you everything. There are secrets I'm keeping. I've lied to you. I can't tell you how or why because it will put people in danger, but I can't do this and lie to you," whispered Rin.

Cleo was quiet for a moment. Rin longed to throw off her morals and pull Cleo in.

"These lies are to protect someone?" asked Cleo.

"Yes."

"Thank you for telling me you haven't been honest. That doesn't change how I feel."

"Are you sure?" she asked.

Cleo's answer was to tilt Rin's head back and envelop her in another kiss. When they paused, she smiled against Rin's mouth. "Yes. I forgive you, Rin," she whispered.

Rin couldn't exercise any more self-restraint. She moved closer to Cleo, and they kissed. Cleo's hands pushed further under Rin's clothes. Soon their clothes were off, and their hands were exploring each other's bodies in the dark. It didn't take long for Cleo's hands to find their way between Rin's legs. She stifled a gasp of pleasure, not wanting to wake their cellmates. As the last waves of pleasure faded, Rin grinned and leaned into Cleo, determine to return the favor. Eventually, exhaustion from a day of working on the Wall overwhelmed them, and they fell asleep in each other's arms. For the first time in a long time, Rin was happy.

Chapter 24

The lights came on in the morning, and Rin woke with a start. Cleo's arms were still wrapped around her. She sat up and rubbed her bleary eyes. Cleo smiled at her demurely.

"Well, at least someone had a good night," said Gai.

Rin jumped and looked over at him, clutching the blanket over her chest. Her cheeks flooded with heat. She had nothing on but Cleo's covers. It was one thing to not be shy about being seen naked; it was an entirely different thing to be seen naked tangled in blankets with another woman. Gai laughed as he stood and left for the bathroom.

Cleo smiled and sat up, allowing the blanket to fall and exposing herself to the morning light.

"Good morning, beautiful," she said, kissing Rin's neck.

Rin's face burned, but she still wanted to turn around and push Cleo back on the bed to continue where they'd left off last night. She settled for a quick kiss.

"Good morning," she said with a smile.

Cleo grinned. Rin stood and quickly collected her clothes, pulling them on. Despite Taylor staring wide-eyed from his bunk, Cleo took her time getting ready. Rin watched her and smiled for a moment before ducking into the bathroom.

That day on the Wall, despite the hard work, Rin felt light and happy. Her mind drifted to the night spent with Cleo, and she smiled. She glanced over at Cleo, digging with her shirt wrapped around her hands to protect them from blisters.

"You've got it bad, huh?" teased Gai.

Rin grinned. She swung her axe into the rock. "Yeah, I guess I do."

That night, during dinner, Jason came into the common room. "Rin, a word when you're done."

Cleo shot her a concerned look. Had they been caught? Gai looked worried also. Rin wolfed down what was left of her food, then walked through her cell and into Jason's office.

"Yes?" she asked.

"So, you and Cleo are getting close," said Jason as Rin stood next to his desk.

Rin's face tinged pink. "She said it wasn't against the rules."

"It's not. Just a surprise. I thought we knew everything about you, but we didn't know you were gay."

Rin shrugged, and the bubble of happiness that had sustained her through the day popped as she remembered her past. "I was too busy committing genocide to worry about romance."

"And you're not too busy for romance now?" asked Jason, leading her into his private quarters so they could talk without the cameras listening.

"I'm going to die soon. I figured I'd make time," answered Rin as the door closed behind her.

"What?" asked Jason.

Rin shrugged. "We're going to destroy the machine that is holding us in this time. That will probably kill us, right?"

Jason frowned. "I don't know. I hadn't thought that far ahead."

Rin was quietly relieved that she wasn't the only one who had failed to consider the consequences of her actions. "Gai thinks it might just trap us here."

Jason sat back thoughtfully for a moment before shaking his head. "That's what I wanted to ask you about. Have you progressed in your plans to destroy the machine? Why were you sneaking around the food fabricator? What's going on?"

"I'm working on it."

"What are you doing to work on it? Why aren't you talking to me anymore?" asked Jason.

Rin was surprised by his questions. "I was offering you plausible deniability."

Jason stared at Rin. "Did I ask for that?"

"The point is that you don't have to ask, otherwise it isn't plausible anymore."

"I don't want plausible deniability. I want to help end this machine that is destroying an entire time stream."

Rin allowed a short pause. It was possible that she had misread him. She chose her next words cautiously, studying his face for the slightest hint it was time to stop talking. "I was concerned that you seemed nervous about the plan."

"Of course I'm nervous about the plan, it involves explosives!" A look of dawning understanding spread across his face. "Wait, did you think I was nervous enough to stop helping?"

Rin was silent.

"I can't believe you would think that! I am as committed to this as you are! Knowing about something as evil as that machine and not doing anything to stop it would make me as bad as the person who built it. I'm not going to stop trying to tear it down."

Rin had been wrong. She'd allowed her scheming to cloud her judgment, and had doubted one of the people who had brought her back from the darkness.

"Well? What's the plan?"

"I'm trying to find the things Taylor needs to build an explosive. He said he could find most of the supplies himself, but he needed a containment method and a heat dispersion method," said Rin.

"Do you have those things?"

Rin shook her head. "I know what I'm going to use for containment. I figured out that I can smuggle a rock in from the Wall. If I hollow out the rock, we can turn it into the explosive and drop it in the cart. They'll shovel it into the fire and blow the machine for us."

"I like that plan."

"The heat transfer is the harder component. He said something like gunpowder, but there don't seem to be any guns around here. We were thinking there might be a heating element in the food fabricator that we could use."

Jason nodded. "That's a good idea." He went to a drawer in his kitchen and shuffled through it, coming back with a thin black cylinder. It was two fingers wide, and the length of a pen. "I thought I might have a replacement heating element for the food fabricator here in my private quarters that I could give you, but it looks like this is all I have. It's an old burnt-out element, but you can replace the one in the food fabricator with that. When maintenance comes to fix it, they won't be suspicious."

"Thank you," said Rin, taking the cylinder from Jason.

"I can give you the code to open the access panel too."

"Thanks, I was going to try to guess it," said Rin.

Jason shook his head. "It'll be easier if I just tell you."

Rin watched as Jason tapped out the sequence to unlock the access panel on his table. She repeated it until she had it memorized.

"Alright, I've got it," she said.

"Good. You better get back to your cell. It's almost time for lights out," Jason told her.

"Thank you," Rin said, holding up the black cylinder.

"It's the least I can do. You need to trust me. I can't help if I don't know what's going on."

"I know. I'm sorry. I won't shut you out anymore."

"Good," said Jason.

Rin slipped the cylinder into her pocket and returned to her cell. She took a shower, brushed her teeth, and got ready for bed.

"Rin," called Cleo.

She looked over her shoulder. She was about to climb into her bunk, but Cleo was gesturing towards her bed. Rin thought about the black cylinder in her pocket. If Cleo found it before they snuck out tonight to steal the cylinder from the food fabricator, she would grow suspicious, but Cleo's bed was so inviting.

"I'm tired," she said.

Gai laughed from where he stood in front of his locker.

Cleo grinned. "We'll sleep. I promise."

Rin smiled and climbed into Cleo's bed instead of her own. If Cleo's hands started exploring, she would slip the cylinder out of her pocket and hide it under the pillow. Cleo wrapped her arms around her, pulling her close. Rin closed her eyes and smiled. She held Cleo's hands, and snuggled back against her, nestling in the curve of Cleo's body. They fit together perfectly. She breathed in Cleo's scent, feeling more relaxed than she ever had in her giant bed back home. If she had to pick between her palace and this small prison bunk, she'd choose Cleo's arms every time. They cuddled close together as their other bunkmates climbed into their own beds and the lights were turned out.

Rin was happy and comfortable in Cleo's arms in the dark. Sleep was inviting, but she stayed awake. Slowly, the sound of breathing in the room fell into the deep patterns of sleep. Cleo's arms went limp as she fell asleep too.

"Cleo, wake up," she whispered.

Cleo stirred. "Is it time?"

"Yes."

The two climbed out of the bunk and crept through the cell in the dark, hand in hand. They pushed into the common room, illuminated by the soft blue glow of the screen.

Cleo held up the panel as Rin pretended to try a few more combinations before she used the code Jason had given her. The access panel fell into Cleo's arms, and Rin stared at the jumble of wires and lights behind it. She had no idea what they were. After a moment, she found what she was looking for: the small black cylinder suspended in the middle of the mess of wires. She reached up and gently unhooked it. It felt heavier than the one Jason had given her. Careful to hide what she was doing from Cleo, she placed the cylinder Jason had given her in the machine.

"I've got it," she whispered, holding up the black cylinder. She slipped it into her pocket and helped Cleo put the panel back in place.

Cleo and Rin snuck back into their cell. They climbed into Cleo's bed and cuddled close. They kissed, but Rin really was tired after two sleepless nights.

"Good night, Cleo," she whispered.

She closed her eyes. She was almost asleep when Cleo whispered, "Rin?"

"Yes?"

Cleo was quiet for a moment longer. "Rin. I think I love you."

Rin squeezed Cleo's hands to her chest. Hot tears welled up in her eyes. Why did she have to meet Cleo here? They'd been born hundreds of years apart! They were working to destroy a machine that would probably kill them. Why did Rin have to find her now, when she could only have her for a short time?

"I love you too," she whispered.

Not long after that, Rin felt Cleo's arms relax as she fell asleep, but her mind wouldn't still. It circled between joy at finding someone she loved, fear for what would happen when the machine was destroyed, and the ever-present guilt reminding her she didn't deserve the happiness Cleo brought. It was right that she should lose someone she loved. How many satyrs had she separated from their loved ones? How many families had her actions torn apart? She deserved this pain, but that didn't make it any easier to bear.

Chapter 25

The next night, Rin took Cleo and Taylor to the closet. Cleo's hand rested surreptitiously on Rin's, providing support. Taylor knew they were together – he slept in the bunk above Cleo and saw them in the morning — but in order to play the part of High Commander, Rin couldn't be too obvious about needing Cleo.

"We have the things you said you needed. Did you get the other materials?" asked Rin, infusing her voice with the imperial might of the High Commander.

"Are you going to tell me the rest of the plan? I'm not building you an explosive without knowing how it's going to benefit me," said Taylor. His admiration for Rin was fading. It was probably hard to continue fawning over someone when you saw them digging on the Wall and being shouted at by guards the same as anyone else all day long. It was a good thing they wouldn't need him anymore once he'd built the explosive.

Rin glared at him. "We're going to sneak out during the blackouts. There's a secret ladder from the Pit to the Tower. When we enter the Tower, it will set off an alarm. We'll use the explosive to distract the guards while we get away."

"Where are we going to go?"

"Back to our own times. The time machine is close to the hatch."

Taylor looked between Rin and Cleo. "What is she doing here? So far you're the one with the plan and I'm the one with the explosive. I don't know why she needs to be involved."

"That's my business," snapped Rin.

"Why does she get to know so much about me, but I don't even know what part she plays?"

"Because I decide who needs to know what," said Rin. She held herself tall, channeling the imperial will of the High Commander.

Taylor glared, then shook his head. "Whatever. What did you get?"

Rin held out the black cylinder from the food fabricator, and a large black rock she'd smuggled away from the Wall. She'd spent her day off hollowing it out with a fork she'd stolen from one of the meals. The chalky rock was easy to carve and had a tendency to crumble and splinter once it was removed from the wall. It had been easy to create a hidden chamber for the explosive.

"Will these work?"

Taylor took the items from her. He pried out the plug she'd carved from the rock, revealing the chamber. "It will be small, but I should be able to make it work." He examined the cylinder, pulling off the end and pouring a black powder into his hands. "Is this why we've been having cold meals?"

"Yes," said Rin.

"It's crude, but I can make this work too."

"How long will it take you to make the explosive?" Rin asked.

"I have the day after tomorrow off. I can work on it then and have it ready to go the day after that."

"Perfect. It will only go off when it's in contact with heat, right? Or will it be unsafe to have it around the cell?" asked Rin.

"It'll be safe to handle. I'll use a trigger that can't be tripped with impact, only heat."

When Rin feigned another blackout, they returned to their bunks for the night. Rin curled up in bed with Cleo, who held her tightly. Rin felt cold. She hated stepping back into the shoes of the High Commander. She hated the person she had been, and pretending to be that person again made her sick. It brought back memories of the horrendous things the High Commander had done and flooded Rin with stomach-churning guilt.

Cleo cradled her and comforted her, feathering kisses behind her ear and on her neck. Cleo's gentle touch reminded her that she wasn't High Commander anymore. The High Commander hadn't had time for love, and wouldn't have been able to love Cleo. She would have had to marry someone who could give her an heir. Cleo's strong warm arms melted the cold of who Rin had been, anchoring her and bringing her back to who she was now.

~*~

Rin waited nervously for Taylor to build the explosive. His day off came, and Rin struggled to focus on her work. Her pick-axe kept slipping as her mind wandered. She almost cut her leg with one wild swing and nearly lost a strike for fooling around on the Wall. Finally, the day's work ended and the inmates were escorted back to the cell block.

"How was your day off?" Rin asked Taylor as they waited for the food window to open.

He shrugged. "Fine. I finished everything I wanted to get done."

"Where is it?" asked Rin.

"Under your pillow. When are we going to use it?"

"In a few weeks; I want to make sure no one notices the materials missing," said Rin.

The line started moving before Taylor could respond. Her hands shook with excitement. In reality, she wasn't planning on waiting a single minute longer than necessary. She would plant the explosive as soon as she could. After dinner, she found the rock under her pillow. She put it in her locker before going to the bathroom to get ready for bed.

The next morning, she slipped the explosive into her pocket while she grabbed fresh clothes and prepared for the day. She fixed her hair in the mirror, noticing how long it had grown. How long had it been since she left the Deep Pit? Months. Had it been a year yet? She shook her head, turning away from the mirror to join the other inmates at breakfast.

She was going to do it. Today she was going to plant the explosive that would destroy the machine. Of course, it would take time for the explosive to go from the rim to the machine. She didn't know how long it would sit in the mountain of ore, waiting to be fed to the fire. It could be months, maybe years before the explosive went off. Rin grinned and ate her food. Months or years that she would be able to spend with Cleo. She would always be wracked by guilt, but she could weather that guilt with Cleo's arms around her.

Rin waited impatiently for the guards to take them to the Wall. As she slid down the incline to her place, she was acutely aware of the live explosive in her pocket. She swung her pick-axe and felled a large enough handful of shimmering black rocks. She scooped them up, slipping the explosive in among them. Carefully, she tossed the entire armful of rock into the collection cart. She was on edge the rest of the morning as people tossed rocks on top of the explosive. Taylor had promised it would only be activated with heat, but she still worried. She didn't stop sweating until the guards wheeled away the cart when it was full and replaced it with an empty one.

Rin's body was weak with relief. She'd done it! She got the explosive into the cart! Now it would slowly make its way down the Pit to the machine, and she could focus on Cleo. She glanced down the Wall towards Cleo, swinging her axe into the rock, shirtless as always. She looked up and saw Rin watching her. Cleo smiled, and Rin smiled back. She took her place on the Wall next to Cleo.

"How's your morning been?" asked Cleo.

Rin let out a shaky breath. "Productive. I finished what I wanted to get done."

"It's gone?" asked Cleo.

Rin nodded and looked out over the Pit. "It's gone."

Cleo slipped her hand into Rin's and squeezed. They didn't know how long it would take, but they had done what they could. They had fought back against this machine that was destroying their time stream. Hopefully, it would be enough. For now, they had time together.

"I love you," said Rin as they pulled apart before a guard could notice them.

"I love you too," Cleo answered.

Chapter 26

A few days later, Rin woke in the darkness with a hand over her mouth. Her groggy and confused brain struggled to understand what was going on. The hand moved from covering her mouth to tugging her shoulder. She was supposed to get up. Careful not to wake Cleo, she disentangled herself from her. She climbed out of bed, the strangeness of the situation bringing crisp awareness to her mind. She followed the hand through the darkness. The door to Jason's office opened, and Rin followed him through. It had to be Jason she was following, even though she couldn't see his face in the dark. No one else had access to his office.

Jason didn't speak until he'd closed the door of his private quarters behind him and turned on the lights. His face was white with terror.

"What's going on?" asked Rin.

He ran his fingers through his hair. "You were right," he said.

An icy stone dropped in Rin's stomach. "Right about what?"

"Not trusting Taylor."

She waited.

"He was a test. I didn't even know about it."

"What do you mean?" asked Rin.

"He was planted by upper management. Apparently, it's standard procedure to place a mole in a cell block after an escape attempt. They want to make sure no one left knows anything or is planning something similar. The people they send have skills that would be particularly useful in an escape. Like knowing how to build explosives. I had no idea. I've never had an escape attempt in my cell, and they didn't tell me what they were doing."

Rin stared at him with cold panic.

"It was a setup, Rin. They're going to come collect you, and everyone else who was involved with Tyler, and take you down to the Deep Pit. We don't have much time. They're coming to get you tonight."

Tears pricked the corners of Rin's eyes. She couldn't go back there. She wouldn't survive! Her breath came shallow and quick. Cleo! No! They couldn't take Cleo to that place! Cleo, who had lived most of her life on the rim of the Pit. She'd taken a risk in helping Rin, in growing close to her. She couldn't be subjected to the lower levels. "Jason," she panted. "I, I can't. Cleo."

Jason put an arm over her shoulder. He helped her into a chair and sat next to her.

"I'm so sorry," whispered Jason.

She looked up at him. "No one knows you were involved. I didn't tell anyone. Not even Cleo."

"I know. Thank you," said Jason.

"You have to keep trying. You have to destroy the machine. Please," Rin begged.

Jason looked down at his hands, then stood and went to a drawer in his kitchen. He came back with a black box, small enough to nestle in the palm of his hand. He sat down and stared at it.

"I was able to get my hands on this."

"What is it?" asked Rin.

Gingerly, Jason opened the box. Inside were two teeth. Rin frowned in confusion. How was a box of teeth going to help them?

"When you stopped talking to me about the plan to destroy the machine, I thought it was because you couldn't get access to the materials to make a bomb, so I started trying to find something. I found this in cold storage among the inmates' confiscated belongings. It's an explosive."

"An explosive that small will destroy the machine?"

"It's extremely powerful, from far in your future, but using it is dangerous. You wear it in your mouth. If you leave it in too long, the poison from it will seep into your bloodstream and kill you."

"Why didn't you tell me about this sooner?"

"I wasn't sure how we would get it down to the machine. Even after you told me about your plan to use the ore, I was afraid the explosive would go off in transportation and wouldn't make it to the machine. Besides, you had a plan that was much better than mine."

"Now I can carry it down to the machine in person," whispered Rin. Her hands shook at the thought of going back to the Deep Pit.

"I wish there was another way," said Jason.

"No, this is perfect. This way, we'll know that the explosive is delivered." She had been a fool to think she could be happy. She didn't deserve Cleo, and now she wouldn't have her.

Jason plucked one of the teeth from the box. He held it out so Rin could see that there was a small button on the tooth. "Both of these teeth will go in behind your real ones. This one has the release. The other tooth is the explosive. You should be able to push the button with your tongue. When you do, the other tooth will come loose and you can throw it into the fire."

"Alright. Can you put them in for me?" asked Rin.

"Yes, but I wish I had some kind of anesthetic. It will hurt," said Jason.

"Don't worry about it," she said.

She leaned forward, and Jason placed the tooth with the button in the back of her mouth. He pushed it down hard into the sensitive gums and ratcheted it against the tooth next to it. Tears streamed down Rin's face as she gripped the table with white knuckles. Jason was right. It hurt. Tears and blood flooded from Rin's face, and she was reminded of the satyrs she'd had tortured.

"One done," said Jason.

Rin couldn't speak past the pain that throbbed in her jaw. She opened her mouth, and Jason repeated the painful process on the other side. When he was done, pain throbbed on both sides, and her jaw felt like it had been ripped off. But she had the explosive. She would deliver it to the machine.

"Remember, you have to work fast or the poison will kill you."

"How much time do I have?" she asked through the tears and pain.

"I don't know. A few days. Not longer than that," said Jason, handing her a cloth to clean up her face.

"They heal us every day in the Deep Pit."

"That might buy you a few more days, but the poison will still kill you, even with healing," said Jason.

Rin wiped her face clean. Every time she swallowed, she tasted blood.

"If this doesn't work, you have to promise you won't stop trying to destroy the machine, after...after I'm gone," she said, her voice breaking. "And do everything you can to protect Cleo. Everything was my idea. It's all my fault. Please."

"I'll do what I can."

Rin sniffed. She was scared of the Deep Pit. She didn't want to do this, but if her suffering could spare Cleo and save the satyrs, at least it would be worth it. "Good."

She wiped the tears from her cheeks. Her mouth ached with an incredible pain, but the pain was welcomed. It reminded her that she wouldn't be in the Deep Pit for months this time. She would destroy the machine or she would die trying, and she would do it quickly. Even if she failed, she only had a few days to live, with the poison already spreading through her body.

"You should take me back to my cell," said Rin.

Jason nodded and leaned back so that he could see the screen in his living room. "Almost time."

"What are you waiting for?"

"Allie's blackouts. I don't want someone to review the tapes of tonight and get suspicious. They might try to stop you before you're able to deliver the explosive."

"Those are still working?"

"She was a terrible human being, but she knew her tech. People have been trying to undo what she did, but there are still traces of her meddling deep in the security system. Whoever had the bright idea to bring her here was an idiot."

Rin ran her tongue experimentally over the two new teeth in her mouth. Just the touch of her tongue sent a spasm of pain with fresh intensity through her jaw, but she didn't stop until she found the button.

"Now," said Jason.

She stood. Jason took her back to her cell, and Rin climbed into Cleo's bed. She wrapped her arms around the woman and buried her face in her hair. Hot tears ran down her cheeks and collected on Cleo's pillow. She forced herself to cry silently without sobbing. She didn't want to wake Cloe. She'd give her one last peaceful night's rest; she might not get another for a long time.

Eventually, she cried herself dry and lay under the covers, holding Cleo and waiting. She didn't fully close her jaw for fear of setting off the powerful explosive. The throbbing pain had lessened. It was still there, but it wasn't what caused her hands to tremble. She was going back to the Deep Pit. The heat, the smoke, the fire. Even with her eyes open, she could see the man throwing himself into the flames. Her lungs seized up as though they were already coated with soot. She was going to die.

Rin didn't know how long she waited, trembling with terror and clinging to Cleo. It could have been a few minutes, or it could have been hours. Suddenly, the lights were on and the door to Jason's office banged open.

"Out of the bunks, now!" a man shouted. Guards flooded into the room around him.

Rin fell out of Cleo's bunk. No acting was needed; her terror was genuine. Her cellmates were startled awake as well. Cleo and Gai were terrified and confused. Taylor sat smugly in his bunk, arms wrapped around his knees like he was watching a show.

"Hands behind your backs!" shouted the guard.

Rin complied, and her manacles drew together, holding her hands behind her.

"Rin!" shouted Cleo, but Rin was dragged out of the room.

"This one's the ringleader," said the guard to the head warden in the hall.

"Of course she is. Nothing but trouble since she got here. Get her up to the Tower for interrogation."

Rin was led through the halls to the elevator and whisked up to the clean white halls of the Tower. She focused on the intense throbbing pain in her jaw to distract her from the sheer terror that threatened to overwhelm her. She was going back to the Deep Pit. She was going to die.

~*~

The guards forced her into the metal chair in the bright white room. Rin's manacles clung to the chair, and she was left alone. The room was designed without a way to measure the passage of time, but Rin could count her heartbeats in the throbbing of her jaw. She focused on that, the one thing she could do in that room. She was left alone in the metal chair for hours. The throbbing never faded. Rin began to worry about the poison. What if they kept her in the Tower for a few days? What if the poison killed her before she had a chance to throw the explosive into the machine? Where would Cleo end up? How long would she be there? Would Jason be able to save her and bring her back to his safe cell block as he had done for Rin?

Finally, the seamless door opened and the head warden walked in. "So, we show you mercy and bring you back from the Deep Pit, only for you to betray that mercy a few months later," said the man, crossing his arms over his chest.

Rin glared up at him. She wondered how much he knew. Did he know that the machine his prison maintained was destroying her time stream?

"That just goes to show our system works and we shouldn't second-guess it. If you end up in the Deep Pit, you belong there."

Rin continued to glare.

"You told Taylor that the explosive would be a distraction at the top of the escape hatch, but you didn't explain how you were going to get from the cell to the ladder. What was the actual play here?"

Rin's mind raced. Of course they wouldn't believe she'd told Taylor the truth. She had to take all the blame to protect Cleo, but she had to do it in a way that wouldn't be too obvious.

"A distraction," snarled Rin, making up a story on the spot.

"For what?"

"I was going to get out of here. Just me."

The head warden nodded and tapped on his screen. This was what he expected from her. As long as she told him what he expected to hear, he would believe her. She had to be High Commander one last time.

"You were going to leave your little girlfriend behind? Why am I not surprised? How was it going to work? We couldn't find Taylor's decoy among the things in your locker."

"I hid it on the Wall. Put it in where I knocked a rock loose. I can get it for you, if you don't send me down to the Deep Pit," said Rin.

The head warden snorted. "There was no explosive. Taylor didn't do anything to the rock you gave him. What were you going to do with it?"

"I was going to injure myself. Pretend like I slipped and cut my arm with the pickaxe. Then I was going to set off the explosive in the clinic and escape from there."

The head warden shook his head. "Sure. That would have worked. Well, you'll never know, will you?"

"I answered your questions," said Rin.

"Yes, it made this entire process run smoothly."

"So, can I go back to the rim?" She knew what the answer would be, but she was afraid the warden wouldn't believe her if she didn't seem to have anything to gain from answering his questions.

He laughed. "Absolutely not. You're going to spend the rest of your short life in the Deep Pit. Because you were so cooperative with my questioning, there's no need to be as gentle with you as we were last time. Don't worry. You won't be there long. It should only take a week or two to burn through you."

Rin felt sick. She needed to go to the Deep Pit, and she needed to go there soon. She could already feel the poison's effects. She felt sluggish and tired, and a fog was rising in her mind. She needed to get to the Deep Pit, but that didn't stop her from feeling the bone-deep fear of that place.

The head warden left, and Rin was alone in the white room again. The poison-induced fog thickened around her mind. Every pulse of her heartbeat sent a fresh dose of it coursing through her body. She couldn't count her heartbeats through the fog, and didn't know how long she waited after the head warden left. But the fog brought with it a kind of comfort. She felt a distance from who she was: Her pain was distant. Her guilt was distant. Everything seemed removed, like her mind was floating on a cloud.

Her hair was cut, again, and she was led down the hall to the elevator. Her stomach flipped as the box traveled down. She knew she should be afraid, but she couldn't remember why. Her jaw hurt. There was a reason for that. It was important, but her distant mind couldn't quite remember.

~*~

Rin dug. Her shovel bit into the shimmering black rocks, and she flung them down towards the fire — the all-consuming, insatiable fire. She didn't notice the sweat pouring down her face, even the rivulets that wormed their way into her eyes. She had always been here. This was where she belonged. Another shovelful of rocks went cascading down the hill, and she staggered from the weight of her shovel. The manacles sent a pulse of electricity through her, reminding her of her purpose. To dig.

Her muscles burned, and pain radiated from her jaw. A fog wrapped close around her mind. She didn't know who she was or where she came from. She wasn't aware of anything that might have existed before the shovel and the fire. The pain had always been there. It reached its tentacles from her mouth to every corner of her body; it pulsed through her in time with her heartbeat. *Pain. Dig. Fire. Pain.*

Rin stumbled and fell to the ground. Her manacles buzzed, trying to force her back to her purpose. *Pain. Dig. Fire.* But she couldn't move. Her muscles ached, and the pain was too much. She lay on the black rocks until someone lifted her off the ground. They said something she didn't understand. *Words. Pain. Fire. Pain. Fire. Pain. Pain.*

Rin was dropped again. The ground moved, and she was dragged into a dark tunnel. No more fire. *Pain. Pain. Pain.* There was a cool blast of air, but she could barely feel the relief from the heat through the pain. She was in the dark for a few throbs before a door opened above her head and she was dragged into a bright white room. There was gentle music. She had been here before. That thought surprised her, the idea that there was a before. Before the pain? No. There was no before.

Voices spoke around her. Something pricked her arm, and for a moment, the fog cleared. Rin gasped for air as the pain radiating from her jaw paused for a moment. She noticed the soot coating her throat and lungs. In that moment of relief, her mind came rushing back to her. The pain was from the poison. The doctors must have injected her with something that reduced its effects. The poison was from the explosive. She had to get the explosive out of her mouth and into the machine before it killed her.

"Can I get a sleep mask over here! She's going to jump off the table!" called one of the doctors.

No! She couldn't go to sleep. If she slept, she'd forget — the fog would be back when she woke. But the cloth fell over Rin's eyes, and darkness closed in around her.

~*~

Rin opened her eyes in the dark. A fog was clouding her mind. Something important — there had been something important. Pain radiated from her jaw, making it difficult to think. She clung to the puzzle.

"Out, now," ordered a guard from the door.

She pushed herself off the table. Her knees shook and threatened to collapse under her weight, but she staggered after the guard. A shovel was pushed into her hands and she began to dig. Something important. Every swing of her shovel pushed the puzzle further back in the fog. Something important. She stumbled. Her mouth clenched closed, sending a sharp pain through her jaw as something was jammed deeper into her gums. The explosive. A sudden moment of clarity cut through the fog. The explosive! Rin still had the explosive. She looked up at the fire. The machine! She was a few steps away from it. She had the explosive. She had to get it into the fire before the fog claimed her again.

Rin's manacles shocked her and she stooped for another shovelful of rocks. Her tongue fumbled for the button that would release the explosive from her jaw, but she couldn't find it. The fog threatened to close in around her again. The explosive was there, but she couldn't get it out of her mouth to throw it into the fire.

The shocks from the manacles threatened to push the clarity from her mind. Already the fog was fighting to cut her off from her memory. Rin scooped up a small pile of rocks and threw them toward the fire. She continued to struggle with the tooth and dig at the same time, but her tongue couldn't find the button. She began to panic. Each shock threatened to cloud her mind, but digging made it impossible for her to find the button with her tongue. The fog was closing in. There was just pain. *Fire. Dig.*

No! There was an explosive. The machine. The tooth wouldn't come loose. Rin stared into the fire as she tossed a shovelful of rocks towards the flames. She could feel the darkness creeping in as she staggered down the slope. Another shovelful took her closer to the fire. She could hardly stand. She swayed as she flung the rocks into the machine. She'd staggered and stumbled down the slope, and was standing at the edge of the fire. The heat made the skin of her face tight. She needed to get the explosive into the machine; it didn't need to be freed from her jaw.

Rin didn't look back at the guard. Her manacles buzzed, but the pain from the poison was so intense she didn't notice the shock.

"Get away from the edge!" shouted the guard.

Rin didn't respond. She stood, swaying on the edge of the machine as the guard's heavy footsteps thundered closer. When the guard reached her, she would be pulled away and sent to sleep, and judging by the amount of poison in her system she might not wake up from that sleep.

The guard's fingertips brushed Rin's shoulder as she tipped forward. He scrambled to grab her, and clutched a chunk of fabric in his fist. Rin hung by her shirt, suspended by the guard. She twisted her body and kicked back. The guard lost his grip, and Rin went tumbling into the furnace. She was enveloped by the unbearable heat — and then suddenly she was sitting under a table on a hard-packed earth floor. There was an arrow on the ground in front of her, and a poisonous wound festering in her leg.

Chapter 27

Fire. There had been fire. Where was she? She was supposed to be dead. The pain in her leg drew her attention. She was in her old uniform, the clothes of her time. She looked up. A soldier slammed his boot into a bloody and bruised satyr, knocking her unconscious. A satyr. She was back in her time. Pain lanced up her leg, drawing her attention back to the injury. She couldn't feel the place where the wound originated, but it was sending tendrils up her shin, and she could feel those.

"You," said Rin, pointing at one of her soldiers. "Get me to the infirmary, and bring the satyr."

Soldiers with shields formed around Rin and her guards. She was carried to the medic's tent, and the satyr was dragged behind her. Rin cringed in pain as the damaged muscles and tissue of her leg were shifted while she was carried. The numbness and pain were spreading. She couldn't feel her foot. When they reached the infirmary, Rin was placed in a bed and the satyr was left in a pile on the floor.

"Put her in a bed too," ordered Rin, through teeth gritted against the pain.

"What's going on?" asked the doctor, rushing in, followed by Captain Delton. His cloak was blood-stained and his face was pale with concern.

Rin turned to her captain. "Stop the attack. Capture anyone who doesn't run. No one is to be harmed."

"Yes, sir," he said. His tall frame crowded the space where the doctor was trying to work.

"Captain," Rin said, waiting for him to look back at her. "I mean it. No one is to be hurt. No interrogation. Nothing. They are to be captured and held unharmed. The satyr settlement is to be left alone."

"Yes, sir," said the captain.

"Dismissed," said Rin.

Doctor Sirona was already cutting away Rin's boots, pants, and armor to get a clearer look at the wound on her leg. Rin cried out as the pain cut further up her leg. Sirona's examination caused pressure and the flexing of injured muscles, worsening the agony.

"That satyr is your patient too," said Rin through her tears, pointing to the unconscious figure in the bed next to her.

"Sir?" said the doctor, looking up from her injured leg.

"Treat the satyr also. I want her to be healed up," she ordered.

Sirona began cleaning Rin's leg, and Rin hissed in pain, gripping the sides of the bed with white knuckles. "I don't like wasting my time healing someone who's just going to be killed when I'm done. I need to focus on your injury."

"I'm not going to kill her."

She frowned. "Still."

"It's an order."

Sirona shook her head. "Fine. I'll work on the satyr when I'm done with you, but you should be focused on your own injury. I'm going to have to take this leg to prevent the poison from spreading to the rest of your body."

"Do it," said Rin.

The doctor ordered her assistants to prepare Rin for the operation. A cloth covered Rin's face, reminding her of the way she was knocked unconscious in Hell. Darkness claimed her.

~*~

Pain. Rin woke up to pain. The explosive? No. It wasn't in her jaw. The pain was in her leg. The explosive — she'd set it off. She'd jumped into the fire and was returned to her own time. Pain. Her leg. The assassination attempt. Rin opened her eyes and looked around. She was in the infirmary. In a bed. She was nestled in white sheets, and her head rested on a soft pillow.

The familiar walls of a tent rose around her. She wasn't surrounded by the matte white walls and strange seamless stone floors of the future anymore. This was her home. The walls were fabric. The floor was wood.

A curtain was drawn around her bed. Next to her was a table, piled high with the tattered remains of her uniform, her dagger resting on top. She was wearing a medical gown. Rin was home. Cleo was gone. She wanted to cry — the woman she loved wouldn't be born for hundreds of years. She would have to be High Commander again, and she didn't have Cleo's hand to ground her. Rin closed her eyes. No. She couldn't cry. The High Commander didn't cry. Still, a silent stream of tears slid down her cheeks. When she was able to compose herself, Rin turned her attention to the challenges at hand. She was back in her own time. She was High Commander again. She had a chance to change the things she'd wished she could change when she thought she would die in Hell.

"Doctor," called Rin.

Sirona came through the curtain.

"Good, you're awake."

"The satyr. Is she alright?" asked Rin.

The doctor frowned. "Yes. She has been stabilized. She's unconscious, but recovering."

"I want her in my sight at all times." She was worried that her soldiers would finish what they'd started and question the satyr to death if she didn't keep vigil over her while she was injured.

"Yes, sir," said Sirona. She called in her assistants, and they began rearranging the curtains.

"Bring me my journal and pen," Rin said, pushing herself up to sit. The pain in her leg flared, and she gasped.

"Sir, stay reclined! You'll pull your stitches and it will take longer for your leg to heal," the doctor said, racing to her side.

"Help me sit. I need to write. Where's my journal?"

The doctor turned to one of her assistants. "Go to the High Commander's quarters and get her journal and pen."

The assistant hurried away.

"Let me examine your injury while we wait for her to come back with your things," she said.

Rin nodded.

The doctor pulled back the blanket that covered Rin's painful leg. From the knee down, her leg was gone. What was left was a bloody, puss-covered stump. The doctor cleaned it with alcohol, and Rin hissed in pain as she twisted her fists in her blankets.

"Apologies, sir. It's healing well," Sirona told her.

"Thank you," she said through gritted teeth.

The doctor helped Rin sit, stuffing pillows behind her back and arranging her blankets to hide her missing leg. A table was extended across her lap, and her book and pen were brought to her. The assistants finished moving the curtain so that the satyr was included in Rin's corner of the infirmary. She watched as Sirona tended to the other patient.

"Will her horns grow back?" asked Rin, noticing the bloody stumps as she pulled back the dressing to clean the injury.

"No. Their horns stop growing after adolescence," answered the doctor. "But that is the worst of her injuries. A few broken ribs threaten her breathing, but as long as she doesn't strain herself while they heal, she should make a full recovery."

Rin felt a surge of guilt. This was her fault. The satyr would live without her horns because of Rin. She opened her book to a fresh page and held onto that sense of shame. As painful as it was, she was afraid of losing it. She was surprised that she could remember Hell, and she was afraid she would forget over time. She couldn't allow herself to explain away the guilt and go back to her old ways, but she didn't have Cleo to hold her accountable. She had to be responsible for her own actions now. She had to remember, so that she could work to undo the pain she'd caused. She hadn't expected to get this chance, and she wouldn't let it slip away.

Rin began writing. She would write down her entire experience in Hell, committing every second of her time there to the page. She would not become the monster she had been. She would not forget Cleo. She would work hard to ensure the satyrs were safe.

~*~

"Sir!" said Captain Delton, pushing through the curtain.

Rin looked up from her journal. She was halfway finished writing her account, and she wanted to get it all down before she forgot the details. There were places where her memory was already hazy. Her time in the Deep Pit was hard to recall beyond general sensations of pain and guilt.

"Yes, Captain?"

"We captured the rebels."

"Have they been harmed?" asked Rin, guilt clenching her chest. She had ordered the rebels captured. If they had been harmed, it was her fault.

"No, sir."

"How many were captured?"

"Seven."

"Have them identify a leader and bring the leader to me."

"Yes, sir," said the captain.

"They are all to remain unharmed," Rin reminded him.

"Yes, sir."

"Dismissed."

Delton left, and Rin bent over her book again. She wondered what had happened to Cleo and Gai. Had they been sent back to their times? Had Cleo been assassinated, or had she escaped her fate as Rin had? Rin had never learned how Gai died. She would never know what happened to her friends. Would Cleo remember her? Would she hold onto her memories the same way Rin had? Or would she only see Rin through history books?

Hot tears burned Rin's eyes. She had to ensure the history books remembered her as a better person. She couldn't bear the thought of Cleo knowing her only as the monster she had been up to this point in her life. She hoped Cleo would remember her. She hoped Cleo would survive being returned to her time and would get the same chance Rin had to atone for the evils she'd done. Rin wiped away the tears. She had to focus on her own time; she couldn't fantasize about the future. She and Cleo had to live separate lives now. Rin had secured a future for the satyrs by destroying the Consolidation Machine. Now she had to stop the genocide she'd started, and ensure they had a chance to enjoy that future.

Rin finished writing her account of Hell and closed her journal, running her hands over the leather cover. She had a lot of work to do to unravel the harm she'd caused.

Chapter 28

The curtains around Rin's bed fluttered open and a satyr was pushed through. He fell to his knees, hands bound behind his back. He was a middle-aged man, a bit older than Rin, not muscled or hard as Rin would have expected from a rebel leader. He looked like he spent more time with books than with weapons. Her captain stood over the satyr with a smug satisfaction.

"This is the one they called out as their leader."

"Thank you, Captain. You're dismissed," said Rin, putting her journal on the table next to her.

"Sir, you need to be protected," Delton protested, glancing toward the satyr unconscious in the bed next to her, as if she would suddenly wake and lunge for Rin's throat.

"You are dismissed. Wait outside. I'll call you if I need you," said Rin.

"Yes, sir," said the captain, standing straighter. A look of fear flitted across his face as he realized who he'd been arguing with.

Rin waited until Delton was gone, then turned her attention to the satyr on the floor. He'd stayed where the captain had thrown him. Guilt surged in Rin's chest. She had been there, now. She knew what it was like to be pushed around by angry guards. To stay on the ground for fear of worse treatment. To wait for the boot that would kick her while she was down.

"Come here, satyr," she said as gently as she could.

The satyr pushed himself off the ground. It was harder for satyrs to move with their hands behind their back than it was for humans. Rin remembered having her hands shackled behind her back. Being led down to the Deep Pit. Down to die. No. No. She was home. She had power here. She would use that power to fix the evils she'd done.

"Come here. Let me see your hands," said Rin.

The satyr kept his head down. He walked up to Rin and turned around. She dug her fingers into the rope. She noticed that her hands weren't hard and calloused any more, as though she'd never held a pickaxe or a shovel. She worked at the rough knot until the rope gave and the satyr's hands were loose.

"There you go," she said, letting the ropes fall to the floor.

The satyr staggered away from her, shooting a scared glance towards the curtains where Captain Delton had disappeared. Then he turned back to stare at Rin as he rubbed his sore wrists. Blisters had begun to form where the rope had rubbed his skin raw. Rin would have to have a conversation with her captain about the definition of 'harm.'

"What's your name?" she asked.

"Tharne," said the satyr.

"You may call me Rin. Do you know her?" She gestured toward the satyr in the next bed.

Tharne swallowed hard and nodded.

"The doctor says she'll be fine as long as she isn't moved too much. She has a broken rib that needs to heal. You can go to her," said Rin.

Tharne stumbled across the room to the other bed. He gently pushed the satyr's hair out of her face. Rin's bed was close enough to the satyr's that she could see Tharne's hands tremble as they hovered over the ruined horns. Rin burned with guilt. How many of this satyr's loved ones had been murdered at her command? She had saved this one woman, but how many had she destroyed? Guilt washed over her. How was she going to stay afloat without Cleo to listen to her and comfort her? How could she survive when centuries stood between her and the one person who understood her? The one person who loved her?

"What are you going to do to her?" whispered Tharne.

"Nothing," she said.

Tharne looked up.

"My doctors will continue to treat her until she's well again, but I'm not going to hurt her. Once she's healed, she's free to go."

"But there will be nowhere for her to go. You'll have destroyed our home by then," said Tharne, with a bitterness that Rin deserved.

"The settlement will be unharmed. No one who was captured or who escaped will be harmed," answered Rin.

Tharne frowned, confused.

She sighed and leaned back into the pillows that supported her. Her stump of a leg ached. She was tired. The guilt sapped her energy and made her want to close her eyes and let someone else handle things. Was this really her life? Was this what she'd built before going to Hell? It would be a long, slow process undoing it.

"Doctor," called Rin.

The doctor appeared.

"Bring a chair for Tharne," she said.

Sirona disappeared. A moment later, an assistant came in with a wooden chair. It was placed between Rin's bed and the satyr's bed.

"Have a seat," Rin said as the assistant withdrew.

Tharne sat awkwardly in the human chair.

Rin closed her eyes and rubbed her temples. The pain and remorse were combining to give her a throbbing headache.

She looked Tharne in the eyes. He was scared and confused. He knew he was going to die. Rin had forgotten what it felt like to be herself in her time. She had forgotten what it felt like to hold power over the lives of others, rather than being the one who cowered, powerless, before guards and wardens.

"I am sorry," she said.

Tharne's eyes widened with shock. Whatever he had expected her to say, that was not it.

She took advantage of his shocked silence and plunged forward. "I have recently endured an—" She paused, looking for the right word. "An experience, that opened my eyes to the horrors of my actions. I am truly, deeply sorry for everything I've done. I intend to spend the rest of my life putting things right, but I know that there are things I can't undo, people I can't bring back. There's nothing I do can erase the pain I've caused. I don't apologize with the expectation of forgiveness. I know that I do not deserve that. I apologize because you deserve to know how sorry I am."

Tharne's mouth hung open. Rin was quiet, allowing him to digest her words. She tried to imagine how shocked he must feel. She had no point of comparison. There were people who had been cruel to her in Hell, but she had deserved their hatred. She had done terrible, unforgivable things. They had been cruel to a monster. Tharne and the other satyrs had done nothing wrong. She had been cruel to innocent people. She didn't know what it would feel like to receive an apology from someone who hated her for existing, rather than for the atrocities she'd committed.

"Thank you?" said Tharne. He looked confused and scared, as if he was waiting for Rin to reveal her trick.

"I intend to draft a law granting satyrs equal rights with humans under the law. Satyr hunting will be made illegal immediately, and I will begin working to help your people rebuild what I have destroyed."

Tharne continued to stare at her mutely.

"I want to fix what I've broken, but I can't do it on my own. I had you brought in here so that I could ask for your help," she said.

"My help?" asked Tharne.

"I have too much power. I need an equal. Someone who has the same power as me; someone who can stop me. I have done so much damage, and I've surrounded myself with people who support me. I cannot pull an equal from within the ranks of the government. I need someone who disagrees with me strongly enough that they would try to kill me. I need someone like you."

Tharne stared at her. Rin waited. "Me?"

"It's a lot of responsibility, and it's dangerous. I understand if you personally don't want to take that on, but I need a satyr. Someone who will force me to undo what I've done. If that's not you, I understand, but I need your help finding someone who will do it."

Tharne slumped in his chair. Rin waited, tracing the lines embossed on her leather journal.

Sirona came through the curtain. "Sir, I need to check your dressing."

Rin nodded.

Tharne had to scoot his chair back to make room for the doctor. She glared at him, then looked questioningly at Rin.

"He stays," said Rin.

Sirona shook her head, but folded back the blanket over Rin's leg. Tharne's eyes went wide when he saw the extent of the damage. Rin hissed in pain and clenched the blankets as the doctor cleaned her wounds before applying fresh bandages and draping the blankets over her legs again.

Sirona moved to the satyr's bed and checked her horns. Tharne stood and watched the doctor as she worked. He asked a few questions, and she answered him. Then the doctor left, the curtain fluttering closed behind her.

"What's her name?" asked Rin. She had been told before she went to Hell, but had long since forgotten.

Tharne was still bent over the unconscious satyr.

"Sochi. She lost everything, her entire family, in a raid a few months ago. She came here ready to die," he answered.

Rin closed her eyes and felt the shame burning in her chest.

Tharne looked up at Rin. "What kind of experience did you have?"

She looked down at her journal. "It's quite unbelievable."

"Everything about the last few hours has been quite unbelievable."

"It involves time travel," she said.

Tharne looked surprised, but not as surprised as Rin thought he should be given what she'd said. "The conversation we are currently having is less believable to me than time travel."

Rin watched her fingertips trace over the embossing. "It only gets more unbelievable from there."

"You have said some incredible things to me. I need to know what you experienced if I am going to entertain the idea that you may have changed."

Rin looked him in the eyes. If he wanted to know, she owed him the truth. "I went to Hell."

Tharne raised his eyebrows. "Don't you usually have to die first?"

"I did die. I was supposed to die. Your assassination was supposed to work," she told him.

"Then what happened?"

"I blew up Hell and came back."

"So. When did you go to Hell?"

Rin gestured vaguely towards her leg. "In the attack. I died. I went to Hell. I was there for two years, and now I'm back."

"In the past few hours, you've lived years?"

Rin sighed. This conversation was getting off track. The story was ridiculous. "Do you genuinely want to know what happened?"

"Yes."

She opened her journal and pushed it towards him. "I wrote down my entire experience. I didn't intend for anyone else to read it; I wrote it down so that I wouldn't forget. But if you want to know what happened, it's all in there."

Tharne watched Rin warily as he approached, as though he was afraid she would withdraw the book and stab him with her dagger when he came too close. He grabbed the journal and sat back in the chair. Rin settled into her pillows and closed her eyes. They were heavy, and she didn't really want to watch him read her journal. She knew it would read like the ramblings of a madwoman. She fought the impulse to snatch the volume back and protect her reputation. She was strong and formidable, not the scared and broken woman in the journal. She forced herself to focus on the satyr in the bed next to her. Sochi. Blood stained her short brown hair, and her long, velvet ears were covered with cuts small enough that the doctor had left them to heal on their own. She had lost everything. The guilt bloomed as a fresh flame in Rin's chest.

~*~

Rin was startled awake when Tharne placed her journal on the desk in front of her. She rubbed the sleep from her eyes and pushed herself up in bed. A twinge of pain went through her leg at the movement. Tharne sat back in the chair next to her.

"Like I said, unbelievable."

The satyr looked pensive. He spoke slowly, choosing his words carefully. "I don't know if what I read was true or not, but it does help me understand."

"Will you help me?" asked Rin.

Tharne nodded his head slowly. "I will."

She sank back in her pillows. "Thank you."

"I need something from you, immediately."

"Anything."

"My people who are currently being held—"

"They are free to go. I'll give the order," she said.

"I want to talk to them in private first."

"Use my quarters. They are the closest thing to private around here. I will send someone to escort you. I wish I could go myself," said Rin, already trying to think of who to send. Who could she trust to protect Tharne and his fellow rebels? Who wouldn't try to hurt them? She struggled to remember the people of this time and place. She used to know her command inside and out, but so much time had passed. She had forgotten many faces, names, and loyalties.

"How much freedom do I have in this?" asked Tharne.

Rin ran her hands over her face. "Complete freedom, but I will need you to stay close at first. Partly because I am worried for your safety, and partly because I am afraid of slipping back into my old ways, and I need someone who can call me out if that happens. Someone who can hold me accountable."

"I understand. I don't know if I'm the best person to help you, though." He glanced at the satyr in the bed next to Rin. "Sochi has more of that fire."

Rin looked at the bed. "The doctor says she can't be moved right now, anyway."

Tharne thought for a moment before speaking again. "Alright. I'll go speak with my people and send them home. Then I'll come back here. I should be here when Sochi wakes up. I am worried what she might do if she wakes up in a bed next to you."

"Doctor," called Rin.

The doctor stuck her head through the curtain. "Yes, sir."

"Send in the captain."

"Yes, sir."

A moment later, Captain Delton was standing at the foot of her bed. He shot a confused look at Tharne, who was sitting next to her, unharmed and freed from his ropes.

"The satyrs you captured are to be released, unharmed," said Rin.

The captain's eyes went wide. "Sir?"

"Tharne," she gestured towards the satyr, "will be staying with us. He has full freedom and may come and go from this camp as he wishes. His rank is equal to mine. Everyone in this camp will obey his orders as if they were my own, including you."

"Sir?" Delton said, his mouth hanging open.

"I will be asking a few of my people to stay," said Tharne.

Rin nodded. "Any satyrs in this camp have full freedom and may come and go as they please."

"Unharmed," said Tharne.

"Unharmed," Rin added.

"Sir?"

"Send in squad six. They will no longer be reporting to you, but directly to Tharne until he no longer needs them," said Rin.

"Sir?" said the captain again. He looked ill.

"Those are all orders," Rin said.

"Yes, sir," said the captain.

"Dismissed."

Captain Delton turned from the bed and pushed through the curtain in a daze.

"I believe you may have broken him," Tharne said, watching the curtains flutter closed with some amusement.

Rin pressed her palms to her temples. "He won't be the worst of our problems. He follows orders. There are others in my command who may decide I am mad and try to put me out of their misery."

"They may find you're harder to kill than they expect," said Tharne.

Rin smiled at that. "Doctor," she called.

The doctor appeared.

"I need a glass of water."

A moment later a glass of water was on the table next to her. Rin drank it thirstily. It tasted different from the water she'd gotten used to in Hell. There was an earthy taste to the water of her own time that she hadn't noticed before.

"Equal authority to you?" asked Tharne once the doctor had disappeared.

Rin sighed and nodded. "It's going to be hard making that a reality just in this camp, let alone the entire country, but it is my intention for you to have equal authority to me in all things."

"How is that going to happen?" asked Tharne.

"I don't know. I haven't had much time to think about it. I didn't believe I would ever come back to my own time," she said.

Tharne watched her with an unreadable expression for a moment. "I am thirsty, too."

"Doctor," called Rin.

Sirona reappeared.

"Bring a glass of water for Tharne, and for future reference, he holds the same authority as I do in the camp from now on," said Rin.

"Yes, sir."

A moment later a second glass of water appeared on Rin's table.

It didn't take long for the sergeant in charge of the sixth squad to stick his head through the curtain. "Sir? The captain said I was to see you. Something about reporting to someone called Tharne?"

"Yes, Sergeant. Come in." Rin pushed herself up to sit, wincing in pain.

The sergeant stood at the foot of her bed. "This is Tharne," said Rin, gesturing towards the satyr.

The sergeant looked confused. "The satyr? Sir? I'm reporting to a satyr?"

"Yes. Tharne has equal authority to me in this camp. Everyone is to obey his orders. You are to report directly to him. I suspect he may need protection," said Rin.

"Yes, sir," said the sergeant. His expression was confused, but not offended. That was why Rin had chosen him. He was loyal, and lacked the hatred for satyrs that was commonplace among Rin's soldiers. Rin couldn't remember much about the soldiers he commanded, but he stood out in her memory. When she first met him, she'd seen his lack of hatred as a liability. Now she saw it as an asset.

"What's your name, Sergeant?" asked Tharne, standing from his chair.

"Niles, sir," said the sergeant, addressing Tharne with the same crisp military respect he used with Rin.

"I have to go collect my people who are currently being detained."

"Sir, I would advise a guard detail."

"Well advised," said Tharne.

The sergeant stood, waiting.

Tharne glanced at Rin.

"He's waiting to be dismissed," she told him.

A bemused smile twitched the corner of Tharne's mouth. "Dismissed, Niles."

The sergeant disappeared through the curtain.

"Am I going to need instructions on how to give orders around here?"

"You can make any changes you want. I like using a verbal dismissal. If I don't, I end up with officers running off to carry out orders before I've finished giving them," Rin said.

Tharne crossed his arms. "You're giving me a lot of power while you're stuck in a bed. I could do a lot of damage without you knowing."

"I cannot be trusted with the amount of power I have."

"You know nothing about me. How do you know I can be trusted with this kind of power?"

She sighed and sank back in her pillows. "I don't know, but this has to be better than that amount of authority concentrated in a monster like me."

Tharne opened his mouth to speak, but the sergeant returned, cutting off their conversation.

"Use my quarters as your own for now," said Rin. "I'm not using them. I apologize in advance, though, if I have to send someone to grab something for me."

"Alright. I'll be back," said Tharne, and he left.

Rin was alone with the unconscious satyr. She looked at the pile of her things on the table next to her. She reached over and ran her hand along her father's dagger, the 'gem-encrusted knife,' as Jason had called it. The pile shifted and she saw her cards. She pulled them from where they were tangled in her jacket pocket and tipped them out of the box into her hands. Memories of playing Pockets with Cleo surfaced as she shuffled the worn cards. Her vison blurred with tears, and she brushed them away. She would have to stand alone now, but at least she had something that Cleo had touched. Rin clutched the cards to her chest, before returning them to their box and putting them back on the table.

She leaned back and closed her eyes. She was so tired. She would rest a moment before continuing to work.

Chapter 29

Rin woke with hands clenched around her throat and a very angry satyr on top of her. She couldn't breathe, and couldn't call for help. Rin threw her arms up between herself and Sochi in a self-defense gesture she'd learned as a child. The satyr was weak, and Rin was able to break her grip. Rin coughed and gasped for air as the satyr struggled to reach her neck again. Rin kicked with her good leg, throwing them both off the bed and crashing to the ground. Rin's leg exploded in pain as she landed, and she cried out.

"Sir!" shouted the doctor, racing into the room at the sound.

"No guards," said Rin. Her voice was hoarse and rasping from being choked, but the doctor heard her.

Sirona raced to Rin's side and pinned the satyr down by the shoulders. Rin rolled off Sochi as waves of pain washed over her.

"Get Tharne," she said through pain-gritted teeth.

The doctor glared at the satyr, who was still scrambling to reach Rin. Sochi must have woken up while Rin was sleeping, saw the object of her assassination attempt in the next bed, and decided to take the opportunity. However, she was weak from her injuries and the doctor was easily able to hold her down.

"I can't leave her alone with you."

"Send an assistant," said Rin.

The doctor called in her assistants. One was sent to get Tharne; the rest were marshaled to put the room back together. Sochi, was lifted back onto her bed. She struggled, but the assistants were able to wrestle her into the bed and pin her there.

Tharne came racing into the room as more assistants tried to untangle Rin from the bloody sheets on the ground. The doctor was shouting orders and Rin was cringing in pain, clutching the blankets around her with a white-knuckled grip as the medics tried to get a clear look at her leg to assess the damage caused by the fight.

"Sochi, calm down," said Tharne, slipping past the medics to reach the satyr's side.

Once Tharne had convinced Sochi to stay in her bed, the assistants who had been holding her down went to help the doctor lift Rin back into her bed. Sirona bent over Rin's leg. She peeled off the blood-soaked bandages and set to work redoing her stitches. Rin held a fistful of blankets and gritted her teeth against the pain. When she was done, the doctor reapplied the bandages. The assistants brought fresh blankets, and Rin was once again situated in her hospital bed.

"The satyr," said Rin as Sirona stood from where she'd bent over Rin's leg.

She glared, but crossed the room to examine Sochi.

Rin glanced around the room as she waited for the throbbing pain in her leg to dissipate. There were more people there than the doctor's medical team and Tharne: two satyrs she didn't know, and three human soldiers from the guards she'd given Tharne, including Sergeant Niles.

Sochi had only sustained minor injuries from their tussle on the floor. She was weak enough that Rin had been able to fight her off, but Rin was equally weakened by her own injuries and hadn't done any damage. The doctor and her team left, but the room was still crowded with guards.

"This is what I was worried about," muttered Tharne. He turned his attention to his guards. "Go back to the quarters. I've got it from here."

"Are you sure?" asked one of the satyrs.

"Yes. Go on. I'll send for you if I need you."

"Sir, I advise leaving a messenger outside the infirmary so that the doctor's assistants don't have to cross the camp," said Niles.

"Well advised. Leave a messenger and go. Um. Dismissed," said Tharne.

The humans and satyrs filed out of the room, leaving Rin, Tharne, and Sochi alone.

"What is going on here?" hissed Sochi from her bed.

"The situation has changed dramatically." Tharne sat down heavily in the chair between Rin and Sochi.

"So dramatically that you defend this monster?" Sochi demanded from the pile of pillows she was now propped against.

"Yes," said Tharne. He looked to Rin and nodded at her. "It might be best for you to tell her what you told me."

Rin swallowed, her face heating with shame. She longed for Cleo's reassuring touch. She had known nothing about Tharne when she'd apologized to him; she still didn't know how her cruelty had touched his life. But Tharne had told her about Sochi. The satyr had lost her family only a few months ago. Had she lost parents? Siblings? Children? Rin felt like a fool apologizing to this woman, but she had gotten a lot of practice swallowing her pride in Hell.

"I am sorry for everything I've done. Tharne told me that I hurt you deeply, and I am truly sorry. I intend to spend the rest of my life undoing the damage I've caused where I can."

Sochi glared at Tharne. "And you believe this?"

"Yes. I have to, because this is our best chance."

"Better than killing her? I thought we were going to kill her," said Sochi.

Rin settled back on her pillows. After her time in Hell, discussions of her death no longer bothered her as much as they once would have.

"If we kill her, another satyr-hating human will take power and use her death as an excuse to continue slaughtering us."

"We already went over this. I thought we all agreed that 'better the evil you know' wasn't a good enough reason not to act!"

"Things have changed. That was before she professed guilt and vowed to institute changes."

"What changes? I haven't seen any changes," said Sochi.

"Look around you, Sochi! You are not dead. I am not in chains. Is that not a change to you?"

"She is toying with us. She wants us to lower our defenses, and then the chains and blades will be back," snarled Sochi.

Rin looked over at the satyr. "You're right. Nothing has changed, yet. I do intend to make things better, but if you'd rather take your chances with Commander Tiken, who is in line to succeed me, then go ahead and kill me. I won't stop you. In fact," Rin reached over to the table next to her and picked up her dagger from the pile of her clothes. She tossed it, sheathed, onto the satyr's bed. "Take this. It'll be easier than strangling me."

Sochi stared at the dagger on her bed. She looked up at Rin and then back at the dagger. Snatching the weapon off the blanket, she pulled the blade out of the sheath to test its edge on her hand, as though she thought Rin had given her a dull blade.

Tharne stared at the blade too. "Like I said, Sochi, things have changed."

"So, what? We trust her until she gets back behind her palace walls where we can't reach her and she changes her mind again? Then we've lost our chance."

"Stay by my side. That dagger is yours. If I slip, if I go back to my old ways, kill me. There will never be walls between us," said Rin.

Tharne and Sochi stared at Rin in stunned silence.

Tharne found his tongue first. "When I said Sochi could hold you accountable, this isn't what I had in mind."

"She's right not to trust me. I already told you I don't trust me," said Rin.

Tharne turned his attention back to Sochi. "Well, are you satisfied?"

Sochi glared at Rin, but she slid the dagger back into its sheath. "Yes."

"To clarify, I am going to leave now and go talk to the others. Are you going to be able to refrain from killing her while I'm gone? Because she might be alright with you killing her, but I am not," said Tharne.

Sochi rolled her eyes. "Yes, Tharne. I won't kill her while you're gone."

"Even if she falls asleep and it looks very easy?" he asked.

"Tharne. Go," snapped Sochi.

Tharne stood, swept one last bewildered look across Rin and Sochi, and left.

Sochi leaned back into her pillows, and Rin did the same. The satyr held up the dagger and examined it. She ran her fingers along the rich engravings and the precious metals and stones inlaid on the sheath. She tested the weight. It was perfect. She inspected the forge. It was flawless.

"It's a nice knife," said Sochi. "You probably have ten more just like it."

"There is no other blade like that," answered Rin.

The dagger was sentimental to her, one of her most prized possessions. It had belonged to her father. He had taught her how to use it and gave it to her when she came of age. The idea of parting with it was more painful than Rin cared to admit, but she had many keepsakes that reminded her of her parents. Their ghosts lingered in every corner of her palace, in tapestries and baubles. The satyrs Rin had terrorized were left with nothing from the loved ones she'd had slaughtered. It was an imperceptibly small penance to give up the dagger, compared with the harm she'd caused.

~*~

The doctor's staff brought food, placing it on the trays over Rin and Sochi's laps. The boiled vegetables and crusts of bread were a far cry from the meals she'd gotten used to in the future, even if it was Hell. She remembered Cleo's smile as they chatted over dinner, and hoped the woman she loved had survived being returned to her time. Sochi kept the dagger at her side while she ate. Rin was hungry and devoured her food. When they had eaten, the plates were cleared away. Rin pulled her journal into her lap and began the work of getting her head around what would need to be done to ensure the safety of satyrs. Sochi was quiet in her bed, and Rin assumed she'd gone to sleep.

"What did you tell Tharne?" asked Sochi, interrupting Rin's work.

"The same thing I told you," Rin said, closing her book and looking over at the satyr, who was fiddling absentmindedly with the dagger.

"All the same things? Tharne heard everything I heard before agreeing to work with you?"

Rin was quiet for a moment. She didn't want to talk about Hell again; it was exhausting and embarrassing. But if Sochi wanted to know, she deserved the truth. "No, he asked me why I changed."

"And your answer to that question won him over?"

"Yes."

There was a pause from Sochi. "What did you tell him?"

Rin sighed and ran her fingers through her hair. "It's unbelievable."

"I want to know."

"I went to Hell," answered Rin.

Sochi stared at Rin. "What?"

"I died. Your assassination attempt worked. I went to Hell for two years, then came back and decided to change my ways," she said.

"So all this is to save yourself from going to Hell again when you die?"

"No, I blew Hell up. I'm pretty sure it doesn't exist anymore," Rin said, pressing the heels of her hands into her eyes. She did not want to be having this conversation.

"You blew up Hell?"

"It's complicated."

"We have nothing but time and each other's company," Sochi pointed out, gesturing around them.

"I wrote it all down if you want to read it," said Rin, putting her hand on the journal in front of her.

"No. I'd rather talk about it. This seems to be making you uncomfortable." Sochi settled back into her pillows with an air of satisfaction.

Rin crossed her arms and glared at the blankets over her legs. Sochi was right. It made her much more uncomfortable to talk about her experience than it did to have Sochi read her journal, but she was in no position to refuse. If Sochi wanted to see her squirm, she would oblige.

"What do you want to know?" she asked.

Sochi wore a self-satisfied smile as Rin shrank back into her bed. She asked questions, and slowly Rin told her about Hell. Sochi jumped around, getting the story out of order. Rin's guilt burned, and she was humiliated as she spoke about such a deeply personal experience. Sochi was not a sympathetic audience. She scoffed at what Rin told her. She prodded for greater detail and lingered on the memories that caused the most pain. Eventually, though, she seemed satisfied and allowed the conversation to drift into silence.

Rin felt raw after her questioning. She sank back on the bed, shame and embarrassment swirling in her. She wished Sochi would just cut her throat with the dagger and be done with it, but she knew that would be too easy. She was reminded of watching the man jump into the fire, a scene Sochi had insisted on revisiting in excruciating detail. Rin remembered wanting to follow him. She'd wanted the relief it would bring, but she didn't feel she deserved relief. Now she wanted Sochi to kill her, but she didn't deserve to take that easy way out.

The task ahead of her was monumental. She had spent years crafting her genocide before enacting it, and then spent years actually committing her atrocities before finally being sent to Hell. It would take even longer to undo that work. This was her legacy. She'd made this mess — now she had to clean it up. She grabbed her cards off the table next to her and began shuffling them. Fortified by the memories they brought of nights spent up too late with Cleo, Rin began planning to undo her own life's work.

Chapter 30

Sochi stood, arms crossed, at the end of the High Commander's bed. She glared down at the woman, watching while the doctor talked her through the details of putting on her prosthetic leg. It was immensely satisfying to know that the monster would live with the false leg for the rest of her life, and it was because of Sochi. It had been three weeks since the failed assassination. Well, if the human was to be believed, the successful assassination. If anyone could believe they died and came back to life, it would be the High Commander. It was a farce. Sochi knew she should write off the entire story, but she had been there. In the moment when the High Commander claimed she'd gone to Hell, Sochi had been watching her, expecting to see her die, when something happened: the High Commander blurred. It looked like she'd moved impossibly fast — one moment, she was staggering back, the next she was already sitting under the table, several feet away. Sochi could have believed it was a trick of her mind. After the torture and the pain, she wasn't thinking straight, and she had been knocked unconscious just a moment later. Maybe the blow to her head had distorted her memory...but she had seen *something*. Could that have been the monster going to and then returning from Hell?

"Alright. Ready to give it a try?" asked the doctor, standing from her stool.

The High Commander hesitated for a moment at the edge of the bed, then slid off and stood for the first time since Sochi had delivered the corrosive poison. She could still remember the feel of the coarse leather pouch that had protected her from the poison as she carried it. The memory made her mouth dry. She was lucky to have managed biting open the pouch without spilling any of the poison, but she'd executed the maneuver perfectly. Every drop of the potion had landed on the High Commander.

She felt immense satisfaction as she watched the monster stagger forward in her first step since the attack.

"Good," said the doctor.

"Fantastic. At this rate, she'll make it to the latrine some time next spring," Sochi said.

The doctor shot her a glare, but the High Commander ignored her. Sochi could say anything to the High Commander now. That was satisfying too. It felt good to watch her flinch at questions and comments. Sometimes she glared and Sochi felt a thrill of fear, wondering if she'd pushed too far and would end up being killed by the human soldiers after all, but the High Commander always swallowed her pride and her anger and answered Sochi's questions.

The High Commander was given a cane, which she used to take another shaking step. The doctor reassured her that the cane was only temporary. As she grew accustomed to balancing with the false leg, she would rely less and less on the cane and would be able to walk more freely. Sochi watched with satisfaction as the wounded monster hobbled around the medic's tent. Eventually, the High Commander wore herself out and sat back on her bed.

"Remove the wrappings on your stump when you aren't wearing the prosthetic. The skin needs to breathe. It's still healing," the doctor told her.

"Thank you, Doctor," said the High Commander as she un-wound the strips of cloth that protected her skin from the harsh metal and leather rig of the prosthetic.

Sochi sat down on her bed across from the High Commander as the doctor left. She reached over and pulled the pros-thetic into her lap to examine it. The human glanced up at it, but didn't say anything. She probably didn't want Sochi touch-ing it. Good. Sochi traced the lines of the false leg while the High Commander took care of her stump.

Sochi had her own prosthetic. In torturing her for informa-tion, the soldiers had cut off her horns, which exposed sen-sitive nerves. When she was well enough to walk, she'd gone to the nearby settlement and had her horns capped. A metal plate covered the exposed nerves and protected them. The capping would have to be redone every few years. She made sure to explain this in detail to the High Commander, because it made her squirm in discomfort. Now she held the false leg the woman would have to wear as a result of Sochi's actions.

Sochi thought of her burned village, all the lives lost. Her family. Her sister. Her cousins, one of them just a child. All cut down and slaughtered in their homes, where they were sup-posed to be safe. It had been a sanctioned settlement. They were supposed to be allowed to live there.

No. She didn't want to think about it. It caused her too much confusion. She'd taken the High Commander's leg, but she'd wanted to take her life. She should take her life, but she couldn't. The woman was too valuable, and something had changed. The monster who had ordered the slaughter of her village didn't align with the broken woman in the bed next to her. It confused Sochi and made the pain of her loss worse.

"So, we're leaving now?" Sochi asked, looking for conversa-tion to distract her from the pain of her memories.

"Yes. We want to get back to the palace before snow makes the roads more difficult for the horses," said the High Commander.

Sochi traced the lines of the prosthetic. Her sister had loved the snow. This would be the first winter she wouldn't get to see it.

"You don't have to come if you don't want to," said the High Commander.

Sochi's head snapped up, and she glared at the woman. "And let you go back to committing genocide? You said there would be no walls!"

The High Commander put her hands up. "I only meant you don't have to go if you don't want to. I'm sure there's a long list of satyrs who would be willing to kill me. I'm not going to stop you from coming, though."

"I'm going. It's not like I have anywhere else to go anyway," said Sochi, focusing on the prosthetic in her lap.

"I'm sorry," said the High Commander. Again.

She kept saying that, and the worst part was, Sochi believed she meant it. She had been prepared for many possibilities when she'd joined the attack on the High Commander's camp. She knew they were unlikely to succeed. She knew they were likely to die without making a difference. She had been ready for those possibilities. She had not been prepared for this. The High Commander's apologies were the furthest thing from what she had expected. They confused her and made her angry. She longed to avenge her sister's death, and now this monster had taken that away from her too. She couldn't kill the woman who had ordered the destruction of her home. That woman was gone, lost to a strange madness — or maybe she was right and she'd been to Hell. Either way, Sochi would have to settle for killing the woman who had replaced the monster, but it would be a hollow substitution.

"I'll kill you for it eventually," said Sochi.

The High Commander nodded as she continued massaging feeling back into her stump. Sochi reminded her that she would kill her multiple times a day. It had caused alarm among the guards at first; now they were getting used to it. Sochi couldn't even get satisfaction from instilling the fear of death in the High Commander. The woman, frustratingly, seemed to want to die.

Sochi played with the High Commander's prosthetic. She heard shouts as the soldiers finished packing up the camp for the coming journey to Highdel. A shudder went through Sochi at the thought of the capital city. How many satyrs had been tortured inside of its walls?

"What is it like? The palace?" she asked.

"Have you ever been to Highdel?"

"No."

"The palace is big and old. It's been built up and out by many generations. Some generations were more paranoid than others, so there are hidden passages and entire secret chambers. The grounds are extensive, with full stables and riding trails. There are plenty of rooms. Tharne will have his own wing. You'll have your own rooms."

Sochi looked up and glared. "No."

"No? You don't want your own rooms?"

"No. You said no walls between us. Remember?"

"If you want to stay in my rooms, that's fine. They're plenty big enough for two beds, unless you also want to share a bed."

"Two beds are fine. It'll be easier for me to kill you in your sleep," said Sochi.

"Ah, yes, because during the day, I can just hobble away so quickly," said the High Commander, glaring at her stump leg.

"You have guards during the day."

She shook her head. "It's up to you. You want to share a room, we can share a room. I thought you'd be looking forward to me not waking you up in the night anymore."

The dreams. The High Commander woke up screaming often. "Do you do that on purpose? So that I won't want to stay as close?"

"What? Wake up screaming in a cold sweat? No, Sochi. I don't do that for you."

The dreams. Sochi had struck a nerve. She decided to keep hitting. "You dream about Hell?"

The High Commander closed her eyes and took a steadying breath. Sochi knew it hurt her to talk about Hell. She felt like she was twisting a knife in the High Commander's gut every time she asked about it. It wouldn't bring her sister back, but it was the closest she could get to avenging her death. There were memories she could prod like a wound and get a pained reaction. The man in the fire. Cleo. The smoke. Whether or not Hell was real, it was still painful for the High Commander to talk about, and that made it worthwhile.

"Yes," said the High Commander. Her body was rigid, like she was preparing for a physical blow.

"The fire? The man jumping into it?" asked Sochi, going to one of the memories she knew was most painful.

The High Commander flinched. "Sometimes."

"What else?"

The woman drew her good leg to her chest and wrapped her arms around it, resting her chin on her knee. In the three weeks Sochi had spent in the infirmary with the woman, she had been surprised by how un-stately her movements were. She didn't sit with a straight back and an imperial gaze. She slouched and folded into casual positions. She even shrank away in fear.

Now, she stared into her blankets, her eyes lost and haunted. "It's not always a memory. Sometimes I just dream that I'm back there, that all this is the dream. Sometimes I dream about falling into the fire, but never reaching it and being stuck hanging over the flames in the smoke and the heat forever. Sometimes I'm digging and the Wall is falling on me. Sometimes it makes even less sense. Sometimes it's just hot and dark and the feeling of guilt and fear."

The High Commander trailed off and continued staring at her blankets. Sochi didn't want to admit it, but she'd seen people like her before. Broken satyrs who had lost everything. They looked off into the distance the same way she did.

"High Commander," said Sochi, but she didn't respond. She was lost in her memories.

The High Commander didn't like her title. She asked Sochi and Tharne call her Rin. Sochi didn't, because anything that made her uncomfortable made Sochi happy, but seeing that brokenness in her eyes was too close to what Sochi felt. It sucked the joy from twisting the knife in her gut. The woman had changed. Sochi relented, just a little.

"Rin."

Still no response.

Sochi stood and walked over to Rin's bed. She didn't look up. Sochi dropped the prosthetic leg on the bed in front of her, where she was staring, and Rin jumped in surprise.

"Did you say something?"

"Rin," repeated Sochi. The woman blinked in surprise. It was the first time Sochi had called her by her name rather than her title. "I'm going for a walk," muttered Sochi before pushing through the curtains and out of the infirmary.

She couldn't stand watching Rin when she was in that lost place. It was too familiar, and too confusing. It made it too hard for her to hate Rin, and in not hating Rin, she felt she was abandoning her sister's memory. She turned towards the trees. The late autumn cold didn't bother her. She let the chilly air clear her head.

The camp was almost entirely packed up. A light dusting of snow had fallen, but nothing that would hamper the battalion's return to Highdel. They would leave in the morning.

Sochi climbed the hill and sat where she'd stood three weeks ago. She had looked out over the camp expecting to die in exchange for the slim hope that she would kill Rin in the process. She had been in so much pain, but at least her goals were clear. Now her world had been turned upside down, and the pain remained. She would go with these humans to their fortress. She would go willingly to Highdel, where satyrs were brutalized and killed. She was a fool, but she still clung to faint hopes. If Rin was genuine, maybe the suffering of satyrs could be ended. Maybe they would be safe in Galilia again.

About the Author

Mary Irving works as a material scientist in research and development. In addition to writing she enjoys drawing and painting both with traditional mediums and digital. She has lived in Western New York, Kansas, North Texas, Maryland, and currently lives in Mid-Michigan. She loves to travel and learn about the local ghost stories everywhere she goes.

Follow me on Twitter: @curious_doodler

And check out my website!
www.curiousdoodler.com

Please, leave a review. Every voice matters!

CPSIA information can be obtained
at www.ICGtesting.com
Printed in the USA
LVHW040014280921
698843LV00002B/172